THE DAY PHILOSOPHY DIES

/ casey maddox

Cover and text design by Tiiu Ruben

First printing, May, 2004

10 9 8 7 6 5 4 3 2 1

Printed on acid-free, recycled paper

Library of Congress Cataloging-in-Publication Data
Maddox, Casey, 1973 -
The Day Philosophy Dies / Casey Maddox.

ISBN 0-9753014-0-3

LCCN 2004103957

Flashpoint Press
P.O. Box 903
Crescent City, California, 95531

FLASHPOINT PRESS
CRESCENT CITY, CALIFORNIA

"NO EUROPEAN WHO HAS TASTED SAVAGE LIFE CAN AFTERWARDS BEAR TO LIVE IN OUR SOCIETIES."

benjamin franklin

<<

one / rewind

"HEY, SUPERSTAR. WAKE UP," says my wife Sarah.

And I mumble something about just ten more minutes.

The lights snap on.

I curse, squint.

"This is an intervention," says the woman standing at the foot of my bed. But it's not my wife. The woman's skin is shockingly white against the black nylon ski mask.

Suddenly I'm wide-awake, jumping up, saying, "Who the hell are you? What are you doing in my hom—Ow!"

She tells me it's only on stun, and if I don't sit down, I'll be lying down. Ten thousand volts tired.

This new reality I've awoken to is slippery. My mind is racing, sliding every which way at once, but I know enough to sit back down on the bed. My entire left side is pins and needles, and I look behind me, reaching back to comfort Sarah.

The bed is empty.

My wife is gone.

I can still feel her warmth on the sheets, and a staccato pulse thump-thump-thumps in my neck. When I look up to ask where is my wife, I notice that besides the petite woman with cold blue eyes and bare lips, there are three men in my bedroom.

My throat is dry, sticking shut with each breath.

Two of the men are videotaping me.

They're all wearing black jeans, black tank tops, black ski masks, and my mind screams robbery.

It screams home invasion.

But the woman repeats that this is an intervention.

"Where is my wife?" I manage to ask, my head tingling, my body going numb.

Her bare lips smile through the mouth hole in her mask and her soft, calm voice tells me I surprise her with how honorable I am. But she doesn't say a damn thing about Sarah.

I'm trying really hard not to lose it, but I am.

I'm freaking out, hyperventilating.

"Look," I tell her, "if it's money you want—"

She tells me step one is that I need to recognize there is a problem.

I have no idea what that means, and I suddenly realize that these people, whoever they are, are insane.

Her smile is real.

She is getting off on this.

My eyes tell my brain that she has a gun, that they all do, but this doesn't really surprise me. What *does* is that the guns aren't shiny and beautiful and sexy like on television: rather they're old and dirty and well used.

I'm having trouble breathing now.

She starts tossing Polaroids at me, flick-flick-flick, one after another. They keep flying at me, bouncing off me, and shocked, bloody faces stare up at me from the goose down comforter.

These are people I know.

Bob, my agent.

Karen, my publicist.

Oh-God-Oh-God-Oh-God, I mumble.

She says step five is that there is no higher power. <<

And she's really starting to piss me off with her calm, Buddhist, Zen Master, Self-Help, Twelve-Step bullshit. I say to her that they've undoubtedly tripped the condo's alarm system and that the police will be here any minute.

Her lips stop smiling.

She tells me that step five applies to them as well.

What can I say to lunacy like this?

I try to calm down, to breathe, to steady my shaking, twitching body, and I ask her, "What do you want from us?"

"Step one," she says, "is to recognize that there is a problem."

I say I do not understand, that she is not making any sense, and that the only problem I have is that there are four wackos with guns and video cameras standing in my bedroom and my wife is missing.

The woman tosses me a big black book, gold letters announcing the title as *The Big Black Book of Recovery: Twelve Steps to Recovery from Addiction to Western Civilization*, and tells me in a calm voice that my wife isn't missing.

"She is ODing on heroin in your bathtub."

"What? But Sarah doesn't do hero—"

"She does now," says the smallest of the three men.

Then he laughs too loud, crazed.

The woman tells me I'm going to have to memorize *The Big Black Book of Recovery*, because there will be pop quizzes along the way.

What do I do?

What do I say?

"Please . . . I'll give you whatever you want. . . . Don't do this. . . . Do you know who I am?"

She laughs, throaty, good-natured, completely inappropriate, then says, "Yes, we know who you are. You are the 124th greatest on-screen presence of your generation."

I can't keep myself from shouting that I won a Golden Sphere for my realistic portrayal of a dyslexic single parent battling colon cancer.

All four of them laugh at me, not with me.

She tells me it was not all that realistic, but that I showed good potential and have been chosen to undertake the most incredible acting job of all time.

I'm barely listening, staring down at the Polaroids still scattered around me. The bruises. The blood. The look of surprise in their glossy, vacant eyes.

I ask if they're dead.

And she says yes. She says my fingerprints are all over the place. On blunt objects, kitchen countertops, broken mirrors, bodies, genitals. She says there's an FBI profile just for me.

The numbness, the shock. I am so tired, drained.

She says that I wet the bed until I was twelve.

"No. No, I didn't."

"Well, now you did."

"Who the hell are you people? Why are you doing this to me?"

The woman tells me that her name is Deirdre, and that she'll be directing me on the sets. Then she points to the three men standing silently in my bedroom.

The tall one is Derrick.

The medium one is John.

The small one is Joe.

She tells me they'll be in charge of camera, sound, makeup, wardrobe, editing. She says they are also security. *Very* hands-on.

I want to scream.

I want to shout and argue, but my mind is blank.

Grasping in its darkness, I say, "I . . . I . . . I'm all booked up. I just signed on for a new reality-TV series that starts shooting later this week."

But Deirdre mock laughs, as if she appreciates my effort, and tells me that eating a rat for a million dollars is not reality, that *this* is reality, the role of a lifetime, and if I can pull this off, then all of my backwards desires will be fulfilled—if I still want them to be, that is.

For a split second, I see all of my desires coming true. I look at Derrick and John pointing their cameras at me, and I know that once the tapes are shown on the evening news, my career will be launched like a satellite.

Superstar.

I say thanks, but no thanks.

And someone says, "Wrong answer." It's the little guy, Joe, I think.

Deirdre tells him something in sign language.

Little Joe rebuts.

Their silent conversation is long and vigorous, and then Joe walks into my master bathroom, shuts the door behind him.

My brain is coming to life again, as I try desperately to figure out what is happening here, how to get out of this, but I'm coming up with nothing.

The sound of water splashing.

A sharp thud.

Something I cannot discern.

And my heart is skipping like a record stuck on a drum solo.

I open my mouth to say something, anything, that I love my wife, that whatever it is they want, I'll do it—if they'll just *please* not hurt her.

But my voice is a faint squeak of air, and then I'm puking up warm acidic bile all over the colorful snapshots of death that litter my bed.

I am shame.

Impotent.

This is *real* terror.

Deirdre just watches me, studying me, so calm, with wide blue eyes and a playful smile peeking through the mask, with the stun gun pointed leisurely toward the thick cream carpet my wife picked out for us two years ago.

My mind begins to scream at me, telling me to do something, to rush her, to fight.

I feel my muscles tense, my weight begin to shift.

The bathroom door opens to my left.

Out staggers Little Joe, with my wife Sarah wrapped in a rug and slung over his shoulder. Her hair, darker than the usual ash blonde from the water it still holds, drags on the floor behind him, and he raises his other hand, pointing.

The loudest sound explodes, filling the room.

The picture window of New York's nighttime skyline shatters into ice-like spider webs.

And I cannot hear my own screaming, just a high-pitched ringing. My throat is burning as I watch the silent movie of Little Joe throwing my wife off of the 50th floor of our building.

Now I'm up.

Up and running.

Heading for the window, for Sarah, for death.

But electricity snaps, pops, enters my body, seizing it, as every muscle in my body locks up, then turns to mush, and I'm falling, praying that momentum will carry me out into the cool night air and put an end to this madness.

I can see I'm not going to make it.

As the darkness washes me away, I hope that by some miracle I will never wake again.

So much for hope.

As the world fades back into existence, slow and bringing the pain, I realize I'm in a car moving smoothly across the George Washington Bridge.

I force myself to remain still, to not change the easy breathing pattern of sleep.

The sound of tires humming.

I crack my eyes just enough to take in a blurry version of my surroundings.

Back seat, small car, and the guy to my right is poking me in my right hip with what I'm hoping is a gun. Orange light floods and drains the car as we pass through the night like a tank of deadly fish. The guy on my left announces that I'm awake.

The dome light snaps on dimly.

The guy in the passenger's seat quickly turns around with a camera, which leaves Deirdre to be the mass of long blonde hair behind the wheel.

Her eyes meet mine in the rearview mirror and her voice, little-girl light and deadly serious, asks if I'm ready.

"For what?"

"To die."

I tell her yes.

But she says, "One step at a time. The first step is to recognize that there is a problem."

She says we have a lot of work to do to make this movie on schedule.

Something in my mind clicks, and I say, "Snuff film."

But she says, "Shockumentary. Going to break the cycle, set the world on fire. Maybe even figuratively."

I almost laugh, but stop.

If I start, I may never stop.

My teeth feel like glass, hollow, delicate, my skin feels like rubber, and I am starving. I say that I am hungry, that I need some protein.

And Little Joe laughs.

No one is wearing ski masks anymore, and I see that Joe has Barbra Streisand's nose, Kojak's scalp, Stalin's mustache. He nudges my right hip with his gun, I'm hoping, as he says, "Protein," and starts laughing again.

Deirdre says she thinks Joe really likes me.

I say the crazy bastard killed Sarah.

This makes all of them howl with laughter.

She tells me he was only following the script.

"What script? You people are fucking insane."

The guy on my left tells me it's all in *The Big Black Book of Recovery* and hands me a copy.

It's a big, heavy book and I grip it tightly with both hands.

The guy who gave it to me, his lips don't move, but he whispers the name "John."

I forgot we were on camera.

I'm not sure if I'm going to start crying or bash John's face with *The Big Black Book of Recovery*. His face is so middle-of-the-road normal that he looks like everybody, nobody.

"Where are you taking me, John?"

"A recovery program upstate," he tells me with a smile.

And I envy, hate his talent for appeared normalcy.

My hands hurt from squeezing the book too hard.

The cameraman in the front passenger's seat asks me how it feels to be a serial killer. He is a tumbling mass of Howard Stern's hair, a spooky smile, a half face behind a hand-cam, a blinking red dot telling me that this moment is now eternal.

"I haven't killed anyone," I say to him, to the camera, "so I don't know. Why don't *you* tell me how it feels, Derrick?"

>>

Deirdre says that's not my line.

My anger is growing, rising, filling me.

I smell gasoline and burning orange peels.

Little Joe laughs and nudges me with whatever. He says I have to find my character, that I've just killed everyone I love in this life and that I've never felt so alive.

"Lies," I growl.

He says there are no universal truths. He says it's a step.

And that's it.

I am hate.

I am rage.

I am slamming *The Big Black Book of Recovery* into Little Joe's face, with who knows how many volts of electricity racing through me, and I think that if I can just kill this bastard, then I'll be able to find my character, I'll be able to do whatever it takes to survive this.

But the lights go out.

A window shatters.

And as The Nothing swallows my waking nightmare, I hear Derrick yell out, "This is really great stuff!"

two / fast forward

NINE ONE ONE ZERO ONE.

Today I'm a surgeon.

I was supposed to be a real estate agent, but the script was rewritten. This happens a lot. I've been shooting on location for about five months now, even though time is a system of control and I'm not supposed to keep track, and today is the first time there has been an add-on scene.

Today is supposed to be a feeding frenzy for human emotion, and I am walking through New York's Bellevue Hospital. I was told it would be crowded, but I was completely unprepared for what I'm seeing, the immensity of the throng of wounded people and their families.

A man's voice rings out above the chaotic din with indignant rage: "America has been attacked! This means war!"

I say nothing, but walk by him in the over-packed halls, then bend over and grab a stethoscope that is lying on the ground. It's been trampled. It is broken, bent, unusable, but I hang it around my neck anyway. It gives me authority; goes perfect with the generic white lab coat Deirdre gave me on the way here.

She said the coat cost her ten bucks at a thrift shop in The Village.

I think you should pick one up, because it's a great investment. You would be thoroughly surprised at how differently people treat you depending on what they think you do for a living, your perceived social status.

People's perceptions are their realities.

True or false, it makes no difference to them.

There are bloody, dirty, hysterical, crying people everywhere. This scene has been typecast as a buffet of sorrow.

I choose a young Asian woman standing in the crowded ER hallway with a vacant look in her almond-shaped eyes. The irises are shiny black pools reflecting my outward façade back to me in miniature perfection.

She is covered in white ash and concrete dust from the explosions, and I notice that her blood has mixed with it to make a kind of pink paste on her dark slacks, in her dark hair, on her fair skin.

It looks totally fake.

I tell you, makeup has been really subpar lately.

"Excuse me, Miss," I say, "Are you hurt bad?"

She stares right through me, saying nothing for maybe a full minute. I'm not even sure she heard me.

But then, in a faraway voice, she says, "I was late for work. . . . I was late and that is the only reason I am . . . I am . . . "

"Miss, are you—"

"Alive," she says, waking up and looking at me for the first time. "I'm alive."

And she actually smiles, can you believe it?

Fresh tears run down the muddy tracks of earlier ones and she is smiling so wide, so improbable. Her teeth are so clean.

I am truly impressed.

She's a very talented actress.

But her happiness throws me off a little. It's not what I was expecting, looking for, told I would find. She's improvising, rewriting her own script, and it makes me wonder if any of my own proposed changes have been accepted, but I stick with the original line and ask her again about the extent of her injuries.

She says that she is very hungry. She laughs awkwardly.

"Great," I say, "Let's go grab a bite. My treat."

But she tells me that thousands are dead and that the survivors need my help. She half frowns.

She is so smooth, so fragile, so I pitch the lunch invite again, and she gives me this look that says she thinks something smells bad, and that it might be me.

Someone grabs my elbow from behind.

I spin around, worried it might be a cop.

But it's Normal John, and so I ask him if it's time for my medicine.

He says, "Script change."

And I say, "Cool. Who am I now?"

In lower Manhattan, the sun is bright and it's a summer-fair type of atmosphere, with all of the excitement.

Except, that is, for the fear and the tears and the billions of tiny particles of World Trade Center floating through the air and covering the entire city landscape.

I'm a rescue searcher now.

Jumpsuit. Hard hat. Breathing filter covering my face, which is good because of all of the cameras that could recognize me.

And Deirdre is suddenly by my side, dressed as a Xerox copy of me. But today she has red hair. Red red.

No matter what she changes, I always know it's her. It's the eyes. They burn into me, even in the dark, late at night, in empty-mansion bedrooms, when she pants dirty words through her clenched teeth. And I would love her if love was not a concept that suggests I am part of something bigger than myself.

It's a step.

People on the street wearing paint masks are handing out ziplock baggies with PBJ sandwiches inside them, and I'm not even remotely sure what my purpose is for being here.

I say as much.

Deirdre tells me it's to teach me how *not* to change the world, that this is just one zealot punching another zealot in the nose, that this is innocent people dying for another's oppressive cause.

"Causes are the worst kind of evil," she says.

I ask her what do I feel? What do I say?

She says there is no script this time.

She tells me to figure it out for myself, because it's a step.

So I watch the people walking by me, holding up pictures

of their most-likely-dead loved ones, crying out names like Bill, Cathy, Jeff, Susan, Robert.

It's a powerful visual image: emotional, depressing.

I tell Deirdre that it's cool, I'm being trained to save lives, take lives, whatever. Ask me how to perform an emergency tracheotomy and I can tell you. Bic pen, remove the filter, hollow of the neck and just punch it through. It takes about seven pounds of pressure. I practice on bananas.

"You really have come a long way," she says.

I tell her I've been good, I've done my research. "Ask me how to kill you with a pocket comb."

She says that day will come, but not today.

And so we walk down into the epicenter of destruction, with its smoking pile of rubble standing five stories high, and I can smell burning flesh in the air so thick that I think this is what hell would taste like, if it was a real place and not just a tool of domination.

three / rewind

THE FIRST THING THEY TAKE is my watch.

And I awake to more pain than I have ever known. Every muscle in my body is shredded, limp, sore. Electric shock is a full-body workout.

I do not open my eyes.

I ask the darkness what time it is.

But there is no answer. And the silence, it surprises me, disorients me. I expected my captors, but am alone. I sit up way too fast, my eyes opening, and the world blurs, doubles, bends, shifts, clicking like the hands of a clock, as my body tries to heave up the contents of my stomach. But there is nothing. My throat fills with a thick, warm, liquidy something, which I forcefully swallow back down.

My body is feverishly hot, covered in cold sweat.

I feel weak, hungry, sick, wet.

Finally the world begins to slowly come into focus . . . and . . . and . . . it takes several seconds for my brain to start processing information. Eventually it registers that I'm in a gigantic room filled with shadows, high slanting ceilings, and it is either an empty mansion or an unused museum.

There are four naked figures standing in the dim light of flickering candles which I cannot yet see, but my eyes are still focusing. I wait for a different truth to arrive.

I realize that I'm also naked, sitting on a dark terrycloth couch that seems to be the only piece of furniture in the room. But for some reason I am not cold, and I am thinking that one of the naked figures is at least two inches below normal, Normal John, I think it is, and I'm thinking of changing someone's name to Not-So-Little Joe.

Derrick is definitely not Jewish.

Deirdre is not really a blonde.

And the reason I'm not cold is that the flickering light is not from candles, but rather a fireplace in a faraway wall behind me and to my left.

The reason for silence, I don't yet understand.

I wonder if I should dare to stand.

Again, I ask what time it is.

Derrick says that time is a system of control.

"I'm hungry," I say.

"Then it is time to eat."

I think it's good news that he's smiling, and so I ask him what's for dinner.

Normal John says the word *dinner* comes with an

intention of time and that therefore language is also a system of control. I'm not entirely certain what the hell that means for me, but Derrick says he disagrees.

They start speaking to each other in sign language, a heated debate, but to me it just looks like two naked guys dancing in the dark corner of an empty museum.

I am utterly confused.

Not-So-Little Joe asks me if I want to know why we're all naked.

I say, "Wait. Don't tell me. Clothing is a system of control, too."

Deirdre laughs, little-girl light, a comforting sound for some reason, and says, "No, Superstar. We had to burn the evidence."

I cannot make out her face too well, but her hard little body is amazing. And I'm kind of glad she's not really a blonde, because I've always preferred brunettes.

What the hell is wrong with you? yells my mind. *She's the leader of the group of four wackos that killed your wife, your agent, and your publicist, and will probably kill you, too!*

But all of this is feeling like a dream now.

The crook of my elbow hurts.

My head feels like a giant balloon tugging on the string that is my spine, threatening to snap off and float away.

I think something is happening here, between me and Deirdre.

I think the word I'm looking for is *Stockholming*, but I'm not really sure.

"Joe is only trying to help you," says Deirdre. "You should always ask why. It's a step."

I ask her why?

She says, "Exactly."

"No. Seriously. Why are you doing this to me?"

She says I'm going to have to start figuring things out for myself, that it's a step.

And I'm getting a little pissed off again, because she's doing that ultra-calm Buddhist, Taoist, Zen Master shit again, answering every question with another riddle.

She says, "Your wife doesn't miss you."

"You killed her."

"Well, she doesn't miss you." Then Deirdre does this feline-feminine-stretching thing that makes my mouth fill with saliva, which angers me because I can't remember my wife's name at the moment.

I look down at the aching crook of my elbow and notice a tiny red dot on top of my bruised vein.

Sarah, I remember.

"Sarah," I say.

And Deirdre says I can call her that if I want to, that I'm the star of the show. Whatever helps me get into character.

"What the hell did you inject into my arm?"

"Freedom," says Derrick, "is why you can't remember your wife too well."

I tell him that's bullshit, that we were having problems, but that I really did love her.

I want to cry, but my eyes are bone dry.

I cannot find my character's motivation.

"You have been programmed to feel this way," Normal John says. "You've been taught to suffer emotionally. You've been taught that emotional suffering is noble." He tells me it will pass, that the steps will help me to get over my addiction, and that he is here to help.

He is so sincere that I want to kill him, all of them, but I'm sitting here naked in this huge room with the fire dying to rosy embers, with the pain growing inside me, gnawing at me, and the world shifts again.

I close my eyes.

"Go away," I mumble, "Just go away."

I hear the snapping of fingers, loud, echoing.

I open my eyes, and Deirdre says something in sign with precise stabbing motions. I can barely make out all four people now—they're just different-sized shadows—but the men leave and Deirdre tells me they're fixing some food.

She says I need my energy, because my recovery is going to be a long and difficult process, and we are going to be having sex several times a day in order to strengthen our working relationship.

I shake my head.

My body betrays me.

And somehow she has moved right up next to me, with her warm breath tumbling out onto my neck as she whispers in my ear, saying that if I cooperate, then everything will work out just fine.

"Be selfish," she purrs, "and everyone will benefit."

I tell her it's not right, that my wife's body is not even cold.

"You've been sleeping for three days. She's as cold as she's ever going to get."

I feebly deny her again, but her hand slides down, rubbing, stroking me, and I exhale, melting, moaning, as she tells me that I am very smart not to upset the producers: a real veteran move, a real professional.

There is a blinking red dot in the dark to my left.

There is a blinking red dot in the dark to my right.

And when she catches me off guard with her mouth, I moan again, thinking that men are not the only pigs.

four / play

"THE VALLEY OF THE SHADOW of death."

Isn't that how it goes?

That psalm they read at people's funerals?

That's how I feel. Cold, alone, waiting to die, as I lie in the empty master bedroom of some uninhabited mansion, without any furniture, lying naked on the floor, in the dark, with a psychopath's smooth-hard-perfect-little body entangled with mine, and that one line repeats in my mind again and again.

"The valley of the shadow of death."

I'm wondering if some minister, dressed in black, holding a gigantic menacing Bible, read these words at my wife's funeral.

Poor Sarah.

Poor beautiful, dead, gone forever Sarah, the only woman I have ever really loved. She was no doubt found in a crushed puddle of flesh and bone, staining the sidewalk a color that will never scrub clean, and by now she is buried softly in satin and dark brown earth.

"The valley of the shadow of death."

The scene plays out in my mind. The somber, tear-stained faces. I am, was, and now will forever be her only family. But her friends come to pay their respects, twice as sad, crying for the both of us, because they think that I am dead as well.

But I'm not. Not yet.

I am in the valley of the shadow of death; in some giant, empty mansion with the naked body of one of Sarah's murderers pressed against mine, and the shame, the guilt I feel pressing down on me brings an aching pressure in my chest, moving up into my face, leaking from my eyes. Liquid shame.

I can't believe I had sex with this woman. Deirdre.

I can't believe she made me come. Twice.

And I wish I were dead, cold and gutted and broken, lying in satin with Sarah, softly swallowed by the earth forever, because I deserve it. Because who knows what kind of sick torture these insane people have in store for me? Who knows when they will decide to kill me?

"Don't cry, my little superstar," soothes the warm mouth against my ear.

It startles me and I gasp, cough, stiffen, before sobbing like a little girl. I can't help it. I am dead and dreaming. My whole life is slipping away.

Deirdre squeezes me, kissing my neck, circling my belly button with a light finger, as she tells me, "When this is all over, everything will be better. You will see."

But my body stays rigid, and I try to pull away from her schizophrenic kindness, repulsed by her gentle killer's touch.

"I hate you," I tell her. "You are insane. You killed my wife and my agent and my publicist, and who knows how many others. You are sick and evil and I hate you."

My words are meant to be filled with rage, but they come out in a pathetic whine, and then I am sobbing even harder.

Deirdre's voice hardens as she says the word *medicine*. She rolls on top of me, straddling me, pinning my arms over my head. She is much smaller than I, but shocks me with her strength.

Bright light spills out from my left.

I squirm, trying to overpower her, but it's no use, and I see Not-Jewish Derrick emerge from the suddenly bright master bathroom with a camcorder attached to his face.

Normal John comes out of the closet, also filming.

And Not-So-Little Joe enters the room from the hallway door, carrying a syringe and a piece of surgical tubing.

I am fighting, panting, panicking.

They surround me, staring down at me, their hard expressions full of intense purpose. They study me, as if attempting to gauge my reaction. The moment stretches on, awkward and too long, silent and pressurized. My heart is fluttering, my mind is shrieking, my naked body trembling, and I'm so scared, so completely terrified, that my brain begins to shut down.

I'm going numb again.

Deirdre smiles, sly, amused, and tells me, "Go ahead. Speak your line now."

I can barely hear my own voice, as I beg, "Please don't do this. Please don't kill me."

Everyone laughs, getting a big kick out of it, like I'm being silly.

Deirdre says the word *medicine* again.

And Not-So-Little Joe ties the surgical tubing around my arm. He taps the syringe. A tiny stream of clear liquid arcs into the air and comes down on my neck, cool and thin and trickling into my long hair pressed into the thick carpet.

He winks at me.

He slides the needle into my arm.

I turn my head. Just a little pinprick, that's what I tell myself, but it feels like a jagged chunk of ice digging into my arm, touching the bone and freezing it instantly. And then someone removes the tourniquet, releasing the pent-up blood, the medicine, and euphoria floods my entire being. My mouth fills with saliva, tasting like sugar and metal, and I gulp it down to keep from drowning.

I think I'm moaning.

I think that maybe I'm smiling

"What kind of medicine is this?" I ask, mumbling, kind of giggling at the faraway sound of my voice.

"The kind that frees you from being a slave to gods that do not exist," Deirdre tells me. And her tongue traces the hinge of my jaw, making my face tingle.

I laugh, dazed, confused, amused, because what she's

doing feels incredible, and what she's talking about makes no sense to me. "How can I be a slave to something that does not exist?" I moan. "You are such a crazy bitch."

And I laugh again.

Deirdre stops licking my neck.

A man's voice startles me, and I open my eyes to see Not-So-Little Joe shaking his head at me. He says, "Wrong answer."

I forgot he was even here. "What?"

"That's not your line," Normal John tells me.

And Not-Jewish Derrick says it's not *how* but *why*, that I should always ask *why* about everything, that it's a step.

Shit. I forgot all about the steps.

I look up at Derrick's half face, half of an encouraging smile, the big black eye of the camera hiding the rest of him, and suddenly I remember we're making a movie here, but about what, I seem to have forgotten.

The red dot is blinking.

"I'm sorry," I tell them, embarrassed at my lack of professionalism, and I ask Deirdre if I could have a chance to look over the script because I'm having trouble remembering this scene, my lines, my character.

Deirdre explains slowly, simply for my simple mind, that I am nobody, invisible, anonymous, that I am just another human animal, but that I am starring in a movie where the character I must help to create will change the world.

"How am I going to change the world?"

Normal John says, "Gradually at first. Then suddenly."

And Deirdre's big blue eyes, so wide and bright, so young and honestly insane, stare down into mine, pulling me into them.

I'm suddenly very interested in this movie, in this character who will change the world. "Tell me again, how am I going to change the world?"

All I see is a blur, leaving my left cheek stinging like a

fresh sunburn the size of her hand. The slapping sound reverberates in the huge, empty bedroom, and the whole thing is so unexpected that my reaction is delayed.

I flinch.

"You're not listening," she growls. "*How* is not important yet. You should be asking *why*. The most important step in your recovery is to ask why about *everything*."

"Why are you doing this to me?" I ask, flinching.

Joe says they finally got tired of television.

It's all turning slow and slightly blurry to me, this whole scene, especially her words, and it takes what seems like several long minutes for me to figure out my next line, because I've never really been very good at improvisational acting. "What am I recovering from again?"

"Western Civilization," says John, and he zooms in for my close-up.

I do my best to give a dazed attempt at what I'm hoping is sex appeal, but I'm not sure how it will translate on screen, because I cannot really control the muscles in my face very well at the moment. I feel sleepy, but I try to stay with the direction the scene is moving and ask, "Why do I need to recover from Western Civilization?"

"Because," says Derrick, his voice turning kind, "it is a culture of domination."

"Domination," growls Joe, "is a policeman. Domination is a priest. It is a president, a gun, nuclear bombs, napalm."

Deirdre says that domination is a nonexistent god, writing laws and appointing punishment.

John adds, "It is selling hours of your life in order to purchase survival from society."

I think I get it. I think I know my line. "Yes. Yes. Domination is four wackos kidnapping me and killing my wife and friends. Right? Right?"

Silence.

Once again, they gaze down at me with a strange mixture of curiosity and humor, studying me as if they're silently weighing decisions they're going to make about me.

I think I now know how a lab monkey feels.

Confused. Afraid. Violated. Alienated.

Deirdre's face softens, flowing into a sly smile. She lets go of my wrists, then straightens up her body. Her soft weight presses firmly into my hips. She wiggles a little, settling in deeper, her smile growing wider, her eyes locked on mine, and her little-girl voice announces, "I knew you were the one. I knew you'd be perfect for this role. . . . You're right. This is domination. And we are here to help you recover from it. But you have to follow the steps. OK?"

Not-So-Little Joe leaves the room, shaking his head, followed by Derrick and John. Once we're off camera, I swallow tears, then look up at Deirdre as I whisper to her, in total honestly, "I don't think I can do this."

Her eyes open too wide as she caresses the face she slapped, her fingertips gliding across my cheek. "If you do not try to recover from your addiction, you will die."

"Why?" I ask.

"Because I will kill you."

My drug-induced euphoria is gone, replaced by an eagerness to recover, a crystal-clear mind—see-through, empty—and I shift beneath Deirdre's weight. I tell her, "The threat of death is domination."

This changes her expression to a sexy hunger. She shocks me with her laughter, clapping her hands like a happy child. She leans forward, kisses my mouth with violence, and slides her hand between my legs, causing a fever to roll through me. She pants breathlessly against my face, saying, "Good for you. I knew you could do it. . . . Step one is to recognize that there is a problem. . . . Domination is a problem."

She is insane.

My eyes are closed.

My hands begin to slide over perfect flesh, hard marble wrapped in satin, *her* flesh, and she guides them to her head. My fingers sink into her warm hair as her mouth slowly moves down my body, as I moan, writhe, lose myself.

And she tells me I'm a pretty bullet, that I'm going to change the world someday.

She says it over and over.

She sends me far off into the distance, flying through the ether, a pretty bullet.

Her bullet.

five / play

"IF YOU HAD ONLY A LIMITED TIME to live, how would you choose to live it?"

This is Deirdre speaking.

It's just the two of us in this scene.

And this is how I wake up: with her little-girl voice in my ear and her hard body against mine, with a hypodermic needle in my arm and a hypothetical question echoing through my still-gelling mind.

Deirdre has blue hair now. Neon blue. Short.

I rub my eyes, rub my nose. When she yanks out the sliver of metal, I rub the tiny bruised vein in the crook of my elbow.

"If you had only a limited time to live, how would you choose to live it?" And Deirdre pets my head, lying against her chest, as she asks me the same question again and again. Again.

She kind of sings it to me over and over, like a small child mindlessly humming a storybook rhyme or lullaby.

Lying here, in the middle of the floor, under a pile of blankets, with my head on Deirdre's hard little breasts, I can see my breath move out in swirling vapors and disappear into the cool air surrounding us. We are in the first-floor sitting room and there is no heat, no electricity in the giant house.

No one has started a fire yet.

I wonder when we will have to move again.

Deirdre's fingers slide through my long hair, scratch my scalp, send electric waves down into my face, neck, chest, back, stomach, hips, thighs, toes.

I moan.

She sings her question with a developing rhythm that snakes its way through my empty mind, haunting me, tugging me.

"If you had only . . . a limited time to live . . . how would . . . you choose . . . to live it?"

"With my wife and friends," I tell her. "The same people you killed." I almost laugh at the tragic irony, but I hold back, because if I start I may never stop. And it scares me, this feeling. To be so close to the edge of insanity.

"You are missing the point," says Deirdre. "I did not ask *with whom*. . . . I asked *how*. How would you live your life if you knew it was only for a limited amount of time?"

"Well, I guess if I knew I only had a certain amount of time to live, then I would seek pleasure and happiness instead of stability." I pause. "I would probably live more for the moment. Lots of fattening foods and great sex, you know? And I would take more risks, worry less about the future, tell people what I really think about them."

"Perfect answer," she purrs, petting me.

But then it hits me what she's getting at.

I sit up with a quickness, saying, "Wait a minute. You're

saying you're going to kill me soon, huh? Why? I told you I'll read your book, I'll do the steps, I'll make the movie, change the world, you don't have to kill—"

"The question," she growls, "has nothing to do with whether or not I will kill you."

"Then why are you asking it?" I whine.

Deirdre raises her arms above her head, stretching out on the floor, her lean muscles flexing, her hands balled into tiny fists, as she yawns and says, "It's in the script."

I try not to yawn, but it's contagious, unstoppable, and my jaws open against my will. It kind of pisses me off. "But *why*?" I snap at her. "Why ask me such a stupid question?"

"Because it's not stupid. It's the only absolute truth in this entire life, and it's an important step in your recovery."

"What is?"

"Knowing and admitting, as well as believing, that you are going to die."

And I look down on her, watching her lie there so beautiful and serious and mentally disturbed. I do not know if she is telling me that I'll die soon, or just someday.

She sighs, says I disappoint her, that I should have been able to figure this out for myself by now. "It is the only universal truth that exists," she says.

"What about gravity holding us to the earth, pulling at us?"

She says maybe it's pushing us, who knows? But, she adds, "The one thing we know for sure is that everything which lives, dies. Everything falls apart. *Everything*."

A confused, kind of hopeful relief fills me. "Well, no shit everything dies. I think everyone knows that."

Deirdre sits up with me, taking my right hand in hers and smiling, gently squeezing it, as she says, "Wrong answer." And slowly, lightly, she glides the short glossy red fingernail of her left index finger across my wrist like a feather, tickling.

The tickle turns to screaming-hot pain.

The blood, so bright and real, is squirting and then just pumping out onto soft blankets and bare skin, so warm and wet and everywhere all at once.

I am hypnotized, watching in horror, only half-believing.

Deirdre says to look at her.

I tear my eyes away from the mess, thinking of screaming.

And she tells me, in a calm voice, "Western Civilization teaches us to always ignore that we only have a limited amount of time to live."

The blood pours and pours, slower and slower.

I am suddenly very tired. So instead of crying out, I simply cry, asking *why? Why? Why?*

"Because there is nothing good on TV anymore," she says.

I'm crying harder, really losing it, going hysterical and pulling, tugging, trying to break free. Finally I yank my wrist from her grasp and squeeze the trickling wound. I turn to Normal John, and he zooms in as I yell, "Please! Please don't let me die like this!"

Suddenly Deirdre is screaming that she's doing this because she realized she has only a limited amount of time left to live, that she refuses to be a wage slave, that she is . . .

Her voice is fading.

I look up, and my lips go fuzzy as I beg Not-So-Little Joe to help me.

He frowns.

Because this is what she has always wanted, yells a faraway Deirdre.

And finally I plead with Derrick, but he doesn't move. His camera just keeps right on filming, the red dot blinking. Nobody moves to help me. They all just watch me, filming me bleed, recording me as I die.

"Cut!" screams Deirdre.

And as I sink back down into the cold, bloody blankets, the three of them swarm around me in a frantic hurry, suddenly trying to save me, attempting to stop the bleeding, but they are too late.

They are far away, in a tunnel of dimming light, and I cannot feel them. Can't feel anything.

Then they're gone.

So am I.

And so are you.

six / fast forward

ANOTHER MANSION, home.

And Deirdre is somewhere in one of the fourteen bedrooms upstairs, on the phone with our producers.

Me, I'm pacing.

The script says I'm unfulfilled, but I'm really just confused. Because even though I've been doing this for several months now, I'm nowhere close to figuring out anything even remotely resembling a plan of action. A goal. A finale.

And it's still kind of eerie to walk through a home with no personal belongings. It feels like I do not belong here, like I am uninvited, but this is how we live. Everything is transitional and leading up to a climax that I'm unable to see.

One of us is always a realtor.

We check the listings, select a home—mansions only. Sometimes we represent, sometimes we don't. We never sell. We just move.

You see, the thing about mansions is that there's usually a lot of room between you and your neighbors, and this is a must for us. Sometimes we have guests. Sometimes they scream.

Don't ask: I haven't seen them yet. >>

Derrick, John, Joe are watching TV, and I stop pacing to catch what's on every channel. I see the plane hit the building for the thousandth time, and then some middle-aged guy in a two-thousand-dollar suit and plastic salt-and-pepper hair comes on the set to announce, with appropriate somberness, that three thousand people are dead.

And this latest body count is being brought to you by the good people at Phillip Morris. They remind us that there are worse things in the world than smoking: *See, we're not so bad.*

Joe laughs, hacking, saying, "That's way twisted. Steel balls, man." And he lights a new cigarette with an old one.

John says that they will definitely pay, but that he has to go to work right now. He's working in a morgue today, and he says that business is booming with this terrorist thing, that everybody is in a recession but them.

He comes over to remind me that I am supposed to join him for a particularly disturbing scene next week.

Derrick turns the camera on me and asks me how I feel about the attacks.

Suddenly everyone is quiet, looking extremely interested in my potential answer, but I just say, "I don't understand why I was a rescue searcher again today. It's really hard work."

Derrick zooms in, telling me that the government is already passing bills and laws and statutes taking away personal liberties in the name of defending freedom. "It's the worst kind of irony," he says.

"Well," I say, "Free thinkers are dangerous."

Everyone appreciates the joke, and it feels good to laugh, but then the intercom on the living room wall pops, crackles, and Deirdre's voice tells us all that she has a major announcement to make.

She pauses.

An invisible remote finger mutes the television.

It's so quiet that I can hear my body working to keep me alive, but then Deirdre speaks, and the wall tells us all that we're heading out West.

Sunshine and drive-by shootings.

Movie stars and police brutality.

It's time to even the playing field, she says.

The script tells us all we're very excited, but I'm just confused, because I have no idea what the hell we've accomplished here or hope to accomplish there, and so I ask, "Why?"

I say it's a step.

The wall tells me that a plan of action has been decided.

Derrick does a funky little jig, following the script, as does John, but Joe says that action is overrated. He lights up another smoke. He sneers. He flips a middle finger at the wall.

For some reason, this ignites something inside me, and I say, "Yeah. I don't think I'm going anywhere unless I know what this so-called plan of action is."

Deirdre's calm voice tells me I've been working too hard.

Shit.

She says that I've lost my focus.

And I can hardly breathe, because I know what is coming.

"You could really use a little R & R," she says.

I try not to cringe. I'm trembling.

Normal John bolts from the room to work with the dead.

Fear and excitement roll through me, hot and spilling.

Deirdre tells me she hopes to see me later, that we can spend some time together, that she really enjoys our unique relationship.

The intercom clicks off.

The house is quiet as death.

Derrick turns the camera on me again, red dot blinking.

And Not-So-Little Joe shows me a snake's smile as he

sets the dirty revolver on the floor between us. "You are so easy to provoke," he says.

I pick up the gun.

It's cold, heavy. I am weightless, electric, trying to breathe, but I am not afraid, because I've been here before. Death, I am hoping, is black and white, an answer not open to personal interpretation, because at least then I won't be so fucking confused all the time.

I cock back the hammer.

I place the muzzle's tiny circle to my temple.

I pull the trig—

seven / rewind

TODAY IS . . . IS . . .

Well, I'm not exactly sure of the date or the time, but I think I've been with these people for a month now, and that makes today my birthday.

I decided this is true upon awakening this morning (evening)—I'm not sure which it is because it's dark and raining outside—but when I mention the special occasion to my captors, I am fully ignored, as if I have not spoken at all.

No one even looks my way.

All four of them are standing around some kind of blueprint spread out on the kitchen countertop. The power is no longer on in this house. Candles are everywhere. It's time to move, they say.

But today is my birthday, and so I push, announcing it again.

Ignored.

I say it louder. Louder. Louder. And then I'm yelling,

"Happy birthday to me," singing it too loud, out of key, basically screaming it, with my throat burning and spit flying from my lips. Because I *want* this, *need* this, the tiniest bit of normalcy.

I finish singing, screaming. I suck in air, swaying.

All eyes on me.

And Normal John says, "Congratulations." He tells me that I was the fastest of three hundred million sperm, the greatest fluke, the accidental winner of the only race that counts for anything. "Bra . . . Vo," he sneers. "Bra . . . Vo."

"But I've been good," I tell him, them. "I haven't tried to escape or anything. I just want to go to a bar and watch the Yankees play a game. I just need to be normal for one night. I think I deserve it."

Deirdre tells me that normalcy is all about perspective. That I have nowhere to escape to anyway, that I'm a serial killer on the run from America's System of Punishment.

Derrick turns on the camera, turns it on me, asks me how that makes me feel.

Not-So-Little Joe says, "It's been a while, but I'm going to back you up on this."

He calls me friend.

He says I could probably use a little R & R, that it might just help me out with this perspective thing.

He smiles so cold that a chill moves through me.

And then suddenly everyone is agreeing, nodding their heads and saying things like, "It's true," and "You really could use some R & R time," and "Good idea."

They charge me.

I'm caught off guard, off balance, shoved to the ground and held there, unmoving.

When Deirdre straddles my stomach, she chokes me so gently that I'm not even worried as The Black closes in to swallow us all.

I am woken with a deep, soft kiss.

A sharp slap.

My eyes fly open and the gang's all here.

I am sitting in a chair—no, tied to a chair—at a makeshift dining room table. Cardboard boxes. A sheet. A candlelight dinner.

Grimy old revolver is the main course.

I'm shaking, and I have no idea what's about to happen. I smell fear pouring from my pores, alkaline, and the fumes rise up like ammonia, stinging my eyes, blurring my vision.

The silence is taking us somewhere too fast, and so I say, "I thought you said I needed some R & R?"

"We did," says Deirdre, her lips curling up at the corners. "Russian Roulette is a great way to gain freedom from taught thoughts of importance."

Joe flicks open a blade, cuts my right arm free, and places the cold steel weapon in my hand.

It's much heavier than the prop guns I'm used to.

Normal John and Not-Jewish Derrick film me from different angles, the first pointing at me, the latter at the wall behind me, and I realize that *that* is where my brains will run down the lazy-white paint if the cylinder lands wrong.

Joe holds my wrist, gives the wheel a good spin, and guides the barrel's tiny black eye to my temple.

He lets go.

Miraculously, I hold it there, holding my breath because for some reason I cannot exhale. My face feels drained, slack, pale.

"How important is that Yankee game right about now?" asks John. "Do you even remember what month you were born?"

His quiet, unassuming demeanor is salt in a wound: *my* wound.

The fear inside me turns, solidifies. I clench my jaw. I say, "April. . . . And fuck you."

I pull the trigger.

Bang!

My heart is not beating. For a split second I am dead, like sneezing, but then I realize that the only pain is from clenching my jaw too hard and that the gun didn't even go off.

My brain says it was something hitting something.

I open my eyes and *The Big Black Book of Recovery* is on the cardboard table in front of me.

Deirdre looks concerned.

Joe starts to giggle, impish.

The other two zoom in for my close-up, as I breathe and smile, as I point the gun at Normal John because he's right up on me with his camera.

Bang!

This time it's not a book; it is real, and the gun flies from my hand. John falls to the polished wood floor.

Derrick screams. He turns the camera on John.

Everybody starts freaking out.

Me, I think the hole in his stomach looks fake. Even when the blood begins to flow from his wound, I think I've seen better special-effects makeup in cheap B-movie slasher flicks.

But the acting. . . . It is superb.

I cannot hear him, can't hear a thing except a high-pitched ring. His silent screams of pain are a powerful visual image. The shock. The horror. I tell you, it is an award-winning performance if I've ever seen one.

And the others are crowding in around him, ripping open his shirt so the camera can get a better shot as they attempt to stop the bleeding.

I lean down, make eye contact with him, and mouth the word, "*Congratulations*."

"Bra . . . Vo," I tell him. "Bra . . . Vo."

eight / fast forward

TEXAS.

Another empty mansion.

Another city tour date.

Another day inside my world, and I'm so alive that I feel half-dead. Truthfully, this isn't really a mansion. It's more like a ranch, which Derrick is supposedly attempting to sell in a recession market. We could probably stay here quite a while if we weren't on a schedule to reach a certain west-coast destination still unknown to me.

"It's hard to keep a secret in the movie business."

This is what I'm told every time I ask how this is all going to end. I'm told that if the finale leaks out, we'll all be fired and there'll be a cheap movie-of-the-week knockoff before we can say *no comment* to the microphones thrust in our faces on the courthouse steps.

What can I do?

I want to finish production, get on with my career, my life, and when in Rome . . . blah-blah-blah . . . whatever.

For some reason, since arriving in Texas, I've been playing all of my roles in the field of electronics. You know, telephone line repairs, meter checker for the electrical company, alternative power sales rep: stuff like that.

Go ahead, ask me to explain electrical current, speed of light, relativity, how to create an undetectable computer virus, how to build up or destroy an electrical infrastructure. After six months, I can explain all of this and much more. But it would absolutely bore you to death.

I think at this point I've become the greatest method actor of all time, and whatever it is they're injecting into my arm with each meal is allowing me to retain it all.

And it's all on tape.

I must be up to using close to twenty percent of my brain by now, but I still cannot bend a spoon with my mind, with my will.

How do they do that?

Speaking of will, I found out something amazing last night when I had a little R & R.

I. Want. To. Live.

What a strange realization that was. It caught me off guard. It's been a long time since I could say that and really mean it.

I do not expect you to understand.

So do not expect me to explain.

Today is kind of a day off.

And I'm standing in the middle of the biggest mall I've ever seen, just me and Deirdre, because the others are off inside various shops and stores. Pretty soon they'll meet back with us, and their pockets will be full of money for the next leg of our journey westward.

It's an easy scam.

It's a lot of fun.

You should really just try it for yourself.

It's called the mall game, and it goes like this: The night before you want to play the game, you steal garbage from giant dumpsters behind the mall. Take the garbage to a quiet place and pick out the tiny pieces of paper that just about everybody throws away directly after a purchase.

The bulk of consumers are the young.

They have no foresight.

Next, separate the receipts into categories. Just browse until you find something small, expensive, out in the open.

Prada shoes? . . . $500.

Nokia HP Pocket PC? . . . $250.

Louis Vuitton handbag? . . . $600.

The feeling of walking out of a department store, looking into the security cameras and smiling, with your pockets full of free money? . . . Priceless.

Pick a busy day, weekends are best, and then just pick the item matching the receipt. Remember to be stealthy. Pick something small. Return it. Get paid. One, two, three.

Deirdre is smiling at me.

It's her way of frowning.

Whenever we're alone together, I want to ask her a million questions. But as soon as I start, she touches me, and hours later I fall asleep with all questions forgotten.

Today she has short, black hair, shining like a fresh oil spill.

"The script is vague," I tell her, "as to what I believe in."

"Believe in nothing that can't believe in you," she says.

"But if we're trying to change the world, topple the system, then what are we? Anarchists? Nihilists? Naturalists?"

She yawns, tells me some of all, all of none.

"I don't get it."

Step three, she says, is to figure it out for yourself.

"Come on. Help me out here. It's important for my character to be marketed correctly, you know?" And I am total sincerity. It's obvious. She knows my acting abilities.

"Do you know of the Situationist Movement in the sixties over in France?" she asks me, indifferent, chewing her lip, not even looking at me.

I laugh. I tell her that in the sixties I was still dead.

"We are the Society of the Spectacle," she says. "We do not play sports, we watch them on television. We don't have affairs with supermodels, we watch soap operas. We do not kill people for fun, we watch movies about serial killers. . . . We look at a sunset now and say that the colors seem so *real*, almost as clear as my new high-definition-plasma-whatever TV." She pauses. "We have become digital dreaming idiots."

Her words excite me. I feel something in the same family of thought as understanding. I think we are Situationists. It seems logical, right? So I ask her.

"No," she says.

What?

She says she likes their perspective, their words, but words are nothing and she is all about action.

And I'm about to ask her to explain, but Normal John flies by us at top speed, with several rent-a-cops chasing him, and Not-So-Little Joe chasing *them.* People stumble out of the way, craning their necks to gawk at the show.

Deirdre starts laughing, then says, "People are sheep, clones, clones of sheep. Mutually molested children of our mother earth."

Derrick walks up, wearing a long, black, leather trench coat and a wide smile. He always looks like a living contradiction to me. Crazy hair, clean, young face, but he's forty. He says he needed pockets to hold all of the free money, thus the coat, and that Joe and John should be in the car by now with our new guests.

And I know that there will be screaming tonight.

And I know that we will be leaving town soon, heading west.

But really, that's about all I know.

nine / rewind <<

DAYS PASS AWAY.

Time has no meaning.

And I cannot ever remember sitting still for this long, all alone, with nothing to do, nothing to distract, nothing but my own thoughts, which become more and more foreign to me as I watch the weather change.

It's raining outside again.

Outside is a faraway world.

I stare out the second-story bedroom window of my exquisitely crafted, unfurnished confinement, the crown molding and the delicate construction of a home built for beautiful-powerful-wealthy-famous people holding me prisoner with every bit as much force as metal bars and concrete walls.

My wrist is healing too fast.

I wonder what the date is for the 211th time.

And the cold, hard rain falls from a sky the color of dead fish. I watch it come crashing down, shattering against the window like liquid glass, tiny shards running down onto the sill and pooling, then flowing over to form miniature lakes below and turning the grand estate which surrounds this chilly, dead status symbol of a home into a green swamp.

Our third home is my third prison.

It's like a TV show, *Houses of the Rich and Famous Gone Bad.*

This room is as spacious and empty as all of the others, and I've been sitting here all day, alone, unclothed, the blanket too thin. I am smiling for no reason other than I like the rain. It has always seemed the weather pattern that most closely mirrors what has always been inside of me: this unnamed sorrow.

Sometimes I hear them moving in the house. My captors.

Someone screamed earlier—violently, painfully, in the distance.

I think today is somewhere into the third or fourth month of my character's recovery from Western Civilization, but I really can't remember. I'm going through some serious withdrawals. What I wouldn't give just to watch the news or *Entertainment Tonight*. And it's not that I've just lost count of the passing days, it's that I am no longer sure when each day ends. Or begins. They all just blend together now.

And I woke up again with a needle in my arm, with Deirdre holding me against her and singing a song that was another question I can't seem to remember now. I no longer fight taking my medicine. I mean, why bother? I just lie there now, letting the warmth shimmer through my veins, happy to still be alive, swallowing the sweet-metallic saliva that fills my mouth each time the syringe empties its manna.

I no longer ask what they're injecting into me.

A wet, gray, dreary light pours into this barren room, onto the floor, not reaching the corners. I watch the water stream down the glass, casting barely perceptible shadows which move like snakes over the thin blanket, over my bare feet, over *The Big Black Book of Recovery,* which patiently awaits my futile attempts at understanding my character.

It mocks me, the big black book.

I'm supposed to be studying right now.

I've been really trying, honestly—reading it, memorizing it, reciting it after dinner for my dysfunctional co-stars—because I want to keep on breathing, but I cannot understand how this can be the script for this movie we're making. Even the brief passages that do not tie my mind into knots are basically theoretical and philosophically overwritten intellectual dogma which would only make sense if I bought into the overall insanity of their conclusion.

It's a lot like reading a Bible.

"Hey, Superstar," says Normal John's voice, calm and crackling from the intercom on the wall behind me. "How's your recovery coming?"

I tell him I'm hungry.

I ask him where Deirdre is.

"She's meeting with the producers. Joe is baking cookies."

I say nothing.

Silence fills the room again.

I know he's still there, still waiting. I know what he wants. I let the blanket fall from me like shedding skin, as I stand up and walk over to pick up *The Big Black Book of Recovery*.

"Do you want some warm cookies?" he asks, sounding bored.

He knows I'm starving.

My mouth fills with water. My stomach growls.

"Read for me," he says, not asking, not demanding, just saying his line.

I walk to the second-story window, watching the plush estate, waterlogged and green, as it expands below in my view. The hedges and shrubs are carved into animals, standing, still, alive. Lions, giraffes, birds, gerbils, and an elephant.

But this is not what has seized my mind.

No.

It is the window itself.

"I'll bring you up some cookies, OK?"

And I'm thinking, don't bother.

"Tell me what you've been studying this morning."

I place a hand on the icy-smooth glass pane. I shiver. Exhale.

"Six thousand years of Western Civilization," I recite, "has reduced you from an individual being who experiences a co-existence with the natural world to a slave who works half of your waking hours so that you can drive a purchased steel car to a borrowed electrified dwelling where you watch digital satellite images on a purchased television set which reports to you things like cloning, new diseases, war, starvation, and the court decisions that might dictate a change in the price of your systematic-survival that your slave wages purchase."

The latch slides easily, quietly.

The cold, wet air rushes in to tighten my skin.

Tiny bumps everywhere.

"There is no longer an experiencing of life, but rather an observation of it. A kind of second-hand living where you see and hear, but only feel in your being through the falseness of imagination. "

I drop the book.

John asks me what the noise was.

I place my foot up on the window sill, and I tell him, "You are a spectator, an uninvolved bystander, connected to the world only through shared digital images and sounds, a type of manufactured experience, a chemical reproduction. Life is a movie and you are just a spectator."

The wind howls.

Someone screams, louder, closer this time.

And I'm trembling, shivering, crying as quietly as I can.

John asks me, "Are you OK?" His voice is filled with concern.

He really is a talented actor.

"The ultimate pleasure," I say, struggling to finish the scene, "lies in destroying that which is destroying you. And of course you are wondering how, right? Well, the answer is easy. First, gradually . . . then suddenly."

Someone screams again, shrieking madly, terrified, loud.

And I figure out why it is louder now. It's because the person screaming is very close to where John is talking from, their fear blasting through the intercom, piercing, making me cringe.

John is rushing through his lines, trying to finish the scene and deal with the screaming. He congratulates me on my dedication to recovery. He says something about cookies. ›

His voice is snatched away the moment I step out onto the slanted roof, as the wind whips through my long hair, as the freezing rain pounds against my naked body like a thousand stinging needles, as my feet slip on the tiles.

The moment stretches out too long, playing too slow, half speed, as my legs fly out from under me and I twist in mid-air, reaching out blindly, changing my mind.

I come up empty.

I don't even have time to cry out, only to think 235 things at once, before I come crashing down onto the hard, slick tiles, the sharp angle whisking me away, and I'm sliding toward the edge impossibly fast.

Then I am free.

For a single moment I am free, flying through the air, the wind, the rain, and I'm thinking: Two stories. . . . Death? . . . Life? . . . Broken? . . . Freedom? . . . Stardom? . . .

I flip, twist, turn, hope for a swimming pool to catch me, as I watch the gravel walkway I couldn't see before come rushing up to meet—

ten / play

"How do you change Western Civilization in an instant?"

This is the question being posed to me.

My mended broken leg is aching from sitting here so long.

I have been with these people for at least six months now. I've lived in some of the most beautiful mansions ever built, but

I've not stepped outside any of them, except for the time I fell out of one. Was that last week? A month ago?

I just don't know.

I go to sleep, wake up, and we've moved.

My confinement is beginning to weigh on me.

I think the term I am looking for is *sensory deprivation.*

You see, I'm never alone, but I'm alone all the time. This is how it feels to be watched 24-7, every day, all day, for six months.

Deirdre repeats her question.

Derrick goes for a longer shot, wider angle, backing up and stepping into the bathtub.

We're all in a cavernous Italian marble bathroom, and the script says I have DBS, dysfunctional bowel syndrome. I can't stop shitting. I have the runs—permanently. I think it's something I ate, something they fed me, but it's not so bad, because I'm sitting on what has to be the most comfortable toilet ever built.

It feels like it was sculpted just to hold my ass.

When I mentioned this yesterday, I was told that the more money you have, the more comfortable that menial tasks are made for you.

I look down into Deirdre's shocking blue eyes. She is sitting Indian-style on the speckled marble floor at my feet, and I'm amazed that the smell of shit doesn't seem to be bothering her.

"How do you change Western Civilization in an instant?" she asks me for the third time.

I have no idea how I'm supposed to answer.

I say that I have been reading, studying, taking notes, viewing tapes, memorizing facts, but this question has not really been addressed anywhere.

Normal John reaches behind me and flushes.

Swoosh.

He winks.

He tells me that this is a single-question pop quiz and that any answer will do, because I'm not being graded and there is no wrong answer, really.

"Then *no*," I say.

Not-So-Little Joe, who's shaving Kojak's head in the mirror above the sink to my left, says, "Amen." He calls me *friend*.

But Deirdre shakes her head.

John says, "*No* is the wrong answer."

"What?" I whine, "I thought you said there was no wrong—"

"I was lying," he says.

"Then *yes*," I say.

Derrick tells me it's not really a *yes or no* question.

"Perhaps it's a question of insanity," I tell him.

Deirdre says, "Not insanity. . . . Possibility."

I shit.

"How do you change Western Civilization in an instant?"

Normal John reaches behind me to flush.

Swoosh.

He winks.

And suddenly I think I get it. I tell them, "Step one is to recognize that there is a problem."

I am greeted with smiles, nods, the pitter-patter of polite golf claps all around, and Deirdre tells me that I'm onto something.

I'm angry to feel so happy about earning their approval, and when Normal John reaches behind me to flush the toilet again I grab his wrist and squeeze. Hard. I tell him to let it stink. I'm speaking through clenched teeth.

Let.

It.

Stink.

He backs off, shrinks away, sits on the floor, as far away as space will allow.

Deirdre asks me if I have recognized that there is a problem.

"Yeah. . . . I guess."

"Tell me," she says.

My mind fills with so many potential answers that it is like hundreds of sentences written over one another. I say, "Well, there's lots of things."

"Like what?"

"Well, . . . the same old problems as always. Destruction of the air we breathe, the water we drink, the food we eat. . . . And, ah . . . people are still starving, killing, hating. . . . Nothing ever changes."

She tells me, "Yes and no. You've missed the point entirely."

She looks disappointed.

But Not-So-Little Joe, who is tweaking Barbra Streisand's nose, trimming Stalin's mustache, says, "Screw changing the world." He calls me *friend* again.

I know better than to agree with him, even though I agree with him, because if I do, I'll be looking down the barrel of a gun, holding my breath and squeezing the trigger to help me re-focus my perspective.

I'm a slow learner, but I'm a survivor.

Deirdre repeats the question.

And I don't know what to say, so I shit another stream of brown water as a means of stalling. I flush the toilet myself, because Deirdre is wrinkling her nose at me.

Then there is only the silence.

The silence carrying us toward something way too fast.

I ask to see the script.

I am told to improvise.

They are all waiting for me, the camera filming, as my bowels release again, and I say that I have never been very good at improv. "Ask me how to build a pipe bomb out of matches, make a silencer from a soda can, create deadly chlorine gas using only common household cleaning solutions. Evening classes have really paid off. I can tell you how to do all of these things, I can explain it step by step, but I do not know how to fix the problems that have been in the world forever!"

They're all looking at me now, which is nothing new because I'm the star of the show, but something has changed in them, in their eyes, their faces. Something hidden but definite.

"For 99 percent of our human existence," says Deirdre, "there was breathable air, drinkable water, edible food: all provided by the earth. It is only recently, through our own stupidity, that these things have changed. So, in fact, this 'forever' you speak of is actually only slightly less than 1 percent of our entire existence on this planet."

Her face is turning red.

"Yeah," I tell her, "I've never really thought about it like that. I've never really thought about much of anything. I mean, I have absolutely no desire to change the world. I really couldn't care less."

As soon as the words escape my mouth, I am regret.

I am fear.

I am waiting for shocked-bitter-angry faces to tell me some new-imaginative-painful way to help me gain the desire to change the world.

But there is nothing.

Nothing but somber heads shaking, and disappointment bordering on contempt, and somehow this is much worse than the insane rage I was expecting.

Their collective calm unnerves me. Horrifies me.

I shit.

They stand as one, and Deirdre tells the others something in sign language, her hands moving fast, the others nodding grimly.

Joe drops the razor.

Derrick drops the camera.

I'm shaking, shitting, close to crying, because I know that I am about to die.

They step towards me, synchronized. The now familiar faces are emotionless, plastic masks.

I can't catch my breath.

I close my eyes, but the dark on top of the silence is unbearable, and my mind screams *death*. It screams *dignity*. So I open my eyes wide and twitching and unblinking to watch the end of the world with—

They're gone.

What?

I blink.

I shit.

I breathe.

But they are gone.

I am not hallucinating. I am all alone in this luxurious bathroom, and I'm so geared up to die that I feel let down.

I try to stand, only to fall. My legs have been reduced to slabs of clay from hours of sitting, shitting. The marble floor is hard, un-giving.

I think I'm bleeding.

But I don't care—bleed and bleed!—because I'm straining, listening, searching for something, *anything,* that will confirm what I think may be happening, what I cannot believe might be happening.

I crawl on bruising elbows to the doorway and peer into the empty hall. Both ways.

I hear the front door tell me goodbye.

Four car doors outside say goodbye.

And my mind is chanting a single-word mantra called *freedom* that grows progressively louder, louder, louder, until—

Until I hear a clock.
Tick-tick-tick.
But time is a system of control.
Tick-tick.
We don't have a clock.
Tick.
Boom.

>>

eleven / fast forward

HOSTAGE.

It is a word that no longer applies to me, defines me. At times, I'm treated better than equal. I am the star of the show. The food is great, and Deirdre is . . . is . . .

Well, she is the most amazing lover I've ever known.

No. Scratch that. Not lover: sex partner. But I would love her if love was not a concept that suggests I'm part of something bigger than myself.

Denver, Colorado.

And my latest role, my latest part in the movie, is at a bank. Huge branch. Home office. I'm the troubleshooter, hired to audit the system, and you might think this is skilled work, but you'd be wrong.

It's a computer program. Interface. Push a button, it's like squeezing a trigger. It's all so easy, detached. Crunch numbers or bones, after a while it's all the same.

I think the reason I was given this role was to teach me something important about the brave new world of old money. You see, money is not real anymore. It is electronic. It is a blip of memory, a bit of colored light floating on a flat black screen. It is billions of dollars stored in a space no bigger than your fingernail.

But that is just a record, you say.

The real money is in the vault, you say.

I said the same, but I was wrong and so are you. Don't feel stupid, just lied to. It's a recurring theme, a lifetime trend. The truth does not set you free, it just pisses you off.

The thing about banks is that they may have a million-two, a million-five, maybe even two mil, but that's it. They cannot cover even half of what's entrusted to them.

So where's the money, you ask.

The truth is that it is out *there*. Billions and billions of dollars, your dollars, my dollars, traveling across wires in a digital code of ones and zeros. It is on the Stock Exchange, in real estate markets, trading-buying-selling, making the rich richer.

But it's not real. It's electronic.

"What would happen if it all vanished? If their system broke down? For good?"

This is the question that was given to me by Deirdre this morning, with a needle in my arm and her hand rubbing my happy place.

And I've been thinking about it all day, pushing buttons, letting my mind stray. It's like homework, research, field study, these roles I've been playing lately, and what I've come up with is this: If the system broke down for good, if all of the electronic money vanished, then the poor would stay poor, right? But the middle would join them, and the rich would be screwed even worse. And maybe an even playing field is not the answer to the world's problems, but it's definitely not a bad idea to give it a try either.

The question I want to pose to Deirdre when I get home is this: How do they expect to create this "system of a down"?

>>

This is what I'm pondering as I walk through the streets of downtown Denver, because Deirdre didn't pick me up from work tonight, which is a first. I'm not sure what it means.

A sign says *Jesus Saves.*

I walk under its sickened blue glow, watching it shine on those Jesus couldn't save, and I laugh because it's my new way of crying.

My laughter causes the trash heap at my feet to stir, crunching, crackling, as a gnarled arm rises from the filth, proffering a well-used paper coffee cup in a wonderfully mocking salute of the Statue of Liberty.

I cannot help but wonder if the owner feels liberated in a country that offers freedom with exceptions, if he knows he is the exception.

The cup jingles its contents.

I stop, reach in, take two quarters, and say, "Thanks. I really need to make a phone call."

A muffled voice buried in the trash says, "Hey, Superstar."

My skin begins to vibrate as I shrink away. My heart sputters awkwardly, because for a moment I had forgotten all about The Bums. I forgot all about what they were going to do to me in that dank, smelly, nightmare church somewhere deep under the city that never sleeps.

But, I'm thinking, *This is Denver.*

The voice asks me if I know what he did to deserve all of this.

"No," I stutter, because I can't think of anything else.

He tells me that he is cold, tired, ugly, and it won't stop raining in his head, but that he is very happy now.

I back up, asking, "Why?"

"Because now that he is dead, now that the prophet is gone, I am biding my time until the time is right. Just like you. Because we know that the apocalypse is near."

I think that maybe he is crazy.

No. Scratch that.

He is definitely crazy.

But he called me Superstar, and I cannot believe that The Bums have that good of a communications network, so I'm thinking this could be a last-second add-on scene.

"What are you waiting for?" I ask, still backing up.

He asks me if I know what is underneath the world's concrete.

I tell him, "Dirt," even though I know it's the wrong answer.

He laughs with effort, sickness gurgling in his lungs, as he tells me, "No-no-no. You know The Word. You were there when the prophet was slain. You know that under the world's concrete it is all beach. . . . All . . . beach."

And these words might mean nothing to you, but I've heard them many times before. I've heard them growled in the dark of empty mansion bedrooms with Deirdre's eyes burning into me like cold, blue spotlights. I was there in the Last Church of the Apocalypse, under New York City, with the knife stained and raised high above me, as I waited to die, and I heard those words.

I am shaking, close to peeing now.

I yell at him, at the trash heap, "What have you done with Deirdre? Where is she?"

Silence.

I'm answered with a familiar sound—a bone-chilling sound—of heavy metal being dragged on concrete. The trash begins to rustle, sink, drain.

My own reaction shocks me, as I dive forward, thinking of Deirdre, and begin to rifle through old newspapers and damp cardboard boxes and funk-filled blankets to discover what I knew would be there: an open manhole, foul smelling and pitch black.

I have this sinking feeling, panic flying through me, with my mind reeling, and I yell down into the dark hole in the concrete, "Where is Deirdre? What have you done with her?"

"Nothing," comes the hissing answer. "She is The One. She has always been The One."

"Then why are you here? What am I supposed to learn?"

No answer.

Quiet darkness.

Frustration.

And then, in the far distance, echoing: "When it's all over, I will see you at the casting call, the curtain call. . . . I will see you at the beach."

twelve / rewind

THERE IS ONLY The Black.

The Black is nothing, everything, folding out to consume the former existence of all things, and yet. . . . Even the thought that encompasses this new reality, if indeed it is real at all, is not a thought, but rather a fact which is inexplicably known to me.

Is this death?

Then comes the pain. A dull thunder, throbbing, growing sharper against the grindstone that is consciousness, until finally it becomes a blade of light slicing through my closed eye-lids, and . . .

And . . .

My mind is sticky, body crusty, as I become aware of my own being, my own presence. The rise and fall of my chest, as lungs take in the air around me, a taste of disinfectant and of sickness lying just beneath it. I feel the ebb and flow of blood sliding through me, the steady rhythmic pumping of my heart.

This is my body on cruise control. Surviving without me, in spite of me.

And the pain swells higher, in hot waves, threatening to crash. The synapses of my brain fire in their ever-present chemical dialog, and I come to realize that something is horribly wrong.

Where am I?

On the heels of that single query, a madness is born inside of me, and the torrent of questions that flows forth is a great flood which cannot be stopped.

Where am I?

What is happening?

Am I hurt, dying?

And what the fuck is my name?

The pain recedes a bit, settling in my head like thick liquid metal, heavy, impenetrable, swallowing The Self like an ancient culture, never to again be uncovered.

Who?

Who am I?

My eyes flutter open, and I peer through the blurry residue of the great void from which I have returned. A harsh fluorescent light greets me, an invisible slap to the face.

Staring up at the dirty white ceiling tiles, I slowly sit up in a bed that is not my own. The only reason I know this is because of the sterile hospital room which surrounds me. If this were a normal bed, a normal room, I would not know if it were mine.

What the hell happened to me?

The single door to my right swings open silently, the sudden movement catching in the edge of my vision, and in walks a woman I recognize from somewhere unknown to me.

Almost immediately she stops. Our eyes lock. Her face is slack in . . . in . . . wonderment? . . . Amazement? . . . Fear?

I study her, as she seems to be doing the same to me, but I do not know her. I have only the vague sense of knowing her.

The hair is spun honey. Long, straight, unimportant, even though I know that it's incredibly soft. Her face is made of slight angles, smooth shadows. Powder blue jeans and a navy blue sweater show me curves and hints of curves, generic beauty.

But those eyes.

The eyes are large, glacier blue, holding some power I do not understand. A question I cannot possibly answer. I do not know what I am to her, her to me, us to each other.

Confusion.

Home sweet home.

She speaks first, asking if I'm OK. Her voice is deep, trembling. Her face changes with the words. It could be hope or fear or love, but I do not know her well enough to tell the difference.

My mind screams so many questions at once that I have to close my eyes, I have to shut down. When I open them, she is standing next to me, over me, and I open my mouth to speak, but nothing comes out. I am right on the edge of something close to a feeling that remains unnamed.

Ten thousand images fly before me. No order, no rhythm, no time. My mind is a hurricane of snapshots from a life I see as being my own.

An ice cube melting in my five-year-old hand.

My mouth feeling furry the first time I called a girl "Baby"

Giant trucks paving over beaches.

The sweet, salty taste of Deirdre's flesh.

A clock we don't own, ticking.

Step six, step three, step one.

Boom.

My wife rolled up in a rug and flying through a broken window towards the piercing, radiant, yellow moon hanging over New York's nighttime skyline.

My wife standing over me in a hospital, asking me if I am OK.

What?

But she is dead. Sarah is dead.

Bob-the-agent: dead.

Karen-the-publicist: dead.

But my mind screams *no*. It screams, *Don't you realize that evil lives in the motherfucking skin!*

I am several long minutes past insanity now. When I hear someone screaming, shrieking, I want to tell my wife Sarah that there is something wrong with everything, and that her screaming is hurting my throat. But I cannot tell her these things, because I am the one screaming.

And she is supposed to be dead.

But she is crying, sobbing, breaking down right in front of me. She looks so fearful to touch me that I think maybe I am hurt very badly.

And I think that if I could just see the script, then I would be able to read the words *Acid Trip* or *Brain Cancer* or *Death*. And if I could just stop screaming long enough to say *cut*, then I could talk with the director and we could work all of this stuff out like professionals.

But I can't.

And we don't.

And I am relieved when I slide back into The Black.

thirteen / fast forward

A small moment of happiness.

I am exactly where I want to be.

It's a strange feeling, contentment, because the fact that I know it will not last, that it never lasts, makes me want to laugh out loud. It's my new way of sobbing. »

I'm in bed with Deirdre, holding her warm-breathing-sweaty-naked-slippery body against my own, and I am waiting for her to fall asleep. She usually crashes out shortly after we finish having sex.

It has already been at least one hour, maybe more, and I'm hoping to catch her somewhere between consciousness and unconsciousness, because I'm about to say something silly. Dangerous. Mostly stupid.

I whisper her name: "Deirdre."

She groans, moans, mumbles something that is nothing, babble.

Perfect.

Here goes nothing.

"Deirdre . . . I . . . I just wanted to say that I love you and—"

Crack.

Her elbow, my face.

I taste blood, and then she is squeezing my throat just strong enough to seriously worry me, to make me see sunspots in the dark.

I stutter, trying not to puke, trying to breathe, attempting to explain myself with a croaking voice, which is barely able to leak out, "I . . . I . . . I . . . I don't know how else to say it, what I feel for you. And it's not my fault that language is a system of control, right? Right? Right?"

Her face is so close to mine that I can feel her lips forming words, her breath tumbling out in a damp, angry rush that sticks to my skin. "What is wrong with you?" she growls, "Why are you trying to ruin this? Ruin what we have?"

I blurt out that I cannot help it if I am a romantic nihilist.

She starts laughing. She lets go of my neck. She kisses me and says, "That would be wonderful, but you can't be both. A nihilist is a romantic who has been crushed by disappointment too many times and realizes that all of the fairy-tale dreams you have been taught to hope for are not real."

"Besides," she adds, "you are neither."

"Then what am I?"

"Nothing, no one. A human animal, just like everyone else,"

I tell her that just won't cut it in today's market, and I ask whether the producers are aware of this decision, because the youth of the world are throwing money into everything, searching for something to identify with, and I could be that something. All I need is a cause, an identity to define my character. After all, we need the young behind us in order to change the world, right? Right? Right?

"Wrong." She says that to change the world I need no one, because -isms bind us, belief systems separate us, and any system that claims to be the truth or the way is a lie.

"What about the steps for recovery from Western Civ—"

"Lies," she says.

"What? I don't understand. Why am I—"

"You don't need to understand," she tells me. "And I don't need to explain. Avoid labels of all kinds at all times. They define. To be defined is to be limited, to be in a cage, a prison."

My head is starting to hurt from all of this thinking.

The lights snap on and I'm snow-blind, blinking, trying to make the whiteout disappear. When it does, I see that the gang's all here.

Not-Jewish Derrick and Normal John continue filming.

Not-So-Little Joe is dressed in beachwear, flip-flops and baggy shorts full of loud colors. He is covered in someone else's blood. He announces that this conversation has already used up enough energy to suck ten thousand gallons of oil from the earth. »

And everyone starts laughing, on cue.

Joe looks at me and calls me *friend.* He says, "Bottom line." He asks me if I feel anger or frustration, sadness or hate about what is happening in today's so-called civilization.

I surprise myself by saying my line with honesty, by saying *yes* and really feeling it.

"That's enough then. It's all you need," says Deirdre, her muscles rippling beneath jiggling skin as she leaves the room.

My eyes cannot keep from following her, watching her, and that's when I notice that Normal John is wearing a three-piece suit. Black blazer, black socks, black shoes, black belt, white shirt, red tie. He is also covered in someone else's blood.

So is Not-Jewish Derrick, but he's dressed as a Rabbi.

Lying here naked, with all of them looking at me, smiling, filming, I ask, just to break the silence, "What's up with all of the blood and the costumes? I didn't see a Rabbi and a business man and beach bum in tonight's script."

Joe says tourist.

John says politician.

And I see that Joe is indeed a tourist, with his farmer's tan, camera and travel brochure. But John I do not get politician from until he removes the camera from his face, and then I notice that someone from makeup has done a masterful job of creating the illusion of two distinct, yet subtle, faces on top of one another.

His second face smiles, the first one looking angry, as he tells me, "Mockery is the second sincerest form of hate."

I open my mouth to ask what the first is, but all three of them say, "Violence."

And Deirdre walks out of the master bathroom, still naked, but with a Miss Earth banner across her chest and open-oozing-bloody-puss-filled sores all over her normally perfect body.

She parades around the room, strutting, shimmering, the others whistling and catcalling, and then she stops, smiles, plastic, as she says that if she had only one wish . . . it would be for world peace.

Everyone cracks up, mock cheering, but for some reason I am the one who feels insane. "What the hell is going on?"

Joe says that it's Halloween.

John tells me that the producers called with a script change.

Derrick says it's a practice run for the end of the world scene.

I am naked, on the floor, exposed, all eyes on me, and I'm covered in drying, flaking, sugary Deirdre, so I decide to go along.

I'm excited: the script says so.

I ask Deirdre, "So who am I?"

She tells me that I am the 93rd greatest on-screen presence of my generation, but that the movie is a long way from being over and I could still reach number one.

It all depends on how good I am at dying.

fourteen / rewind

MY SECOND DAY in a life revisited.

I am burned, disfigured: too ugly to be alive.

Two detectives are questioning me about Sarah's disappearance.

And I'm on a morphine drip, controlled by a button in my hand. It leaves a stale, greasy taste in my mouth and a foul smell in my nose that mixes with the scent of my own charred flesh, but other than these two minor complaints, I think that morphine may be a new necessity for breathing.

I squeeze the button.

The cops shimmer, as if under water, moving slowly, and it takes them like ten minutes to say three words.

Where . . .

Is . . .

Sarah?

I laugh, because it is basically impossible not to, and tell them, “Sarah was here yesterday, but I think she’s gone now. I’m not exactly sure where to, though.”

I am told that my wife was most definitely *not* here yesterday.

I let my eyes move about the room, but I can’t see the director anywhere. I haven’t seen the script for this scene, so I improvise: “You see, Little Joe, before I knew he was not so little, threw my wife out of the 50th floor window of our condo, wrapped in a rug. She was ODing on heroin, even though she never did heroin, and that was what? A year ago? The same night I was kidnapped at gunpoint to make a movie that would change the world. And I hadn’t seen her—I thought she was dead—until yesterday when she came to see how I was doing.”

The cops say nothing as they write everything down in their tiny spiral notebooks, but their faces show serious doubt as to my credibility.

The euphoric feeling I had is now fading.

I squeeze the button, slide a little further from their reality, and I say, “Honest, officer. It’s true, she was here.” I have to giggle, though I’m not sure why.

They consult their files.

They look at each other, passing a tiny nod.

The younger fat one stands up to not-so-gently slap a handcuff around my surprisingly unburned wrist, then anchor the other end to the hospital bed rail.

The older fat one remains seated.

"You have the right to remain silent. . . ."

I squeeze the button.

"Anything you say can and will be used against you. . . ."

I squeeze the button.

"You have the right to an attorney . . ."

Blah-blah-blah.

I'm not even listening anymore, just floating far away, with the biggest smile on my suddenly not-hurting face.

And time plays a trick on me.

I close my eyes, then open them, and the detectives are wearing different clothes, standing in slightly different places. The pain is rumbling, growing, sharpening, and I squeeze the button, but nothing happens.

Squeeze.

Nothing.

Squeeze.

Nothing.

The young fat piggy says, "Hey there, Superstar. Looks like your little dope baggy is empty now."

I try to look, but the tiniest movement is pain beyond pain. I am a sack of rotting, half-cooked meat and bones being tossed to and fro on an ocean of razor blades. I open my mouth to scream, "I have recognized that there is a problem!"

The piggies frown.

"I did not kill my wife or my agent or my publicist. But I waive my rights and give you permission to kill me right now!"

The older dick finally speaks: "No shit you didn't kill your agent and your publicist. They're out in the hall with your lawyer."

My mind screams *what*?

And I scream, "What?"

In walks Bob-the-agent and Karen-the-publicist, right on cue, with a woman I know from nowhere.

Bob, swarthy, in his knock-off Armani Suit.

Karen, past-her-prime whorish, in her favorite Gabardine-by-Prada.

But the unknown woman is all business. Pantsuit: gray, wool. Briefcase: full. Dark brown hair pulled back tightly in a bun. She's wearing thick horn-rimmed glasses, and even though she is not exactly beautiful or stunning, more like plain-Jane pretty, I still feel the stirring of an adolescent librarian fantasy.

I am happy to find out that my genitals are not burned.

While Bob and Karen begin their sycophantic fawning over me, the librarian tells me that she is my lawyer. She instructs me to say nothing to anyone about anything.

I find her domination comforting.

I'm probably in need of some serious therapy. I think the word I'm looking for is *deprogramming*, but I'm not sure. The only thing I am 100 percent sure of is that I need some more morphine.

I scrunch my face, grimace, let the pain show, and plead with my eyes, mouthing the word, "Morphine."

And Karen, who used to not return my phone calls for weeks on end, totally flips out. She points over my shoulder somewhere and starts yelling that I need more medicine.

I laugh at her choice of words: *medicine*.

She runs out of the room, shouting at people in the hall.

Bob, who's been my agent for years and periodically treated me like a pariah, leans in close and whispers into my ear. He says that this is fantastic, that I've really hit the Big Time, that this kidnapping thing is the best career move I could have made and that the press is en masse outside the hospital. I'm all over the news, and the phone is ringing off the hook.

He says, "Babe."

He says, "It's finally happening. You're going to be a star."

I'm thinking I cannot wait to fire them.

I'm kind of sorry Deirdre didn't kill them.

This whole thing—the entire scene—feels like I'm being kidnapped all over again.

fifteen / fast forward

TEXAS.

I've been dreading today's scene ever since I awoke.

You see, every night I slide into a dreamless sleep, holding Deirdre's soft, easy-breathing flesh in my arms, and I wake up holding a single sheet of freshly typed paper: the script of my life for a day.

It tells me who I am, my name, occupation, likes, dislikes, subtle forms of neuroses and/or mental hang-ups common in today's society.

I have grown to look forward to what each day's script has in store for me, but today's frightens me. It has only two words, centered, stark black ink in a sea of white.

Field. Trip.

Once upon a time, in a whole different life, these words would have excited me. You might think now that two little words—two innocent words—should not inspire such dread, but I assure you that there is no such thing as an innocent word.

All words bear intention. That is their nature.

I get up.

I shower.

I head downstairs to join the rest for breakfast, hoping my fear is unjustified, yet waiting for it to blossom in full.

I tie off my arm, and Deirdre injects me with whatever I have been eating for breakfast for the better part of two years. I'm not exactly sure what it's called, but I've developed a very sincere appetite for it. >>

I want to ask what the script means, but she's busy on the phone. She yanks the needle out of my arm and listens intently.

She silently mouths the word, "Producers."

Normal John and Not-Jewish Derrick are arguing over the benefits of a Jesus who did not get crucified versus one who did, and I have no desire to have my opinion requested of me, so I look away.

I look out at the pool.

I've seen very little of Not-So-Little Joe lately. He is writing "very subtle yet important letters" in an outside cabana that is off limits to the rest of us. Thick plastic covers the closed door, and stolen crime-scene tape dangles like yellow party streamers from its frame. Every time I see him emerge from his isolation, I feel like I'm under water, holding my breath, because he's dressed in deep sea diving gear and jumps into the pool.

The pool is also off limits.

This morning I watch it happen again, as it has all week.

I don't think Joe sleeps.

I think the word I'm looking for is *dedicated.*

But it might be *demented.*

He emerges from the cabana room, dressed like a man on the moon. He jumps into the pool, sinks, thrashes around, strips down, climbs out, and walks through the sliding glass door to plop down for breakfast.

Meals are the only time I see everyone at once.

This morning Joe has the same as always: nine candy bars and a six-pack of Coke. He administers the shot himself. He catches me studying him and flips me the bird, calls me a homo. He asks me when I'm finally going to just fucking die and leave him alone. He scowls, because that's his way of smiling.

I ignore who he is, because his personality is not meant to be taken personally, and I ask him who he's writing to out there.

"Only the finest," he says. "Congressmen, senators, representatives, donkeys and elephants, because they're all the same. And I wrote Tom Brokaw, because I'm tired of seeing that well-practiced faux concern in makeup-accentuated bags under his eyes."

Deirdre hangs up the phone, even though I never heard her say a single word, and tells me that I have Tourette's syndrome.

What?

She announces it is time to go.

I scream the word *Fuck* fifteen times, with extra emphasis on the *F*. Spit flies from my mouth. I do not breathe. I almost pass out. But then I'm fine, because to me it never happened.

The words echo out into the silence of the museum.

This is Tourette's syndrome.

This is our field trip.

It feels really good to have my earlier premonition of dread thoroughly confirmed. I'm more than just uncomfortable here, because I am no doubt only a few moments, at best, from being proven a complete idiot.

You'd think that I would get used to it.

I don't.

We've just entered the museum and the overweight, overaged security guard is walking toward us with a very large frown drooping on his face. No doubt he's unaccustomed to hearing the F-word bounce off the stone walls of his hushed-word place.

My problem is this: I do not "get" art. I hate it. It always has to be explained to me, like I'm a child, and then usually the explanation has to be explained, too. It is just way too much brain activity for something that does nothing for me.

Deirdre explains my mental condition to the rent-a-cop,

and he looks at the Rolex on my wrist, the casual Yuppie-wear we are all dressed in. He decides that we are good, normal, rich, civilized, sophisticated people.

He doesn't know that our wardrobe comes from dead people.

Hey, you can't take it with you, man.

The cop apologizes, says to enjoy our visit.

And I let out with another violent string of obscenities. "Fat-pig-shit-dick-ass-licker." I smile and tell him, "Thank you so much, office-sir."

He's not sure whether to punch me or walk away.

Clicking heels announce our departure, and I cannot help but think of the fact that some poor bastard spends several hours each night waxing this vast expanse of black-and-white-checkered floor, only to do the same the very next night.

You see, tomorrow it could be me.

I never know what the script has in store for me, who I will be, and this makes me think about all of the terrible jobs people do for a living. *For a living* people do things you'd rather die than do yourself.

We stop at the first wall of paintings, which to me looks like a bunch of rectangular windows looking into a cartoon world of people and landscapes, and I'm waiting for the intellectual banter of brush-stroke, light, symmetry, arrangement, abstract thoughts of hidden meaning.

But Not-So-Little Joe snorts and lights a smoke, saying, "The no smoking sign really moves me."

"I've seen better graffiti," says Deirdre.

John says he feels nothing.

Not even hate, adds Derrick.

Their words make me so happy! The Tourette's kicks in. I stamp my foot, snort, say the word *Shit* thirteen times, using several inspiring variations, and then breathe deeply.

Joe smiles. He says, "Shitalicious, that's a good one."

Deirdre asks me, "What's up with joy?"

What?

"Happiness is not an expression that agrees with your second face," she tells me.

And so I explain the whole thing to them. The dread. How I don't get art. I even go so far as to say that art equals shit.

Oops.

Everyone turns to ice.

I shiver.

Deirdre has this blank look in her eyes that makes me angle my hips to protect my stomach.

Joe says, "No. . . . *People* equal shit, and you're one of them."

But the violence reaches me from somewhere unexpected.

Not-Jewish Derrick slaps me right in the mouth.

I stumble, flail, and drop to my knees on the very un-giving marble floor. The taste of my own blood, coppery. My lips have that fresh-from-the-dentist feeling of swollen numbness.

I am anger.

I stand up, square up, ready to fight it out, and say, "I'm tired of being knocked down, tired of being the group's stepchild."

Derrick's face is so full of rage that he looks like a painting, somewhat cartoonish, as he pulls out his grimy gun.

People scream.

I scream.

Derrick points death in the general direction of my face.

And I am a little brave, mostly stupid, basically uncaring about dying, because to me this is taking a stand for something, even if I'm unable to name just exactly what it is.

The fat old security guard is waddle-running toward us, struggling to draw his weapon from a holster half-buried beneath a thousand steak dinners.

Derrick's dark eyes are indecisive, but then his jaw sets.

Bang!

I hear the shot, see the spark, feel the air rush past my face, and I turn in slow motion to see the rent-a-cop standing stalk-still, his hands up guarding his face, with his pants down around his ankles.

Sadly, he is a briefs man.

Deirdre screams something.

All the other people in the museum get down on the floor, on their bellies, hands on their heads.

My ears stop ringing as Deirdre points two fingers at her eyes, the front door, then flicks them too rapidly for me to read.

Normal John takes off running to the entrance.

Not-So-Little Joe takes off in the other direction, down the hall, disappearing around a corner, heading somewhere deeper into the museum.

I'm still standing, doing nothing, freaking out.

Deirdre announces to the museum patrons littering the floor that we're all going to have an impromptu art class. "Your input is welcome," she says kindly, "but ignorance will be severely punished."

I just can't stop breathing, can't stop cussing, can't stop thinking that this day is about to end even worse than it began.

Field. Trip.

sixteen / rewind

PLASTIC SURGERY.

I'm told this is my only option, if I want to look even remotely human again.

I say I'm pretty sure I do.

This makes Bob-the-agent very happy. For the last hour he's been telling me that image is everything, that beauty is respect, and that an ugly, burned hero is not a hero at all.

I let him go on because I hate him. I like to watch him squirm, sweat, do everything except hang himself, just to get me to agree with him on the slightest details, the most obvious decisions.

This hospital room has become my temporary home, part-time conference room, permanent prison, and it is always filled with people I love to hate—the single exception being the naughty librarian who is my lawyer. She is sexy and smart. She spends far too little time here with me.

I can't remember her name.

Bob is on the phone with a plastic surgeon.

Karen-the-publicist is showing me pictures on a laptop: pictures of hair, ears, eyes, noses, lips, chins. She tells me to pick one of each.

My librarian-lawyer is saying, "We will not waive time. We'll rely on due process and the right to a speedy trial, because the district attorney has no witnesses, no body, no evidence to convict you of killing your wife."

I say that I didn't kill Sarah, in fact I don't even think she's dead anymore, because I just saw her last week.

She looks at me through those ugly-thick-black-sexy glasses and says, "You're on a lot of morphine right now, but I believe you."

I'm thinking that I'm not so sure if I can believe *her*, because if lying is acting, then lawyers must be the best actors on earth.

Her cell phone rings and she politely excuses herself to answer it. She turns her back to me.

Karen shows me a picture of mismatched features, a face

that kind of resembles a unisex Rick Springfield. «

"The eighties are over," I tell her. "Can we get on with it?"

The nurse walks in, checks my vitals, scolds me for turning off my heart monitor, clicks it on.

And beep . . . beep . . . beep . . . goes my heart on morphine.

The nurse winks at me and leaves the room.

You see, she caught me masturbating last night because my heart rate increased. And even though she is butt-ugly, I let her finish the job for me. She said I have nothing to be ashamed of, that people who've been through traumatic experiences and are badly injured often masturbate until they start feeling better, because it allows them to have the illusion that they're still in control.

And even though she borders on hideous, I think I'll let her do the same good deed for me tonight. It's not that I have any illusions of control, it's just that I'm really bored.

Karen shows me a flat usual image of what I'd look like if Tom Cruise and Charlize Theron were my parents.

I tell her the color is a little off, laughing.

She starts to fiddle with it.

Bob comes over to say it's perfect.

But me, I'm not so enthusiastic. "Yeah. . . . I guess. . . . I mean, it's better than my first face, but what about the rest of me?"

I'm told we've only just begun.

I sigh, hit the morphine button, and slide. Flooding warmth. Everything shimmers, then clears.

Karen shows me pictures of sexy legs, bare asses.

I say, "The masses are asses." But I laugh alone, which angers me much more than it probably should.

I feel out of place here, with these people.

I hit the button, slide a little further away, say I don't want to look at these digital parts of people anymore, that I need to get some rest.

Bob says a little R & R might do me some good.

And beep-beep-beep, goes my heart as my mind pulls a trigger.

My fantasy librarian, real-life lawyer, clears her throat too obvious, too loud, and everyone's attention is hers.

To me, she always looks like she wants to smile at me, but won't allow it. The corners of her wide mouth, her thin lips, are always in the process of a smile that never quite shows. And there's nothing at all familiar about her, which in itself seems rather familiar to me.

It's hard to explain.

I'm trying to remember her name.

And she tells us all, "There may not be a trial after all."

I cannot even begin to relate to you the relief I feel. My faith in the Justice System is basically the same as my faith in God, that if they exist at all, it is only to punish me.

Bob and Karen look like parents who've lost their favorite foster child, the one with the biggest government check, because their faces are half-hidden anger, and both of them ask just what exactly has changed.

My lawyer actually frowns at them. She turns her eyes to me, resumes the almost-smile, and tells me that apparently the group of individuals who kidnapped me, killed my wife, held me captive for almost a year and then tried to blow me up . . . well, apparently they've sent a videotape to her office.

What?

Bob and Karen are Siamese twins, joined at the money clip. They ask what's on the tape, their voices melt into one. It's kind of creepy.

My lawyer looks at them the same way I would if I still had enough facial features to express disdain, disgust, mistrust.

There are no mirrors here.

When I tried to smile as the nurse changed my bandages earlier, Bob grimaced and Karen ran for the bathroom.

My lawyer tells us all that the tape remains unviewed. >>

And then everyone is looking at me, like I know what this is all about, as if I know what is on the tape.

I click the button, watch them shimmer, slide away, and I'm thinking that this woman, my sexy lawyer, never said her name. In fact, I haven't heard anyone say her name.

They are talking amongst themselves, a long way away. And the name that is forming in my brain, tickling my tongue, I leave it unspoken, choosing to swallow it down, letting it fill my chest with a strange mixture of hope and dread. Tingling.

Mmmmmmmm.

Delicious.

seventeen / fast forward

THE IMPROMPTU ART CLASS is in progress.

Deirdre enlists the help of our classmates/hostages to strip the wall near the front entrance of crappy motel paintings and replace them with several that Not-So-Little Joe brought back with him from scavenger trips deep into the museum.

I stand, shaking, cursing.

Deirdre tells me to look, but not see.

She says to speak what I feel, not think.

And there is a painting of a man which is almost childishly rendered. It is all manic blues and yellows. It looks messy and frantic and the guy in the painting has a bandage wrapped around his head. He looks cold, ugly, beyond depressed, and it reminds me of The Bums who have been stalking me ever since that terrible night in a church somewhere deep under New York City.

What I feel I can't say, so I just start laughing because

there are no words to describe.

Joe starts laughing with me, not at me.

Deirdre joins in.

Even some of the captive class—

"Freeze!"

Everyone does, silent, except Joe. He just keeps laughing, harder and harder, louder and louder, as the two police officers who are crouching down in the hall repeat their command to freeze, then tell us to lie face-down on the ground with our hands spread wide.

I freeze, stare, watch a shadow behind them grow on the wall, rising, moving, the size of a nightmare.

The sound is so sudden, so loud that it hits me with a physical force, hurting my brain, stopping my heart, as a city bus comes barreling, crashing through the front entrance of the museum in a storm of flying glass and twisted metal door frames.

Everything inside of me stops.

Everything around me explodes in chaos.

And bullets start to fly in all directions, slicing through the air too close, ricocheting off of stone walls like tiny pinballs bearing the gift of death.

The bus is on fire.

The lights go out.

It starts raining.

Suddenly I'm running for the hole in the wall that only moments ago was a stylish glass entrance. I'm joined by twenty or thirty people moving together as one massive, pushing, stumbling pack of animals high on the scent of fear.

This is herd mentality at its finest, in action.

I run through rain, fire, over glass and bodies, and when I finally emerge from the smoke it is like walking onto another planet, the sun blinding me with its warmth from ninety million miles away and no one screaming or running.

I blink.

I breathe.

>>

Normal John is waiting at the curb in our new stolen car. He's sitting in the back seat, pointing a camera at me and reading a book.

What?

I want to scream and yell at him, but I can hear the distinct sound of sirens not so far away, and growing louder. I jump in the driver's seat.

Black wire touches red.

The engine coughs, spits, roars to life.

Normal John says, "Idiot." He tells me that I'm in Deirdre's seat.

I do not even bother explaining about cops and sketch-artist renderings of our likenesses being on tonight's evening news, because I'm aware that step five says that there is no higher power, and so I just say, "She said it's cool."

He goes back to his book.

The sirens are closer, shrieking.

I'm gunning the engine, standing on the brake, and waiting.

That's when I see her. Deirdre. Strolling out of the smoke and the flames without a care in the world. She's wet from the sprinklers, strutting, sexy, saucy, strong, deadly, with a gun in each hand and a police cap on her head, smiling.

This is fun for her, says my mind.

Derrick and Joe are just behind her, their arms full of wet paintings, leaking, running, as they calmly walk, unhurried.

The bus, buried halfway in museum, explodes.

Deirdre tells me that I am in her seat.

I crawl over the headrest, sit down on the hump in the back, and Joe throws the ruined paintings onto my lap.

Derrick hops in front, giggling.

The car slowly pulls away from the huge monolithic stone building full of burning art, and in the heavy, breathing silence I begin to laugh also, because I'm thinking of the crazy bastard in the picture with the bandage around his head and the two little words that introduced him to me.

Field. Trip.

It's an indescribable feeling.

You should really just try it for yourself.

eighteen / rewind

THERE IS NO NIGHT AND DAY.

The lights click on, the lights click off, but it is a fake representation of reality. I had the nurse remove the clock from the stark whiteout that is my room. This had nothing to do with time being a system of control. It was banished for mocking me.

People come and people go.

This makes very little difference to me, because sometimes I am here and sometimes I am not. I like to push the button and let the morphine wash them away, take me away. I am not really sure which one of us is leaving anymore.

But today is different.

Kind of.

I had morphine for breakfast, but I haven't clicked the button since. And I don't know how much time has passed in your world, but for me it feels like days. The pain is now a dull knife attempting to cut its way out.

The reason for my determined state of semi-soberness is that I want to be able to see what I'm about to see as clearly and with as many wits about me as possible.

Bob and Karen are already here, sitting in plastic chairs like angry schoolchildren in a time out, and for once they are gloriously silent.

I don't want to give them an excuse to speak—I don't want to open conversation with them—because their sullen expressions over the fact that I may not have to go to trial for the supposed murder of my wife is a priceless beauty to me. But there is a question I must ask them before my sexy librarian-lawyer arrives with the videotape.

I stare at my heartbeat, reduced to green blips on a black screen. I weigh the silence. I ask the question. "My lawyer's name. . . . What is it again?"

Bob says Sheila.

Karen says Lilly.

And they look at each other with furrow-browed confusion that causes me to burst out laughing, sharpening the pain. I yelp and hit the button, then slide away, smiling, warm, happy, with all thought of clear-headed thinking clearly gone.

In walks my multi-named lawyer.

Between the falling-from-the-sky-without-a-parachute feeling in my stomach and the sixth-grade-she's-so-pretty butterflies in my chest, I'm really enjoying this part of the movie.

I wish I knew where all of the cameras were.

Maybe Not-Jewish Derrick is above me in the ceiling shooting a wide-angle filter shot, or maybe he's not there at all. Maybe the camera is a button on somebody's shirt, or the vase which manages to kill its flower every time I fall asleep, and is filled fresh every time I wake up.

I'm still trying to figure these things out.

Bob and Karen ask my lawyer what her name is, adding faux laughter, as if they are embarrassed that it has slipped their minds.

She looks right at me, with that all-business façade and her almost-smile, and says she has returned to her maiden name, Miss Blue, like the color.

This is too rich. I crack up again.

She has brown eyes now.

My mind screams the same three words over and over again: *I know you. I know you. I know you. I know you.*

Karen asks her what her first name is, saying that she had thought it was Lilly, but that Bob had said Sheila.

Miss Blue says, "It's Sandy. Like the beach. Sandy Blue."

"She needed the money," I say. But nobody laughs with me, they just stare at me, and here comes the pain again. I hit the button, slide a little further away.

Miss Blue clears her throat, pulls the videotape from her briefcase, and walks over to slide it gently into the VCR.

Someone hits the lights.

Darkness.

It is time for our feature presentation to begin.

My mind races, playing hundred of tapes, scenes, thousands of hours that were shot during the ten months I was captive. I'm hoping to see Not-So-Little Joe throw Sarah from the 50th-floor window of our old condo, but the tape might also show me and Deirdre having sex, or me shooting Normal John the first time I had some R & R, or me laughing and joking with my captors after I take my medicine.

Most of this would not look good to a jury.

My heart monitor is beeping way too fast, too loud.

Miss Blue comes over in the dark and shuts it off, then stands next to me, so close I can smell her skin. She does not smell like the beach, and my mouth is watering.

The screen flickers to life, jet black, promising.

Everyone leans forward. No one seems to be breathing.

Suddenly my wife appears, holding a newspaper under her chin, smiling for our benefit because it's obvious she has been crying.

What?

She is as beautiful as she always was.

I inhale the scent of Sandy Blue, so familiar.

Sarah begins to speak: "I'm sorry. I'm a mess, I know. I've

been crying, Babe. I just found out that you're alive and I'm so happy, because I thought you were dead. I mean, I saw them kill you, babe. . . . Or at least I saw them kill someone. . . . It looked like you. . . . "

She stops and looks off camera, nods, looks back.

"I really miss you. I hope you are doing OK, because they said that this was for the police, that you are in trouble for my disappearance. . . . They said to tell you that, that, that they don't want you in prison, that they're not finished with you yet. . . ."

Fresh tears roll down the tracks of old ones.

My eyes are drooping, heavy.

"Please don't worry too much. I'm treated well here. In fact, I'm the star of the show, you know. . . . I . . . I . . . Please don't be angry, but I've met someone very special, different. . . . I was all alone and I—"

Click.

She's gone.

I am unable to speak, or breathe, or think, because my mind is so full of everything that it amounts to nothing.

Bob and Karen are arguing.

Miss Blue leans over me in the dark, with her breath touching my bandaged face. She says, "I have a message for you."

nineteen / fast forward

IT'S OUR FIRST DAY OFF, no shooting, and I'm drunk.

All four of us are.

I'm sorry the cameras aren't rolling, because this is bound to be an eventful trip. There is no script.

The reason for a day off is one of necessity. Our field trip to the museum caused a manhunt throughout the state of Texas.

Right now—this second—laserjet copies of our artist-rendered likenesses are riding around in the cars of state troopers and blasting across television screens. The only good news is that human animals are still pretty stupid.

The sketches they're hunting look like two million people.

But Texas was just a step, or at least that's what I've been told, and so we are moving on, leaving on a dark highway, in the middle of night, in the middle of nowhere.

This is anonymity at its finest.

We don't exist.

And this is the first home we have ever had that is not a mansion—and it's fully furnished—but I'm having trouble getting used to watching cacti and the desolation that is a desert night fly by our window at sixty-plus miles an hour.

But the wine helps.

Even though I can't seem to shake that Dorothy-flying-to-Oz-in-a-house-being-carried-by-a-tornado-the-size-of-her-concussion sensation, I still think that this is the best idea Derrick has ever come up with.

When I asked him how he thought of it, he said, "Reality is the best fiction. I got it from a novel by Chuck Palahniuk, called *Survivor*."

It's a great idea. I mean, you see them all the time. These sections of prefabricated houses, built to order, furnishings and all, sitting on double-wide trailers and moving down the interstate with thick plastic covering the open-wound side.

Take a knife. Make a slice. Climb right inside.

It's just that easy. One, two, three.

We did it, and so can you. But there is one problem. You see, you'll have no idea where the house is headed. But let's be honest, at this point isn't it all pretty much the same?

There's no electricity and no water, but I broke up a coffee table from the living room set and got a cozy little fire going in the fireplace. This worried Normal John, but I told him that if people see it they'll just think it's an advertising prop. If the truck driver sees it . . . well, his part in the movie will be a short one.

Not-So-Little Joe is laughing at me.

Everybody is getting to the point of total wastedness.

Joe is so drunk that he keeps on scowling at Normal John and Not-Jewish Derrick and saying, "Primatizo!" Then he laughs too long, too loud, obnoxious, and does it all over again. And again. And again.

"Primatizo!"

The funny thing is that it just keeps getting funnier, and even though I miss Deirdre, I am cracking up without understanding the joke. It's like being a part of a boys' night out. Derrick is passing out joints. I smoke, cough, guzzle cheap red wine right out of my very own bottle.

I'm actually relaxed, having a great time.

Then I ask Joe how old he is.

He stops laughing, starts smiling, tells me to fuck off.

The sudden change in the mood is drastic, as I try to explain, saying, "Since you didn't really throw my wife Sarah out of the window of our condo, I don't want to kill you anymore and I actually kind of like your individuality, and I'm just wondering if you were around for the sixties, you know, peace-pot-and-microdot, Woodstock—"

He cuts me off, his face—in fact his entire bald head—turning red as he tells me that Woodstock was nothing but a giant Irish wake for the revolution. "It was the end."

I am unscripted, surprised.

"We had them," he growls, "We had the most powerful system of government in the whole world running scared."

Genuinely interested, I ask him what changed.

The rage subsides and the sorrow becomes evident, as he

says, "Everything, nothing. People are sheep. Talk is cheap. This is an era of pontificating intellectual cowards, philosophers, and when the words get old they no longer take the next logical step, which is action. . . . Action!"

And John shouts, "Action!"

Derrick yells, "Action!"

I get caught up too, yelling the word and asking who-what-where-when-how?

Joe says that I forgot to ask why, that I should always ask why about everything, because it's an important step.

"But I don't care about the why," I whine.

Joe looks away, scowling, hitting his joint, drinking his wine. "That's too bad, because we're all waiting for exactly that to happen."

I'm really enjoying the inclusion. I'm feeling the effects of the high and I want to argue the stupidity of it all, but Deirdre's cell phone rings in my pocket and I scramble to answer it, because I'm hoping it's her calling to say something I know she will never say.

"Hello? Deirdre?"

Nothing.

Static.

Then Tom Waits's voice asks me if I know what is under the world's concrete.

And I know that it's not Tom Waits, that it's the Bum-Messiah—leader of the Bum-People who are stalking me—resurrected from the dead. But I'm so dazed that I give him the answer he craves: "Beach." Then I ask him how he got this number, and if he's called it before.

His gravelly, bluesy voice tells me, "My child, as this world nears its glorious end, our global experience, predicted almost from the beginning of the experiment, will arrive at its obvious conclusion. . . . And systematic oppression, personal depression, planetary devastation, will all be neutralized by the Blessed Apocalypse, returning us to the freedom of Chaos." >>

I cannot believe he is alive, on the phone, calling me his child, after what he tried to do to me.

His broken voice, so different from Jesus' face, tells me, "Control of the current downward spiral will never be regained, but we are Survivors, we will live on until the sun consumes us."

"What the hell do you people want from me?"

"Respect for individual life will only be available by revolution or death, as life on this planet has become very unnecessary."

"But why are you telling *me*?"

"The hand has five fingers, capable, powerful, perfect for creation or destruction. You must choose to do one or the other. You can act or pray, but it will all end the same way."

"But how am I—"

"Open your eyes."

"But—"

"Close your mouth."

"I don't under—"

"Raise your hand and make a fist."

Click.

Tom Waits is gone.

Deirdre is gone.

It's just the four of us, but the others are passed out and so it's really just me, riding down the midnight highway in a severed, brand new chunk of assembly-line housing that is taking me to a place I've never been, never will be again, because I think that I am somehow going to be responsible for bringing this life we all live to yet another spectacular end.

twenty / rewind

HOME SWEET HOME, where it all began.

Crime scene, first scene of the movie.

Everything is exactly the same, only cleaner, which does nothing to comfort me.

A maid has been coming twice a week in my absence. The rent was paid by check, by mail, in my name, and I'm wondering why Deirdre did this if she didn't expect me to leave them, to come home again.

Obviously this is not the case.

This must all be in the script, every bit.

The bedroom window looks like it was never broken, like it never swallowed a body with wet hair, a body wrapped in a bathroom rug, a body that is still missing, and I'm wondering who it was who took that fifty-floor flight.

And how could it go unreported?

And who cleaned it all up?

There are so many questions, so many pieces of a puzzle that seem to fit nowhere in the picture on the front of the box.

And I am not used to all of this familiar furniture.

I am not used to being alone, home.

I'm not used to seeing the new me—version 2.0—in the mirror. It's an odd feeling to only vaguely recognize yourself, to smile and see someone who resembles you, only different, slightly askew, smiling back from the mirror's reflection.

I wonder if it's a two-way, if I'm being watched, filmed, studied, monitored. It's more than a possibility.

I'm trying to get in character, be my old self, because Deirdre's prophecy about all of my backward desires coming true is about to come true. My appearance has been re-created, altered, built to exact specifications and acceptable standards of preferred beauty, and I'm making my first public appearance in the morning.

Unveiled. Launched.

Superstar.

What I should be is nervous, overjoyed.

I feel small.

And *The Big Black Book of Recovery* is staring at me from the bedside nightstand, like a Bible in a hotel room, meant to convict, meant to remind me that there is someone watching everything that I do and that I should behave. Or else.

I look in the mirror and tell them, "I don't have time to read right now. You-know-who is coming over tonight. Need I explain more?"

I decide not to.

The phone rings, on cue.

I pick up the bathroom extension, start running the water into a tub where the dead stranger soaked, and say, "Hello?"

Blood is thumping in my neck, my temple. I'm holding my breath, because it could be anybody. I haven't seen the new script. But I exhale, because it's just Barney-the-doorman calling to let me know that, per my request, he has shown the only person on my personally approved visiting list to the elevator.

"A Miss Sandy Blue is on her way up," he says.

I thank him and remind him, once again, that there are to be no interruptions, that no one else is to be let up, for any reason.

Barney gives me this I-know-what-you're-up-to laugh, and asks me what he should do if "The Missus" shows, then laughs again at his own stupid wit.

I bust out laughing also, because he has no idea what I'm up to, and because I never even gave a thought to my wife showing up. So I tell him, "If she manages to escape, then by all means let her in."

He starts to say something else, but I don't even hear him, because I'm hanging up the phone, draining the unused tub, walking out into my bedroom to dress in casual star-wear.

I haven't seen Miss Blue in two months. Tonight I get my message. Even though I know what it is already, I'm very excited she's back from vacation.

I give my face a final check in the mirror, because it will be her first time seeing it and I—

Paralyzed.

The entire world stops.

My skin shrinks, squeezes, as my eyes register a subtle yet menacing change in the reflection of bedroom scenery behind me.

The Big Black Book of Recovery has been moved.

It's lying face open on the goose down comforter.

I consciously tell myself to breathe unconsciously, to relax, to blink, as I study the reflection for something else, but there's nothing else.

I look through and past the reflection, right into the cameras, which are maybe/probably there, and I tell them I don't have time to read right now.

On cue, the doorbell rings.

I say, "See?"

I turn around, grab the book off my bed, notice it was opened to page 181, and place it back on the nightstand, trading it for the small, shiny, new pistol that Bob-the-agent gave me on my release from the hospital.

The doorbell chimes again.

When I finally reach the door, finally disengage the three new deadbolts I had installed, it is Sandy Blue, as promised.

I blink.

I breathe.

I smile.

I say, "Hello, Deirdre."

twenty-one / fast forward >>

NORMAL.

It is a word I have feared for most of my life. To be like everyone else, a stereotype, a bit player, and yet that is what I do now day after day.

Ad infinitum.

Ad nauseam.

The only thing keeping me from being one of those people you read about who snaps, who gets gunned down by snipers while indiscriminately practicing Social Darwinism with a rifle from a bell tower—the only thing keeping me society's version of sane—is that I know it is only a role for me. It is a single day in someone else's life as an armpit of society.

But even that . . .

Well, I won't stoop to cliches of straws and camels' backs, but let's just say that I definitely passed on a few proposed script changes to our producers through Deirdre.

Of course I am ignored. Again.

Today I'm so normal that I could die and no one would even notice. Today I am a clone of 23 million people, young people—pimply-faced, under-paid, over-educated—working in dead-end jobs at restaurants in which they themselves cannot afford to eat.

To me this is insanity.

Not-So-Little Joe does my makeup, costume.

He takes my gun.

He sends me on my way with a scowl that is really his way of smiling.

Deirdre drives me to work, silence coming along for the ride, and as she drops me off, I ask if there is anything I need to know for today's shooting.

"Yes," she says. "You are a well-practiced, highly polished ass kisser. You are completely normal."

My feet are killing me.

My cheeks hurt from too many smiles of mock gratuity for the five-dollar tips I must split three ways.

If you have never been a food presenter, or a dish remover, or any other sycophantic form of life serving upper-class, self-described debutantes at an overpriced, snooty, French bistro . . . then you do not know how appealing the thought of murder can seem.

I do.

My feet alternate between throbbing pain and mushy numbness. When I ask my swarthy, obese manager where the employee lounge is so I can take my state-law-required thirty-minute lunch break, he laughs.

He says *employee lounge* in the most absurdly fake French accent I have ever heard. And then he laughs—obscenely.

He says my employee lounge is two trash bins out back, and that my thirty-minute lunch break is a ten-minute cigarette break, but not for another two hours yet, when things slow down.

I smile.

I want to help him die.

I do the math in my head, realizing that even if I worked sixty-hour weeks, minus taxes, plus tips, I'd still be barely above the poverty line and could not afford to eat here on the day off I do not have, wearing the elegant clothes I do not own.

The manager's jowls quiver in authoritative anger, as he yells at me to get back to work.

And I'm searching for the nearest blunt object, but decide that reaching in my pocket is much quicker.

He barks another order.

I pull out my pocket comb.

"Chop-chop," he commands.

And I smile wide, because he has no idea that his part in the movie is about to be over.

Go ahead. Ask me how to kill someone with an eighty-five-cent unbreakable comb. I can tell you.

Better yet, watch and learn.

Action!

twenty-two / rewind

SANDY BLUE frowns.

It's Deirdre's way of smiling.

She asks me who's Deirdre.

For a moment I'm taken aback, but then I realize she's only staying in character, sticking with her roll of being my lawyer, that I'm the one acting unprofessionally.

I apologize, lie, invite her in.

Of course I know it's really her—Deirdre—even though the makeup job is phenomenal. I just know.

When she begins to babble on about my new face, I just can't take the inane conversation. Blah-blah-blah, whatever.

I raise my hands in the general direction of my living room ceiling, and I yell, "Cut!"

"Cut. Cut. Cut."

I look back at Deirdre, at the big brown eyes, trying to glimpse the blue hidden beneath, and I tell her, "Look, I know it's been a while, and please don't kick me in the face, but I've really missed you."

Her usual almost-smile cracks wide open, as she says, "It's only been two months." She laughs. It's unfamiliar.

I tell her that we can do the scene later, but that I want her now, this instant, right here, pressed up against the picture window with the lights on and the cameras rolling, just like old times.

She gives me a strange look.

I kiss her, hard, open, hungry.

She responds with equal enthusiasm, hiking up her skirt, standing on one leg, wrapping the other around my waist, her heel digging into the back of my thigh.

I pull off her mask, and—

She says ouch.

Something is wrong with everything. I stop pulling on the flesh of her face-that-is-not-a-mask. I look into her big brown eyes that are not really blue.

Sandy Blue says no. She tells me that it's OK, that I just caught her off guard, that she likes it rough.

What?

I'm confused and it takes me a moment, but then it dawns on me that Sandy Blue is the real deal, my actual lawyer, my adolescent naughty-librarian fantasy come to life.

You see, I was expecting Deirdre, but I'm thinking this is not so bad really.

The phone rings—not mine, hers—and she answers it with her left hand, rubbing my crotch with her right, scratching, digging.

I'm wondering how rough is rough.

Her brows furrow—she doesn't speak—and she holds out the phone in my direction, says it's for me.

What?

I snatch it impatiently, put it to my ear, and tell Bob or Karen or whomever that this is not a good time for me.

But Deirdre's voice tells me that time is a system of control.

And this is what vertigo must feel like, because I'm swaying, stumbling backward to land on the white leather couch.

Sandy Blue takes off her horn-rimmed glasses, tosses them over her shoulder, licks her lips.

Deirdre says she really doesn't care for my new face.

"Then you shouldn't have burned off the first one."

"I didn't really like that one very much either," she says.

Miss Sandy Blue pulls chopsticks from the back of her hair, shakes her head, and the tightly-pulled bun comes tumbling down in long, dark, shiny locks.

Deirdre says to look at Miss Blue.

I tell her I'm already there.

"Do you see me?" she asks.

"No, not really. It was just the name that made me think—"

"No," she growls. "Now. Can you see me now?"

Suddenly I think I do, because I'm thinking that Deirdre is the tiny red dot of light dancing on Sandy Blue's ear. "Oh God," I mumble, but before Deirdre can correct me I tell her that I'm aware about step five saying there is no higher power.

But Deirdre says no again.

She tells me that tonight I get to play God.

Sandy Blue kicks off her shoes, unbuttons her blouse.

Deirdre tells me, "It's time for a pop quiz, Superstar. You are going to quote from *The Big Black Book of Recovery*, page 181, verbatim, or I will redecorate your living room in Sandy Blue red."

Sandy Blue wiggles out of her long, black business skirt. Green thong. Pierced navel. Centerfold's body. She blows my old fantasy away with ease, and I want to stand up, walk to her, take her, but I can't because by the time I reach her she'll be a corpse.

Or will she?

I ask Deirdre where's my wife.

Deirdre tells me I have ten seconds to begin quoting.

Sandy Blue is now dancing to music I can't hear, her hips swiveling, her smooth, tight flesh blanking my mind.

"Five seconds."

I close my eyes, but still see Sandy Blue. I force her to fade into The Black and I struggle to recall the pages I was made to read hundreds of times.

"Word for word," reminds Deirdre.

I take a deep breath.

"Time's up."

"You are not free. . . . You are a domesticated animal conditioned not to trust yourself, not to trust your passion, taught to control your experience of life. . . . You have been tricked into accepting the humiliation of working for pay as an inescapable reality, taught to see things as personal resources to be used up, while measuring your life's worth by levels of production and consumption. . . ."

I open my eyes just a slit, peeking.

Sandy Blue takes off her bra.

"You . . . You . . . You have been conditioned to expect disappointment and suffering, to see it as normal. . . . You have been brainwashed into accepting the tedium of civilized survival rather than the easy fulfillment of a natural life. . . . You are not free. You must break society's conditioning, its control over you, so that it becomes a role you can play to survive in the midst of civilization, as you undermine it every chance you get. . . ."

Sandy Blue peels off her thong. Completely smooth.

Deirdre tells me that I'm not finished yet.

But I've lost my thread, my chain of thought caught somewhere in the green thong that flies over my head. I close my eyes. I breathe in deeply.

"The humiliation of having to follow someone else's rules, of having to sell your life away by the hour in order to purchase survival, of seeing your usurped desires transformed into digital images used to sell you commodities, this should fill you with rage. . . . Try and explore the extent to which you can live freely without isolating yourself and the rage will grow."

I pause and have a momentary lapse of memory. Peeking out through slitted eyes, I see Sandy Blue on all fours, crawling toward me, naked, wild and growling like a jungle cat.

"God is cruel," says Deirdre.

Click-clack!

The action of a rifle's bolt slamming home a round blasts through the telephone, hurting my ear, giving me a chill, and my memory returns.

"Explore outside of the lines, the rules, and you will automatically expose civilization's inherent opposition to the freedom it claims to defend. . . . Dare to destroy whatever destroys your passion. Dare to become an individual. Dare to be truly free."

Sandy Blue reaches me, head on my lap.

I'm all out of words, hoping it's enough.

She unbuttons my pants.

Deirdre tells me, "This is the first time God has ever surprised me. But there is one more question."

Sandy Blue is gnawing, gnawing, gnawing.

I half moan, half say, "Yes," but I'm not sure which woman I'm talking to. It works for both.

Deirdre asks me if I believe the words I just quoted.

To me this is the worst kind of question, because there is no right answer. I'm watching the tiny red laser dot crawl around Sandy Blue's scalp in my lap. I'm trying to figure out for myself if a high-velocity bullet will go right through her and into me.

I'm thinking *yes*.

Sandy Blue does something amazing with her tongue.

And I'm yelling, "Yes."

Deirdre calls me *God* again, says she cannot really trust my answer due to my track record throughout history, and that I'll be retested soon.

I moan. I say, "All right. You be God next time."

She just laughs, familiar, cool, and tells me, "You don't want that, Superstar. If I'm God, *everybody* dies."

Click.

Deirdre's gone.

The red dot blinks out.

It's just me and Sandy Blue and whoever moved *The Big Black Book of Recovery* earlier, and I'm wondering how long they will let me live this life before they take me away again.

And for what purpose.

twenty-three / fast forward

HEAR THE SILENCE about to break?

I can feel the change in me, as I watch the pasty face of my sophistic French manager go slack in recognition of the violence about to come his way.

He manages half a flinch.

I strike his temple with my comb, hooking the first tooth—the strongest tooth—on the artery I know swims shallowly beneath the surface of thin skin.

This part of the movie is in slow motion: the deed clicking by in single frames, sequential photographs of death blossoming to life.

A giant blood flower blooms.

I yank, ripping, tearing. The thick red mist fills the air, coating my skin so warm, but quickly turning cold. And then I am just standing here, breathing in the air he no longer can, never will again.

The tiny office is a silent car wreck. The door half open,

and each person walks by without a glance, lost in his or her own miserable existence. >>

I close my eyes.

My relationship with time and space is altered.

My equilibrium falters as I sway on my feet, feeling slow and feather light. The noisy bustle of the busy restaurant kitchen is far away, muffled, lost in a sea of blood that is pumping, pumping, pumping through my veins too loud, so fast.

As I float away, crack the surface, return to the now, the fake French accent of my snooty dead manger asks, "Did you not hear me?"

What?

The smell of copper turns to orange peels and gasoline.

I open my eyes and there he is, his fat face frowning, ungrateful, unaware, as he re-barks his orders of "Chop-chop" and says something in French that sounds made up.

I'm drenched. Not blood. Cold sweat.

My cheeks ache from holding a smile that feels insane, inane.

I want so badly to do what I just did, but I'm unsure if it would live up to the beautiful disaster of my fantasy. So instead, I say the words I've always dreamed of saying.

"Fuck off! I quit."

I'm looking for shock and outrage, but this man gives me smug laughter, his immensity jiggling at humor I can't see.

He says no problem, that I will be replaced before tomorrow's shift, and tosses green paper—maybe forty bucks—at my feet.

That's it.

I change my mind. I pounce.

I'm killing him all over again, for real this time, and everything is going along just fine, like the fantasy, until I reach out to strike, but the stupid people walking by the half-open office door are not oblivious to my actions, and they grab me with strong arms, pull me, drag me away before I can finish the scene.

Zap!

Electricity races through me.

My bladder releases.

I'm sleepy.

I've been here before.

I should have known they would be watching me, filming me, because we're making a movie here after all, but the script said I was completely normal and so I forgot all about it.

As I'm dragged out the back door, past the rank-smelling trash bins that would be my employee lounge if this were my tragic life, I see two ski masked figures dressed in black, dragging a tall man elegantly dressed in a tuxedo.

Joe and Deirdre with our new houseguest.

Derrick's breath is on my neck, in my ear, as he whispers that it was a really beautiful scene, a perfect diversion, that I am the best thespian he has ever worked with.

I lie limp in his arms.

I want to ask him how many actors he has worked with, how many they have kidnapped and entered into their Twelve Step Recovery Program for Addiction to Western Civilization.

Are my wife and I the only ones?

Will our separate plot lines meet in the end?

Do I have to wait until the curtain call to see her again?

But I'm way too tired to bother, and I'm not so sure I want to see Sarah again anyway after what she did to me in New York.

I think I'm very close to a full recovery.

I'm ready for the next step.

twenty-four / rewind <<

HOME.

FBI.

This meeting has been requested, denied, ordered.

My press conference? Postponed until tomorrow. Again.

The poor FBI agent is hopelessly typecast. He is a clone of every other agent you have ever seen on television. Black suit. White shirt. Black tie, belt, shoes. Short brown hair. Clean-shaven.

Those stupid sunglasses.

I direct him away from the large picture windows because I don't feel like reciting dogma to save his life. We head over to the dining room table that I never use.

I introduce him to my lawyer.

Sandy Blue is dressed for the part today, all business, wearing a brown pantsuit and those thick, ugly, sexy glasses. Her hair is up, pulled back in a tight little bun. She allows a small untrusting grin, a stern nod hello to the agent. As we all sit down at the table, she scribbles something on a yellow legal tablet, slides it over to me, and begins her defense lawyer babble concerning matters of innocence and protection against self-incrimination.

The legal tablet tells me that she needs a spanking.

I mock cough, hide a smile, dry swallow two Percodan, and ask the agent if this is going to take long, because I have things to do, important things.

He snoots, unappreciative.

He opens his briefcase, removes some file folders, and says we can get started right away, but that his partner is the real expert and is running late. "He'll be here any minute."

Sandy Blue tells him that his partner's tardiness does not affect the length of this meeting, because she has a very important oral deposition to take as soon as we're finished here.

I'm trying not to smile, but my palms are tingling.

I'm wondering what Deirdre is thinking right now, where she is, what the script has in store for us today, because I'm thinking that this meeting with the FBI is not a good thing.

The agent says that he and his partner believe we all have information that can be beneficial to each other.

I think the term he is looking for is *quid pro quo.*

I think he flubbed his line, but I don't have a script.

He holds up an 8 x 10 photograph.

I am shock.

He asks me if I recognize the man in the picture.

"Well, . . . yeah. That's Not-Jewish Derrick, right?"

The agent frowns, writes something down, and tells me that the man's name is really Derrick Johnson, a young man that our government considers to be extremely dangerous. Potentially.

I laugh in his face. I can't help it.

Sandy Blue says, "My," that she will not stipulate to the use of the word, "Our."

I catch my breath and ask him why Derrick is considered to be extremely dangerous. *Potentially*.

The FBI tells me that Derrick is a genius, off-the-charts smart, and that as a young man in high school he was courted by every industrialized nation you can think of. And some you can't.

"So who got him?"

"No one," says the agent. "Because Derrick Johnson disappeared almost twenty years ago without a trace."

"Disappeared how? Ran away? What?"

The agent hesitates, says it was originally ruled an abduction.

Sandy starts rubbing my knee under the table, tiny circles.

I try to speed things up, telling the FBI that I don't have time to chase him around the English language.

He frowns again, writes something down again, and tells me that I would be better off talking to his partner about the Johnson case, since he was the original agent assigned to it.

He says, "Let's move on."

Sandy Blue says, "Yes."

I say nothing, because her nails are sliding up my thigh, nice and light, way up high, but I'm beginning to wonder if Sandy Blue knows more than anyone else in the room.

I'm wondering who else is in the room.

Between the windows, hidden cameras, microphones, who knows?

"Are you feeling all right?" asks the agent.

"Oh, yeah. For sure. So who's next? Deirdre? Show me her picture and tell me who you think she used to be."

The agent looks a little confused, a little excited. He asks, "Deirdre who?"

Man, I hate working with nonprofessionals. I mean, this entire scene is probably going to have to be reshot.

"Come on," I snap at him, "What do you mean 'Deirdre who?' She's the leader, man. Haven't you read the script?"

The agent is so excited he doesn't even take offense. He puts pen to paper and asks me to describe her head to toe, beginning with her hair.

"Blonde, red, black, short, long," I tell him. "It's always changing." Then I'm on a roll, going into great detail about her shocking blue eyes, tiny nose, pouty lips, precise chest-waist-hip measurements, hidden freckles, and when I finally finish, I realize I have just described Deirdre with way too much affection, longing, hunger in my voice.

Sandy Blue has stopped rubbing my leg.

The FBI is smirking at me.

I quickly change the subject, asking him, "What about Not-So-Little Joe?"

The agent's smirk morphs into cold hate, as he holds up a picture which stuns me, and says, "Joseph Orimer died thirty years ago."

"Yeah? Well, his ghost is a real asshole then."

The agent is saying something about Vietnam and L.R.R.P.S. I hear the phrase "well-trained killing machine," but I'm not really paying attention, because the photograph he is holding up is changing my truth.

Not-So-Little Joe, mid-twenties, with long hair and beard, is holding a newborn baby in his arms, and he is smiling so wide, so happy, that it seems it could not possibly be the same man I met.

But that is not what has my mind spinning, smile growing.

No.

It is the realization that I am looking at a picture of Deirdre and her father.

Knock-knock-knock!

The sound jars me, brings me back to the here, the now.

The agent says, "That's probably my partner."

I'm having serious doubts about it.

Knock-knock-knock!

I think that this entire scene is about to be rewritten.

twenty-five / fast forward

I AWAKE FROM MY TEN-THOUSAND-VOLT NAP unrefreshed.

Everything aches.

I am cold, alone in a bare, luxurious bedroom of yet another empty mansion. When I sit up, everything bends, blurs, shifts, solidifies, and I try not to gasp, try not to panic.

Unsuccessful, I suck in air too fast. My eyes too wide, mind racing, I try to somehow rationalize all of this blood. >>

I'm not bleeding.

I calm down.

Chunks of image and sound fill my head: Fields of grain rolling past a living room window. Mountains. No more furniture to burn. Montana. This house. Normal. Restaurant. An eighty-five-cent unbreakable comb. Blood. Zap.

Right.

I remember Derrick complimenting me and saying the word *diversion*, and I remember Deirdre and Joe dragging the limp form of some distinguished-looking gentleman across the dirty parking lot.

I look beside me and find what I'm hoping for.

The script.

A rewrite.

Outside the window it's still night.

What I read really excites me in a big way, because this is the first time I will be doing a scene with one of the houseguests the others bring home with them.

I never see them.

Sometimes I hear them scream.

I shower, shit, and then shave for no reason because I get to wear the full costume. Pants, tank top, boots, ski mask: all black. I cannot really describe to you how it feels to put on the mask, to adjust the holes to line up for my eyes and mouth: how it feels to be no one.

You'll just have to trust me.

Or try it for yourself.

I head up the stairs to meet our very important guest. The script has informed me that just in the last year this man took more lives than lupus.

That is quite an accomplishment, I think.

I can't really remember what lupus is exactly, other than it kills a lot of people. But I would not be surprised if it turns up on a pop quiz later on in the week.

When I reach the upstairs landing, I'm unsure which way to go, as long halls stretch out both ways leading into darkness, and all I can hear is my own pounding heart and ragged breath, as I—

A scream rips through the silence with shocking violence, real terror beyond what fear can only imagine. It washes over me with a physical sensation both sickening and exhilarating.

I release the breath I was holding. I shudder. I turn left, walk softly down the carpeted hall, enter the darkness, wait for another scream, strain to hear something less.

And there it is.

Muffled voices. Polite conversation.

Giggles and heavy breathing.

What?

I try to open my mind as wide as my eyes. I open the door. And what I see does not really register right way. Two hundred lit candles, four ski masks, and a naked man with a butcher's knife.

They all stop whatever they were doing.

All eyes on me.

But I have no idea what's going on. The atmosphere is all friendly-pillow-fight, without the pillows and without the friendly, but still the game-like atmosphere.

And the tall, naked guy—clean-shaven, distinguished silver hair cut perfectly, manicured fingernails ash-white from gripping the large knife too hard—is actually *smiling* at me, can you believe it?

>>

Deirdre's lips, at their sexiest peeking through the mouth circle of her mask, tells me that I am late.

Not-So-Little Joe says I'm really missing out.

The naked guy, who is the picture of GQ-businessman, even with his expensive tuxedo lying scattered in pieces about the room, moves lightning quick, swinging the knife at Derrick's face.

Derrick ducks, spins away, giggles like a child.

GQ-Man keeps his smile, looks at me, calls me Terry, says he will never give up his chairperson's seat on the commission. "You pussy," he sneers at me, "You can't even do the deed yourself, you little backstabbing bit—"

Normal John zooms in for my close-up.

Joe says, "Pussy."

Then everyone is laughing at me, calling me a pussy, only I'm the one who feels insane because I am always on the outside looking in.

I step inside the room and shut the door, determined.

I open my mouth to say something quickly forgotten.

GQ-Man charges me, naked, sweaty, screaming like a banshee, with the knife raised high as he comes right at me.

And I was wrong.

Everyone moves, clearing a path to me.

It was not fear I heard earlier.

He's a blink away.

It was rage.

Fight or flight.

twenty-six / rewind

THE PERCODAN are kicking in nicely.

My mind is tracking logic sideways through a cloud.

I try to widen my drooping eyelids, scratch my itching nose, grab hold of a question that keeps slip-slip-slipping away.

Knock-knock-Knock!

Sandy Blue gets up to answer the door.

The FBI agent asks me again if I'm feeling all right.

His voice snaps me back, and I ask, "How did you know who kidnapped me?"

The agent shuffles papers, says it has been part of his partner's theory for the last twenty years or so, but that none of the others ever returned to confirm it.

"Others? What others? How many others?"

He tells me it's impossible to know for sure, that thousands of people disappear in this country every year and that close to 80 percent are never recovered.

I think *recovered* is an odd word to use for people.

The agent shrugs, says, "You should really wait and talk to my partner, but I think the probables number somewhere around thirty-four."

What?

I'm stunned.

I'm hurt.

I thought I was special.

Sandy Blue walks into the dining room, accompanied by another cloned FBI agent, dressed in the same clothes, the same stupid sunglasses, and it takes me three full seconds to realize that my understanding of life is nothing more than a poorly educated guess.

I am utterly speechless, thoughtless.

I cannot explain.

I shake the new agent's hand.

I shake Normal John's hand.

My face is twitching, rectum clenching, stomach rejecting the protein shake I had for breakfast, and I vomit all over Normal John, the FBI agent who has been chasing himself and his friends for the last twenty years.

My knees buckle.

I grab onto him, staring into his plain face, as he grabs onto me. Something in my mind snaps, because I cannot—will not—take this insanity any longer.

I snatch at his waist, snatch his gun, pull it from the holster as I fall to the floor, and I point it up at his fading smile.

I pull the trigger.

Click.

I pull the trigger. Pull, pull, pull, but it's click-click-clicking, because the gun's not working, not loaded, just a prop. For a split second nobody moves, the movie is on pause.

All hell breaks loose.

The first agent pulls his gun.

Sandy Blue screams, runs, jumps on him. Her legs wrapping around his waist, she is punching him in the face, growling like a lioness.

Normal John tries to run, but trips, falls.

I scramble over to him, grab his neck and squeeze as hard as I ca—

Bang!

Something shatters.

Bang!

Someone screams.

John and I freeze.

I roll over to see Sandy Blue straddling a dead man, a bright red stain growing amoeba-like on the thick cream-colored carpet that my wife picked out.

She climbs off of him, stands, points the gun at me.

"No! Don't shoot me! It's not in the script!"

But Sandy Blue stands a different person before my eyes. Her hair gone wild, clothes askew, hundreds of tiny new blood freckles speckling her face, she says she is not going to shoot me, but that I should move away from the other agent just the same.

I stand and quickly get the hell away from Normal John.

But John looks nice and calm, collected, like this is only another day in one of his less exciting lives, as he says, "Pop quiz, Miss Blue."

Her eyes narrow, the gun no longer steady in her hand.

John asks her what is under the world's concrete.

"Beach," she says, lowering the gun, deflating.

My mind is trying to expand, but there are just way too many combinations of different realities with this new information.

Sandy Blue points at the two hundred pounds of cooling meat at her feet, and asks if he was—

"No," says John.

She actually sighs; she's that relieved.

John speaks too loudly to no one who is here, "We need a recycle team. Stat."

Sandy Blue wipes her face and frowns at the blood on her hands. She looks at me and says, "I'm going to go and take a shower now. Are you coming? I could really use that spanking."

I manage to tell her that John and I have a lot to discuss.

"Wrong answer," says Normal John. "The scene is over."

"Bullshit, John. I want some answers."

But Normal John tells me that if I want answers, then I should pick a religion, because they have it all figured out. Just ask them and they'll tell me.

Spit is forming on his lips. He's yelling.

“Or,” he says, “If you want to keep on breathing, keep on acting, you can go give Sandy Blue her spanking.” >>

For some reason unknown and unexplained, I choose to live.

twenty-seven / fast forward

FIGHT OR FLIGHT.

I want to run, but I have been trained to kill.

Taking a life is really the easy part; it's knowing the right time to do it that's tricky. The right person.

My dilemma is this: I know nothing about our new houseguest, GQ-Man, except that he has taken more lives than lupus in the past year and is currently running at me, naked, sweaty, screaming like a banshee, with a knife raised high in a white-knuckled right hand.

Time is broken and I ignore the knife attempting to hypnotize me, the man's rage attempting to rattle me, and I watch GQ-Man's waist because that is what I have been trained to do.

All upper-body movement comes from the waist.

I bend my knees a little, sinking down, standing my ground, and you might think I'm brave, but you'd be wrong, because at the last second I change my mind.

I run.

I turn and I run like the fucking wind.

I scramble down the hall, stumble down the stairs, in real time, at top speed, and I can hear GQ-Man huffing, puffing, grunting so close behind me that it makes my scalp vibrate.

Lungs burning, I turn left.

I turn right.

Left. Right. Right.

I'm flying through empty rooms with no furniture to use for obstacles, with everyone screaming, yelling words I cannot make out over the sound of stampeding feet.

Left. Left. Left.

I fear I can't go on much longer. I fear that I'm slowing down and will soon feel cold steel stab into my back, sliding against my spine like fingernails on a chalkboard.

So I do the only thing I know to do, the same thing I have done ever since grade school when being chased by someone bigger, someone who gains and gains and gains until they are right up on me so close that I can feel their heat, their breath, their bad intentions.

I fall.

I drop to the ground, throwing myself backwards, and—

Crack!

My head, his knee.

The world dims, tilting like a ship at sea, as I watch GQ-Man come crashing down hard and awkward against the hallway carpet far away.

He does not move.

He slides further, further, further, and then he's gone, and so am I.

I am freezing cold, but when I open my eyes I forget all about it, because the big night sky of Montana is filled with more stars than I have ever seen in my entire life.

I am reduced to childlike awe.

This lasts less than one second.

Something is definitely wrong with the picture of the world that my brain is attempting to agree with. The sky is a long rectangle high above me, running the length of my body, bordered in a deeper black.

I breathe in the cool night air, but it does nothing to clear my confusion. I am damp, cold; I smell earth, fresh and overwhelming.

Shink!

Dirt falls from the sky in a separating pile that lands on my legs, and fear spreads its wings in my chest, catching my breath, as—

Shink!

Dirt falls from the rectangle sky, landing on my stomach.

I jump to my feet, jump for the rectangle of night sky above me, scramble up cold, moist walls made of dirt which threaten to give way, to throw me back down to be buried alive.

But someone grabs my hand.

Someone grabs my wrist.

And I am pulled up and out, the sky growing huge and panoramic, as I roll onto the hard, frozen ground. I jump to my feet and ask, "What the *fuck*?"

Not-So-Little Joe is holding a shovel. He says, "It's a miracle!"

Everyone laughs, even Normal John, who is holding what seems to be an empty squirt bottle in each hand.

What?

Derrick's on the camera, solo. He zooms in for my close-up, asks me when I'm going to ascend to heaven.

I show him two fingers: middle, both hands.

Deirdre wipes my face with her sleeve, gives me a violent kiss, and says, "You almost ruined everything."

What was I supposed to do, I ask.

She just smiles, tells me I run like a girl.

"Ha-ha. Very funny."

Normal John clears his throat, asks if we can get on with

the rest of the scene.

Joe slaps me on the back and says, "This is going to be the most disturbing scene ever filmed." He turns to Derrick, looks right into the camera, and warns, "Viewer discretion is advised."

Everyone laughs on cue.

I'm not laughing: basically terrified.

Deirdre asks if everything is in place, set up, ready to roll tape.

John shows her the empty squirt bottles.

"What about the skin?" she asks.

Joe says, "Secured. Five thousand and *one* uses for super glue."

I am totally lost, excited, close to pissing my pants.

Deirdre smiles at me mischievously and tells me to close my eyes, that she's got a surprise.

I search those big blue eyes, but she is too good of an actress, because all I see is sincerity that means absolutely nothing.

"Don't you trust me?" she asks, sticking out her bottom lip.

"No."

Joe chuckles, says I'm learning.

Deirdre tells everyone to get ready, saying that she and I will release him.

I ask her, "Who? Him? That crazy asshole with the knife?"

She tells me he wasn't crazy, just cruel.

The three guys walk off toward the house, laughing, making strange grunting noises.

Deirdre takes my hand in hers. The simple gesture melts me, shocks me, scares the crap out of me. I mean, she's never done anything like this before. Even our nightly sex is hard passion: an invisible step away from violence.

I'm thinking that maybe I'm about to die.

This is her way of saying goodbye.

The grave I woke up in was just my size. >>

Nervously, I ask her what had been in the empty squirt bottles that John had.

"Buffalo piss," she says.

"What?"

Walking together in the darkness, she squeezes my hand and says, "America once sustained herds of Bison numbering sixty million head. . . . Can you imagine what it must of looked like to see them moving across the open plains?"

"Yes, I can," I say, "But it's still amazing."

"There is only one free-roaming herd left. It's in Yellowstone National Park."

I'm following what she's saying and am somewhat saddened by the tragedy, but my eyes are searching the darkened grounds of the mansion, because something is about to happen and I have a very bad feeling about it.

We walk hand in hand, like lovers, a word that Deirdre would never use.

I know something is wrong.

As we walk toward the tennis courts, she tells me, "Each winter, the bison migrate out of Yellowstone and down into the valley to graze, because it is natural, it is survival, it is what they've always done."

Crash!

The fence surrounding the tennis courts shakes as if hit by a car, and I jump so violently that Deirdre stumbles into me, almost falling to the ground.

Crash! Crash! Crash!

I flinch again, and Deirdre giggles as she puts her lips to my ear and whispers, "It's just Chuckie. He's horny." She licks my neck.

I'm wondering what's up with her tonight, what's got her in this mood. And who the hell is Chuckie?

She tells me to stay put, and dances away in the dark.

The tennis court lights blast on, hurting my eyes. They close involuntarily. When I open them again, I am once again reduced to childlike awe.

Chuckie is a bison the size of a minivan.

All I can think of to say is, "Whoa."

Chuckie is shaggy, dirty, and ugly, yet somehow majestic.

Deirdre walks right up to the fence and talks to it like a child, "Hello, Baby. . . . Yeah. . . . Hello there. . . . Soon, Baby. Soon."

"Soon what?"

Joe's old voice yells from the house, "Come and get it!"

Crash!

Chuckie butts his head against the cyclone fence again. His nostrils flare with each inhale, shoot out great gusts of steam on the exhale. I notice that he is excited as only a man can be.

I feel something like embarrassment, because Chuckie is hung like a . . . like a . . . well, like a two-thousand-pound buffalo.

Disgustingly large.

Scary large.

Then, with Chuckie's flaring nostrils and huge erection, I think I know what is about to happen, but my mind tells me there is just no way.

No. Way.

Deirdre says, "Beef is a huge industry for the state of Montana. There is a disease called brucellosis, which can cause pregnant cows to abort. It doesn't hurt the cows, and they're probably just as happy to not have children who will grow up to be taken to slaughterhouses."

The guys are yelling from the house, asking what is taking so long, chanting, "Release the beast."

But Deirdre pays them no mind, continues right on explaining her rationale for the insanity that is about to ensue, saying, "Some of the bison test positive for *exposure* to brucellosis, which doesn't mean they have the disease, just that they've been exposed. And even though there has never been a case of bison spreading the disease to cows—scientists don't even know if it's *possible* for bison to spread it to cattle—the Montana Department of Livestock and the National Park Service kill bison who leave the park."

I remember GQ-Man calling me Terry, telling me he will never give up his chairperson's seat on the commission.

I remember Normal John's empty spray bottles.

Not-So-Little Joe saying that the skin is secure with superglue.

I ask Deirdre a question that is more of a statement: "The piss, it's from a female, in heat?"

My answer is Deirdre's smile.

She opens the gate.

The ground shakes, and my bones vibrate as Chuckie-the-bison barrels past me so close that I can smell his stench, feel his shaggy hair brush against my shoulder.

I thaw, slowly turn around, and watch as the massive animal rumbles off into the darkness with surprising speed. I feel Deirdre slide her hand into mine with that same foreign gentleness she has shown since I rose from the grave.

"What's wrong?" I ask her finally.

She puts her head on my shoulder, saying that she never thought the movie would make it this far, that she's never been so happy, that she's just not used to it.

A scream shatters the night, tearing through it.

I have never heard a human being scream so loud, with such all-out abandonment, such all-consuming terror and pain, as GQ-Man is doing now.

The moment seems to last forever, the scream stretching out like taffy, longer, longer, longer, until finally it breaks.

Finally he breaks.

I know that every time I hear the word *buffalo* for the rest of my life, I will hear that same scream.

I shudder.

Deirdre lets out a small sound of contentment on my shoulder.

twenty-eight / rewind

MY HEAD HURTS so bad that my hair aches.

My mind has been working overtime since yesterday's meeting with the FBI. The thing that really surprises me is that my kidnappers are real people. They have mothers, fathers, friends, jobs.

Of course, this is true of all movie actors.

I was supposed to meet Bob-the-agent and the newly hired Team Image this morning, but I think I know how to get rid of my headache and so I blew him off.

I'm riding in Sandy Blue's car. It's a total hunk of crap, but I needed a ride in a nondescript sort of way and she volunteered.

Sandy Blue is yet another enigma in my life.

I don't really know much about her except that she likes to be spanked, lightly bit on, talked dirty to in a soft voice, tied up with silk scarves—nothing too far out of line really. Butterfly bondage, she calls it.

But I know she is one of *them.*

And cruising down to the Village, as an unspectacular rain gives this city a much-needed shower, I silently contemplate the beginning of a conversation I have very little desire to take part in.

You see, my problem is this: I always have the overwhelming urge to know people, who they really are, but then when I find out, when they open up and spill their guts, I hate them.

Knowledge leads to definition, disappointment.

But this silence is way too mundane, it makes me nervous, and so, against better judgment, I ask Sandy Blue where she is from originally.

She frowns at the rain, says that her story is remarkably unremarkable and that the bookstore is only a block away.

I'm a little pissed off, mostly relieved.

Hey, I tried.

Heathen's Voice, reads the sign.

As I walk under it, through a glass door littered with flyers announcing worthy causes to support, I have a smile, because everything looks exactly as my small mind pictured it would.

Mostly young, mostly long-haired men and women dressed in layered earth tones and Birkenstocks.

A fireplace. Couches.

Dim. Cluttered.

The overall aroma is an odd mix of books, burning cedar, herbal tea, bran, and clean but unperfumed flesh.

The dozen or so patrons give us second glances, a few thirds.

Someone snickers.

I walk to the register because I have no idea what else to do. I mean, I've never bought a book in my entire life.

Sandy Blue strolled off to browse, I guess, because I'm standing alone when the girl behind the counter looks up from a thick, dog-eared book to say good morning.

She is almost gorgeous, in a supermodel-waking-up-in-drug-rehab sort of way. Unpolished. Unkempt. When I say hello to her, she looks me over with a tiny smile that says I must be lost.

I tell her, "I'm looking for a book called *The Big Black Book of Recovery* or *Twelve Steps to Recovery from Addiction to Western Civilization*."

Her smile changes to something along the line of holy shit. "Way cool," she says.

She tells me she's never heard of it, but if I find it, she would really like to read it, too.

The more I study her, the more I realize that she is naturally beautiful, so I look down at the book she is reading, wondering if I can wing it enough to strike up a conversation.

It's a Bible.

I'm at a loss.

"You're reading *The Bible*?"

She laughs, sexy, unabashed, then says, "Sure. It's my favorite novel of all time. If you change God's name to Lex or Naz or Willy, then he becomes a very well-written villain. He makes Hannibal Lector look like a choir boy."

Her eyes are clear, like glass, like she is blind, but she is reading a book and I decide to play a hunch. I tell a lie, explain to her that I am also looking for a book I once read, but I cannot seem to remember the author's name. Only the first name: Deirdre.

She stops smiling.

She says there is no such author.

She returns to her favorite novel.

Her sudden rudeness surprises me. I clear my throat and say, "Excuse me. I could really use your help here."

But without looking up, she tells me that all of the help I will ever need can be found on the shelves behind me.

I'm thinking, *What is her trip?*

Someone taps me on the shoulder.

I spin around, my breath catching, and suddenly I understand the reason for the poor service, because Bob-the-agent tells me that he doesn't appreciate being blown off. >>

Shit.

I tell him that I'm developing my character, that I have a life, that he wouldn't understand, and, "How in the hell did you find me here anyway?"

He says I'm under surveillance for my own protection.

I mock cough the word, "Bullshit."

Sandy Blue walks up with a stack of books for me to read. She places them on the counter and tells Bob that stalking is illegal.

"Yeah," I say, "So get lost. Kick rocks. Pop the clutch. And if you have to watch me, then you should do it at a much greater distance."

Bob looks seriously pissed off, the plastic professional smile twitching, as he says, "I was. I mean, I will. But Team Image just called me, freaking out, because you were missing and the press conference is in less than twenty-four hours."

As I stare at him, hating him, I can't help but wonder why I feel like the least involved person in my own life story.

My mind takes a step.

It asks, *Why?*

twenty-nine / fast forward

CHICAGO, late night.

Another beautiful mansion, empty.

Deirdre is still outside with the guys, burying another houseguest in a back yard that is temporarily ours.

I was excused from tonight's scene, left unscripted, and I'm bored, waiting, watching TV, eating chocolate, and drinking instant coffee. But it's all just a mechanical process because I'm busy thinking.

Deirdre has been acting strange lately, as if she is struggling to stay in character; and at night, in the big, empty bedrooms, she wants me to be the man.

This is a problem.

You see, I've never been very good at that.

But she is soft, slow and submissive, and she kisses me with such feeling, such unspoken emotion, that I am suddenly more than willing to believe in things that don't believe in me.

Then they bring home another houseguest.

Deirdre directs the scene, gives the cue to scram, all the while keeping her new true-smile. This boggles my mind.

I'm thinking I might just risk my life tonight.

I think I'll ask Deirdre some questions.

The television is built into the wall. It's flat and gigantic, and it tells me that 62 percent of Americans are obese, that it's an epidemic. The following clip says we are spreading freedom by bombing the crap out of yet another country. The next segment is about the unveiling of an invention called the *It Wheels* which will supposedly revolutionize civilization.

And I'm laughing hysterically, because it's my new way of screaming.

"Beautiful people telling beautiful lies," I mumble.

Derrick's voice says, "Exactly." He plops down on the carpet next to me with a big bag of turkey jerky and a box of pineapple juice. He tells me, "The press is the hired agent of a monied system." He tells me that the historian Henry Adams said that.

I tell him, "I've never heard of the guy, but that doesn't surprise me because history is completely ignored in today's society." I smile for the camera, because I'm thinking it's a pretty decent line for being unscripted. >>

But Derrick says, "Wrong answer."

What?

He tells me that history is far worse than ignored or forgotten, that it is rewritten daily, romanticized to the point of being one long love story.

Whatever.

I nod and ask him if they're finished shooting outside.

He announces with a grand smile that his brothers are fed.

"Life feeds on life feeds on life feeds on life," I sing.

He smiles with half of a mouth, says that's his favorite song.

Not-So-Little Joe yells from the kitchen that we are out of Cokes and cookies 'n' cream candy bars. He says it's my turn to type.

You see, we never buy food. We just type letters to eat for free. It tastes better, like free money spends better.

You should really try it.

Write to any food corporation—Hershey, Kellogg, Coca-Cola, Procter & Gamble—using a plausible but fallacious company letterhead. Tell them you are seriously considering the purchase of 50,000 units of their product for your dummy-prison, dummy-retirement home, or dummy-hospital, and that you would very much appreciate a sizable sample of the product for a test run.

Bingo.

Free food, your choice, delivered.

It's that easy. One, two, three.

I tell Joe I typed them last time.

"So what?" he yells back.

So I say fine, whatever, I'll do it later tonight, and I ask him where John and Deirdre are.

"John's working late at the office," he says.

"What office?"

"The one tonight's houseguest no longer works at."

"Deirdre went with him?"

He doesn't answer.

It takes me forever to exhale.

"No," says Joe. "Deirdre is upstairs taking some much needed R & R, and she asked to have some priv—"

"What?!"

"It's true," says Derrick, "She really has lost her focus lately."

Before I can think or feel or speak, I am up and running, yelling out her name in my mind. I take the stairs two at a time, knees bouncing off my chest, and I run down the hall towards our—

Bang!

I stop at the bedroom door, blood rushing, temples throbbing, knees weakening, as I spray it with chocolate and coffee that flies from my mouth in a great warm gush.

I want to open the door.

My hand weighs a lifetime of sorrow.

I reach the knob, twisting, but it's locked.

I feel so tired, so hollow.

I watch the chocolate coffee run down, slow and thick, like blood on a bedroom wall, and I close my eyes, start to sway, to fall, but—

Crash! Crash! Crash!

I'm kick-kick-kicking in the door. It flies open. I look inside, breathing in the taste of smoking gun, and I want to run, but I can't. Because there, in the vast empty room, in the middle of the floor, she is lying so crumpled and still that I'm looking for the stain.

Unmoving, I whisper her name.

"Deirdre. . . ."

"No words," she growls.

The joy I feel is like insanity, as I run to her, fall to her, hold her, squeeze her, tell her that I thought she was—

"No! Words!"

I let go, back off.

She rips my pants open, down, off.

Her mouth hungry, hands demanding, she commands me without making a sound—just a look in those eyes that is far beyond driven. Jaw clenched. Brows furrowed.

And as my body bends to her will, her movements, I feel something unnamed grow inside of me, beneath the joy as it evaporates, beneath the pleasure as it consumes.

I do not understand it. I cannot explain it.

But I know that it will never go away.

I will never forgive her for making me feel this way.

In a word: *raw*.

But then the pleasure swallows me, her, the world, and I am left on the floor, sweaty, bruising, drained of my life force, with a stupid smile on my second face.

Something inside me is dead.

thirty / rewind

I AM THINKING SANDY BLUE will not kill me.

Her breathing begins to slow.

Everything is happening for reasons I can't fully nail down, and the last thing I need to do is fall in love with this woman.

After all, she is one of them. And she's no Deirdre.

But this sexy, amazing, living-fantasy of a woman looks up at me in the dim lighting, a thin sheen of perspiration beginning to bead on her naked form. Even though we are finished having sex, she retains that fragile expression normally reserved for the moment just before she climaxes.

I'm lying in a puddle, in the bed my wife picked out, in the bedroom where I thought I saw her die, but there is no other place I would rather be than right here, right now, staring at Sandy Blue's face filled with that fragile expression of pain-hope-fear-trust.

My mind takes a step.

It asks why. Why am I so happy right here, right now, in this moment?

The answer: I miss my wife, I miss Deirdre, but I do not miss Sandy Blue.

I know that seems like an oversimplification, but it is the truth. It makes me snicker, makes me feel small.

Sandy Blue puts her head on my shoulder and says, "Ohio."

I almost say, "What?" but my mind interrupts, explaining that the only logical reason for her to say this is because I asked her earlier today where she was originally from. She had said that her story was remarkably unremarkable, and I had let it go at that, because my heart has always been a tiny blood clot, an annoying scab. Before I met Sarah, I used to pick at it with strangers incessantly, so that it never healed, never went away. It was always getting infected by someone, like open wounds tend to do.

I thought getting married was a lifetime cure.

Sandy Blue is my new disease.

In Ohio, she wanted men, Sandy Blue tells me.

She wanted men with bad breath and self-inflicted scars on their arms. She wanted men with burn marks on their chests from falling asleep while smoking in bed.

She wanted men who were sick and had no health insurance, no medicine. She wanted men who smelled of hair grease and black dye, whose sweaty heat would smother her in the back seats of broken-down cars up on blocks in their front yards.

She wanted men who were fat and bald and washed their cars more than their bodies, men who sold or did drugs, men who had tattoos of unattainable women on their backs.

She wanted men who were stupid and smelled of cheap beer and even cheaper deodorant. She wanted men with gaps in their employment histories and their teeth, with no futures and forced smiles. She wanted men who were junkies, who pulled over their rented cars in suburban neighborhoods to vomit before running home to their wives.

She wanted men who repulsed her when she kissed them.

Sandy Blue wanted men, because she was told to.

She wanted them to call her up. She wanted them to fuck her and mention her with fondness to others. She wanted them to straighten up and wash their cocks for her before sex.

She wanted them to recognize that she was the one single solitary fine thing in their miserable broken-down lives, and to thank her, sobbing with gratitude with their faces in her lap, while she waited for the stoplight to turn green.

She wanted to be inside them much deeper—*much deeper*—than their unspectacular penises could ever be inside her.

She wanted to keep them, feed them, clean them up, dress them up, so that she could finish their sentences for them in front of their parents, so that their oldest friends would pull her into the dark corners of dank bars with sticky floors and old, sad songs on the jukebox, just to spray her with drunken spittle while proclaiming to her how good she was for them.

"What a savior you've been," they would say.

This is what Sandy Blue wanted.

I remain silent. I know this story. It makes me angry and sad to remember how it felt to live someone else's accepted life.

"Do you know why I wanted men?" asks Sandy Blue.

I know that she does not want me to answer her.

She wanted men because she was not all right, she says.

Because in a room crowded with people she felt alone.

Because there was nothing good on television anymore.

Because she fell asleep in the shower for too long, too often, and she felt nothing all the time back then.

Because there were huge dead voids inside of her that nothing could ever hope to fill.

Because she hated not knowing if she was really alive.

Because it helped her to figure out how to act, what to do with her hands, what to say to other people, and it let her ignore large chunks of her life for long periods of time.

Because she could not stop thinking, dreaming, starving for something she couldn't quite name.

And because for small amounts of time—for a single heartbeat even—Sandy Blue craved that feeling we all crave: of being featherlight, like a little girl being carried sleeping from a car into a house, to be put to bed by a loving father.

But finally, Sandy Blue wanted men because sometimes, when she was all alone, she wished she were dead.

Poor Sandy Blue. I hold her tight against me, just squeezing her, squeezing her, because I know where this story is going, the way it goes for so many young women who are told what to want and whom to obey.

Sandy Blue swallows tears and tells me what I already knew: It did not work out well for her.

She got everything she was told to want.

She got so many men.

She got fucked, beat up, cheated on, proposed to, lied to, gang raped, pregnant, and had abortions.

She got high.

She got drunk.

She got more men.

She got black eyes, broken noses, and knife wounds, and she got tired of the foul taste of cum from the men who ate avocadoes. <<

She got fading consciousness and the sound of sirens, and she got the stench of emergency room disinfectant with the blood and the pain.

She pauses.

I wait.

But then one day, Sandy Blue tells me, she got smart.

She asked *why*.

"Why do I want men?"

She got a girlfriend.

She got silk on silk.

She got genuine affection and multiple orgasms.

She got faithful, caring, and nurturing.

She got twice the wardrobe.

She got ridiculed and fantasized over by all of the men she never really wanted.

She got a pain-free smile that felt real.

Sandy Blue got married.

The happy ending that I know is coming fills me with a thick-fuzzy-growing pride for her, as I kiss her scalp, her warm hair. It kind of reminds me of Sarah and me, how we both found a gentle solace in each other's arms.

But then I remember that Sarah is gone and Sandy Blue is not with her wife, and I am hoping that she will say divorce, but the odds are against it.

She got hate-crimed.

Sandy Blue got widowed.

As the tears pool in my eyes, filling up, spilling down, Sandy Blue's voice turns to sharp ice.

Sandy Blue got a gun.

She got even.

She got famous.

I stroke her scalp, thinking I'm a goner. I can feel the disease multiplying, growing, infecting my brain, affecting my thought process, creating a chemical imbalance.

Hey, don't laugh: love's killed more than cancer ever will.

"And here I am with you," she says, her voice returning to the smooth sound that I am beginning to crave during the day when we are off shooting different scenes.

"Wait a minute. . . . Tell me how you met Deirdre."

She never met a Deirdre.

She started running.

She started considering America's newest version of suicide: serial killing.

She started stalking homophobic rednecks, good Christians in the Bible Belt.

"But how did you get involved in this . . . this movie?"

She got kidnapped.

"What?"

"Kidnapped. Just like you," she tells me.

"Then how can you not know Deirdre?"

Sandy Blue sighs and tells me, "It doesn't work like that, because if it worked like that, then it wouldn't work at all."

What?

She says it's more like a pyramid scheme, or a chain letter, or that movie where they pay it forward, where each new link creates its own links, which in turn create even more links. "We all know someone. Nobody knows everyone."

My mind is attempting to expand, but I don't understand.

"No one knows how many people there are," she tells me, "or what the name of the organization is, because there is no organization. No numbering, no hierarchy, no communication. No label to wear."

This whole thing is insanely interesting to me, and it is even more interesting to me that I am part of it. "Well, how many have you met?"

"The FBI agent? The one you called John? He was the third. The other two kidnapped me.

I'm kind of bummed out by her answer.

I was hoping for much more.

"But there is a rumor," she says, "that we are all going to meet after civilization ends. A kind of curtain call, at the beach."

Yet another piece that seemingly fits nowhere in the puzzle. I am starting to wonder how much of my information is basically misinformation.

"Are you going to be there? At the beach?" asks Sandy Blue in a sleepy, sexy voice, starting to slip away from me.

I pet her head, the long hair, the soft skin of her cheek. "Yes. Yes, I am. Me and you."

I tell myself I am not lying, but it feels like a lie.

thirty-one / fast forward

ANOTHER DAY.

Another city.

Another mall.

Everything I see does nothing to prove to me that I'm anywhere I've never been, yet it's true, and here I am.

Here is Tucson, Arizona, and *am* is running the same old scam to raise more money for our push Westward.

I enjoy the scam, the inept beauty of it. It's like a game and I am always its undisputed champion, because I always finish first. Always.

Do you want to know my secret?

Shoes.

When you dig through the stolen trash the night before, go for the shoe receipts. Foot Locker. The Athlete's Foot. Big 5. Copeland's Sports. Red Wing. Mervyn's. Macy's. Nordstrom. Because, you see, more stores sell shoes in a mall than any other item and they're expensive.

Plus the service is good.

You sit down and a salesperson gets you exactly what you ask for, exactly what's on the mustard-stained receipt in your pocket. When they bring them to you, you say yes. You say that your son/daughter/wife/husband/dad/mom/best friend will absolutely love them for their birthday/anniversary/appropriate holiday. As the sales person moves on to someone else, you walk over to the register with the box of shoes that you are now returning because your brother/mother/friend absolutely hates them.

You show the cashier your piece of trash and get free cash.

It's just that easy. One, two, three.

It's a great feeling.

You should try it.

Not-So-Little Joe calls it living in the cracks.

Everyone else calls it stealing.

So, I pull the shoe trick twenty-seven times and I'm done. First again. I sit down to watch the rest of the world die slowly, obliviously.

It is the biggest shopping season of the year—the misspelled Holy Days, Christ Mass—and America is doing what it does best.

Consuming.

Life's soundtrack is being pumped into the surrounding air we breathe by unseen speakers, the same old tired, jolly tunes we've all been hearing since we were old enough to be lied to, but my day is a little less joyful when I find out that I am no longer the champion of the mall game. >>

Not-So-Little Joe is sitting on a bench, drinking coffee from a paper cup and watching kids climb onto Santa's lap.

What?

I get up, walk over, sit next to him, and ask in a nonchalant sort of way just how in the hell he managed to beat me.

"It was easy," he says. "I didn't play."

"What do you mean you didn't play?"

He smiles at me—it's his angry face—but he says nothing and goes back to watching the fat, old, mythological pedophile with the big white beard.

"Not playing is cheating," I tell him.

Joe sighs, sips coffee, keeps watching Santa, his voice telling me that if he's not playing a game, then he cannot be cheating, because rules only exist in the game.

I think maybe he's talking about something else, like maybe everything else, but I'm not sure. I'm never sure.

I say that I—

"Shut up," he growls.

"Why? So you can watch fucking Santa Claus? Don't you hate what he stands for? The consumerism, materialism, the overall deception taught to us early on and forever?"

"Just shut the fuck up for a minute," he growls, smiling. "It's about to happen. I think this is the one."

And that does it. I'm quiet as stone, watching Santa, because I don't want to miss whatever is about to happen.

I'm thinking gun, sniper, fire, blood, death for jolly old Saint Nick.

I watch as a little boy—maybe three or four years old, just a bit part actor—gets pushed from the front of the line toward the fat red-and-white saint. A green midget lifts the boy up and places him in Santa's lap.

"*Ho-Ho-Ho!*"

The poor child, the little boy, starts screaming, crying, scared to death, scarred for life.

Joe is laughing so loud that people stop, stare, frown, form very un-Christmas-like words with their mouths.

When Joe finishes laughing, I ask him why.

I tell him that it's an important step.

"It's priceless," he tells me, "that kids, before we mess them all up, know something is wrong. They recognize that there is a problem."

"Yes," says Normal John.

He's sitting right next to us, but for how long he has been there I have no idea, because whenever we are out in the world around normal people en masse, he just blends right in. I never see him coming.

I don't bother saying hello to him anymore.

I don't think he likes me since I shot him.

He says, "Pop quiz."

I know right away that he's talking to me.

He tells me that since nine one one zero one, sales in teddy bears have quadrupled, puppy sales are twice that, and that religious articles are being bought at an all-time high. . . . Why?

Cakewalk, I'm thinking.

I'm smiling.

I tell Normal John that fear is the basic element of faith and that the threat of death by way of terrorism or everlasting pain by way of hell spawns the desire to believe in something greater than ourselves. A need for security. Answers. Comfort in our—

"That's enough," says Joe. "You're trying too hard." John agrees, saying that the single word answer *fear* would have sufficed.

But Derrick, who walked up to catch the tail end of my answer without hearing the question, says he disagrees, that he thinks my politics are coming along rather nicely.

Everyone laughs.

"I hate politics," I whine.

"Well, it's true," says John. "Language is a system of control."

Another kid starts screaming in terror on Santa's lap.

And once again, Joe laughs too loud, rude loud.

I'm tired. I want to leave. So I ask whomever in general, "Where is Deirdre?"

Joe says, "Gone."

What?

Derrick says that she went on ahead of us, because we're running a little behind schedule, but that we'll meet up with her again once we reach San Francisco.

This news bums me out big time. I miss her already. I ask angrily, "Just what in the hell is Deirdre doing in San Francisco that is so damn important it couldn't have waited for the rest of us?"

All three of them answer me at the same time.

"Building another bomb."

thirty-two / rewind

WALDORF ASTORIA.

My long-awaited press conference.

And you should really pay attention, because I'm about to come unglued. I might just break down right in front of you. Because I need this to be all right.

It is not going well at all.

The location was chosen by Karen-the-publicist for the

elegant class it exudes, but the immense throng of reporters is closer to resembling an angry mob than a group of polite luncheon guests.

This is not the open-armed acceptance I have been repeatedly told is my right.

My mind whispers *Salem Witch Hunt.*

It says *Spanish Inquisition.*

It *screams* that they know I'm a fraud.

But Karen brings order with her plastic smile and a voice doctors use at insane asylums, asking them once again to follow the format, reminding them that I have just been through a very traumatic experience, and telling them that I am still extremely grief-stricken by the abduction of my wife.

I swallow laughter and hide a smile, because I'm pretty sure that Sarah is screwing her own personal version of Deirdre and I still have Sandy Blue's DNA all over my skin, under these new clothes selected for me by Team Image.

I'm fighting a severe case of the irony giggles.

I'm staring at the giant bouquet of microphones piled high on the table in front of me like dead, black flowers.

And whap-whap-whap-whap-whap-whap, a thousand camera flashes blind me like small bolts of lightning.

The tiny, hidden speaker in my ear instructs me to choose the reporter in seat 41 of row 6 for the next question.

I ignore it.

I need to win these people over.

I choose the older woman from *The Times* who started the ruckus, asking her, "Could you please repeat the question?"

Raised eyebrows let me know that I've scored with the move.

Too many sneers mock me still.

The woman from *The Times*, past her prime yet still oozing power, flounders a bit, surprised that I have called on her again. But she regains her composure and asks me for the second time if I could please comment on the rumor that I had sex with one of my kidnappers.

"Yes, I did."

The crowd explodes into fragments of questions.

The flashes blind.

The voice in my ear, Bob-the-agent, screams, "No!"

I point somewhere I cannot even see anymore, off to my left, saying, "Next question please."

As things calm down and my vision clears, a man from *The Press Democrat* asks me if the sex was forced or voluntary.

And that's it. I can't keep in the laughter any longer. My face twisting, the laughter leaks out in tiny, pressurized squeaks.

The voice in my ear screams, "Cut mics!"

The bouquet dies.

The bits of giggle stay my own.

Karen stands up, grabs the podium, yells at the crowd that this line of questioning is just too painful for me, but that the full details will be available in my upcoming book, due out this fall.

What?

I mock sob, mock cough, and pop my third Xanex in an hour.

Karen selects reporter 41, row 6, for the next question.

The bouquet of microphones revives with a whine.

Reporter 41 of row 6 is a man with obvious issues of Tom Brokaw idol worship. He asks me why my wife and I were chosen as victims: why we were the only ones.

"Who's to say we were? If I had not survived the explosion, no one would even know these people exist."

Score.

They are all nods and dawning excitement, realizing that this could be cause for paranoia among the normal people who feast on their hype.

I'm smiling.

I've got them.

They're all mine.

But then the same asshole asks me what these people wanted, what was their message or cause, their purpose for doing this?

I'm screwed.

My mind fills with pictures and words, but no answers.

I mumble, "Step one is to recognize that there is a problem."

Utter confusion on his face, all of their faces, and I can't stop smiling because I know how it feels.

Plus, the Xanex are really kicking in now.

The numbered people get excited, bombard me with questions.

What is step two?

How many are there?

What do they cure?

What is the goal?

Karen, still standing at the podium to my right, gives me the thumbs-up behind her back as she yells for order.

She selects number 224 of row 8, another woman, not so old, with *The Sun*, who asks me what is step two.

"Always ask why about everything."

Several others yell out, "Step three!"

"Step three is to figure it out for yourself."

Five hundred reporters chant, "Four! Four! Four!"

"There are no universal truths. Reality is subjective."

"Five! Five! Five!"

"There is no higher power."

This one stumps them for a minute, but then they are begging me for step six.

I'm having a total blast!

But now there's a problem, because I don't know step six, because I never made it that far in my character's recovery. Tick-tick-tick-boom. Remember?

But they are all waiting. The entire world is waiting for me to explain something that they fear is insane.

I wish I had a script.

The tiny speaker in my ear screeches, hurting my brain. I wince, hold in a girl's scream.

And Not-So-Little Joe's grumpy voice says, "Shithead."

He tells me that step six says you are not who they say you are, even if you do what they say you do.

I hate the fact that I am smiling at the sound of his menacing voice, and I want to repeat the step for everyone, but I've lost my momentum.

Karen is yelling that it's over, that further details will be revealed in my upcoming movie, based on actual facts, due out this summer.

I'm beginning to wonder who is signing all of my contracts, because I have not signed a damn thing since I returned.

Not-So-Little Joe's voice is gone, and Bob-the-agent comes on, telling me that they had some technical difficulties, but that I improvised superbly.

I'm not listening.

I'm searching the mass of reporters who are not dispersing, who are complaining, hanging around, demanding to know more, because I'm looking for Not-So-Little Joe or Not-Jewish Derrick or Normal John or maybe even Deirdre. But I do not see them.

My eyes snag on a stain in the polished fabric of the crowd.

A teenaged boy, grungy clothes, greasy, long, black hair, holding what looks like a radio with a long silver antenna extending up from it.

My mind says *no*, not a radio, a transmitter.

He is out of place, doesn't belong, and once I see him I cannot look away. His presence excites me, flooding my body with butterflies and chemicals.

He retracts the antenna and puts the transmitter into the inside pocket of a dirty green Army jacket that looks older than he is.

I study him.

He jumps up onto one of the tables and yells, "That's fucking bullshit!" at the top of his lungs.

Someone screams, "He's got a gun!"

But he just points a finger at me, calling me a liar.

Security swarms.

He yells out, "Free speech!"

I can't help but laugh at him, because he is so young and so wrong, as large men wearing blue blazers with embroidered crests on their chests slam him down to the expensive imported carpet.

The cameras flash, capturing his struggle.

I make my escape.

But before I leave, I tell Karen-the-publicist to make sure that no charges are pressed against the boy.

She shows me a bitter taste on her face, asking me why.

"Because . . . I want you to bring him to me."

thirty-three / fast forward

THE WORLD IS CHANGING before my eyes. Or rather my eyes are changing the world I have always watched, but never seen.

Everything is more beautiful.

Everything is more fucked up. >>

I am not all right.

The Bitterroots, green beyond green, fly by our new living room window in a blur and I can't stop thinking about things I don't want to think about.

Mainly bombs.

Deirdre is building one somewhere and I have a bundle of questions to ask her when we meet up again in San Francisco, because when I ask John-Joe-Derrick to explain, I am told to take a step.

You can guess which one.

But I can't figure out for myself why blowing up a bomb is going to change the world for the better. I can't understand what this is supposed to accomplish. And no one will honestly tell me what the end goal of what we are striving for really is.

Right now, riding in a brand new piece of assembly-line housing, drinking cheap red wine from a styrofoam cup which will decompose much slower than the flesh I live in when we are both thrown away, I am becoming more and more frustrated with my own ignorance.

Trust me: there is nothing blissful about it.

Just another lie.

And don't bother counting them, I've tried. It's easier to try and count truths—they're far fewer—but don't forget to subtract when they're exposed as lies.

Subtract any number from itself and you'll get the same.

Not-So-Little Joe is smashed, plowed, so drunk that his smile is true. He's doing the Primitizo thing again and his laugh stopped being funny an hour ago.

John and Derrick are pretty much wasted as well.

But I've been sipping.

And they've been gulping.

Because I've got a plan. I've got one bullet in my gun.

When Joe pauses to drain his cup, I ask the vibrating living room, in a very believably uncaring manner, just what we are going to blow up in California that is going to change the world.

Silence.

The hum of our house's tires on pavement.

John and Derrick look at Joe.

Joe looks through me, contemplative, as he tells me that we are going to blow up the bomb.

"No shit," I say. I laugh because I am beyond pissed, and because I don't know what else to do—there's no script. But I laugh alone. Until I hear its hollowness.

Silence.

The hum of the tires, of monotony, of sixteen wheels carrying us toward a better world, tragic death, whatever lies between.

"No. Seriously. What's the target, guys?"

Derrick says tell me.

John says tell me.

And Joe's snake eyes sparkle as he makes a decision, as he tells me, "Tomorrow . . . Philosophy dies."

"What?"

"Philosophy *dies*."

Once again, I'm completely lost. I don't get it. I can't track the path of what I think must be logic, so I ask him, "Who's going to die?" Because I don't know what else to say.

Derrick shows me his half of a smile behind the handcam and tells me that it's not so much a matter of life and death really.

John agrees, saying it's much more radical than that.

They are all drunk, smiling, enjoying their favorite pastime of tying my mind into knots, and I think it's time.

"Action!"

I pull my gun, shiny, new, unused, and I point it at Not-So-Little Joe because he won the "most dangerous" contest in my head. My heart beating louder, the room growing colder, I let myself shiver because every bit of strength is going toward keeping the weapon steady in my hand. >>

I'm trying to appear as deadly as I can.

But the image—the silence, the terror I was going for—is murdered by the three of them laughing at me. Not little laughs, but great big guffaws, holding their stomachs, tears streaming as they struggle for breath.

Finally I begin to laugh with them, but differently, like someone who is not me. Like someone who is insane.

I smell gasoline and burning orange peels.

My skin is impossibly hot, my blood a liquid fever, and I feel like I'm caught in a dream, moving slowly, but when I cock back the hammer—Click!—silence returns, reality turns.

Three dark eyes, well used, pointing back at me.

What do I do?

What do I say?

Not-So-Little Joe smiles wide, angry, as he tells me that this is a side of me he really enjoys seeing, but that I'm wasting a potentially great scene.

"Dying is for finales," says John.

The gun is shaking in my hand now, and I'm thinking that maybe my plan was not so well thought out, because all three of them are pointing their guns at my face.

But a thought blindsides me from nowhere and my face smiles.

And I cannot explain to you what an epiphany feels like.

Trust me, you'll know.

"If I die, then all of you die with me. . . . The whole world dies with me." And when I say it, Joe lowers his gun to show me a smile that is really just a smile.

He congratulates me. He asks me if I am ready to die now so that the world can die with me.

"No. Not yet."

"Then why pull a gun," asks Derrick, "on three armed men?"

And here we go. This is where I win or lose, live or die, gain respect or accept my position within the tribe, because with the three of them staring at me and two guns still pointed at my face, they are now waiting for *me* to explain something to *them*.

I've got one bullet in my gun.

"Well," I say, "It's been a while since I could stand on my own two feet again. . . . And it's been *forever* since I saw any of you take some R & R. . . . And don't you think that the day before you change the world is a perfect time to sharpen your focus?"

Silence. The humming. Drunken thinking.

I watch their contemplation in furrowed brows.

"Who's first?" I ask.

No-So-Little Joe stands up, swaying.

My heart stops, skips, slams in my chest too loud, clumsy.

Joe says that he will go first.

I point the pretty new gun at the smooth forehead, an inch from his shaved scalp, and I'm wishing that someone else could go first because I don't think that Deirdre will be too happy about me killing her father.

thirty-four / rewind

THE BOY'S NAME IS STINK.

I don't ask him why—he's appropriately named.

When I let him into my condo, he walks through the tastefully decorated living room with a look of distaste on his young face, asking me how I can feel comfortable up here, 500 feet off the ground, surrounded in glass and furniture made by dying slave children.

What?

I tell him the couch is Italian leather, Natuzzi, and that the love seat is Versace.

He says I'm blind, but that he forgives me.

I ask him what the hell he's talking about, but he doesn't answer me, just ignores me, strolling, casing the joint. He looks so young, so tough, a walking filth heap in his stained army jacket. Ripped jeans. Black boots, falling apart at the seams.

I'm wondering when he last washed that long, greasy, black hair hanging in his face. I ask him why he was at my press conference with a transmitter.

He stops casing, turns to me frowning, saying that he just can't understand why I'm killing this planet, and that the scabs on her face are a fucking disgrace.

He says he blames me.

"Me?"

Yes, he says, he blames *me*.

I want to ask why, but the phone rings in my pocket and I reach in, pull it out, flip it open and hit the button, waiting for the red dot to appear.

I start to say hello.

Deirdre tells me to get rid of him.

"I've really missed you," I say.

She sounds pissed off, horny. She says, "Now."

I'm smiling, tingling. It's so nice to hear her voice, to feel her intense sexuality tickling my ear-brain-spine-stomach-thighs, and I tell her that I'm just doing what she taught me. I'm rewriting the script.

She says wrong answer.

She says I'm committing murder.

The tingling chemicals, the adrenaline, the excitement, the fear rolling through me is wonderful. She's a special woman. Does it to me every time.

But Stink, he's looking at me with a smile of non-innocence, secret knowledge. He asks me if it's *them.*

"No," screams Deirdre, "tell him nothing!"

But I'm already nodding, and the phone whines—ice-pick sharp in my ear—piercing my brain like a cold needle, with Deirdre's voice filling my home at such a godlike volume that it would take me two breaths, if I were breathing, to realize that she is still only a resourceful animal.

I drop the phone.

Her voice—too loud, too powerful, exploding from my living room stereo speakers—rattles my eyes in their sockets, as she screams that she will not allow this to happen.

Stink raises his arms to the ceiling and shouts hallelujah! He asks the flat plaster sky if it knows how long he has waited for this to happen. To hear her voice. How often he cried, alone, motherless, waiting for her to return.

"You *bitch!*" he screams.

I just stare at him with my mouth open, thinking he's as crazy as a shithouse rat, thinking he's as good as dead.

But Deirdre is a big, beautiful balloon of rage with all of its air seeped out, empty, withered, as she whispers the words "no," and "don't," and "please."

Me? I just can't believe what's happening.

Stink's laughter sounds as dirty as the rest of him.

My mind is blank, its silence filling my head, my living room, my world.

Stink tells the ceiling that he never loved her, can't remember loving her, can only remember wishing he could someday tell her he hates her for what she has done, not done, will do, not do.

"Can you hear me?" he screams. " I hate you, Mother! Hate!"

I am numb, cold.

Silence unfolds.

And the red dot appears from nowhere, somewhere, thin air. The cruelest magic trick. It crawls around on the boy's filthy army jacket like a deadly insect, landing over his heart and waiting. Waiting. Waiting to explode.

Stink smiles and spreads his arms out to his sides like wings, like a crucifix, as he says, "Yes, Mother."

I'm waiting for Deirdre to say that he's lying, insane, or mistaken.

I'm waiting for the click-clack of the rifle's bolt to awaken.

But Stink says, "Mother."

He says to go ahead and kill him, because it's what she does best, right? Right? Fuck men and call them angels; lie, create. Destroy lives and call it necessary. Kill your son and call him the Christ. It's what she does, right? So do it!

Silence.

Nothing.

I'm waiting for death to bloom.

Nothing but heavy breathing seeping from stereo speakers.

Stink turns his back on the tiny red dot, on his mother, on the sparkling night skyline outside the picture windows, as he walks over and turns off my stereo.

It doesn't come back on.

The phone doesn't ring.

The red laser dot has vanished.

I'm shocked, unbelieving, trying to make it all fit, so I ask the boy if he's really Deirdre's son.

I whisper, shaken.

Stink just smiles and asks if that's her name now.

I can't even answer him.

"My mother is a legend," he tells me. "She is a myth, and that left me nothing."

My mouth finally moves again, asking him to tell me everything about himself, his life, his mother.

He frowns, scowls, says that who I really need to talk to is his father.

Again I can't speak. My head is feeling so heavy, my body suddenly weak, and I could not agree more.

Someone is knocking on the front door.

My heart stops, speeds up, and I spin around.

The door slowly slides open and Sandy Blue walks through, with a disappearing smile on her face, a bottle of Dom in her left hand, silk scarves and our favorite giant candle in her right.

And I am stuck on pause, frozen, a deer caught in the headlights, or a lover caught cheating, sweating, red-faced and breathing heavily.

Sandy Blue's brown eyes squint as she frowns.

Our favorite large candle and the two scarves hit the ground.

She steps out of her heels, steps into the foyer, shuts the door and—

Crash!

Tiny bits of green glass in her hair, Sandy Blue turns around with the jagged bottleneck clenched tightly in her fist. With her knees bent, her curvy body rigid, she is ready to pounce. She looks like an animal, crazed, hungry, trapped.

The good news is that she's not looking at *me*.

The bad news is that I really need to talk with Deirdre's son before he dies.

thirty-five / fast forward >>

THE GUN'S A CHUNK OF ICE in my hand. Heavy. Cold.

The trigger's a razor blade, stinging, as my finger grabs a hold.

Not-So-Little Joe is calm, breathing, waiting for me to squeeze, as my stomach moves, churns. Fear rises into the back of my throat. It tastes an awful lot like bile.

John and Derrick stand on either side of us, record lights blinking to let me know this moment is captured, eternal.

I try to hold Joe's gaze, but I can't. My feet are unsteady as our chunk of assembly-line housing crawls through mountains I've never seen. Outside the taped windows it looks so serene, so green, but in here it's so electrified with tension that I want to scream. I bring my gaze back to him.

"Do it," growls Joe.

I try not to close my eyes, but they close on their own as I pull the tiny metal sliver of trigger and—

Click.

I exhale.

"Again," says Joe.

And without thinking about it, without wanting to do it, I pull the trig—

Click.

Joe asks me if I am satisfied with his focus.

Throat swollen shut with fear, I nod my head like a broken doll.

Joe tells John that he's next, and they switch places, with Joe taking the camera to his own eye and John standing ramrod straight in front of me.

But Derrick says no.

He says he wants to go next, in the middle, because the

historical pattern of going last in games of chance is not too good.

He looks unsure, unhappy.

But Joe overrules, saying that this is taking too long, that there is wine to drink and a world to change, and we should really just hurry up with it all.

Half of Derrick's face disappears behind a hand-cam, his mouth mumbling something I can't quite hear, something I wish I could hear.

I turn to stare into the normal face of Normal John.

But this time it's not so difficult, maybe because I already shot him once, and so I just let my breath out as I pull the—

Bang!

Tingling hot pain shoots up my arm. Hand numb, wrist throbbing, deafened by the shot, blinded from the flash, I am lost to the world for a moment of indeterminate length.

I can't see, can't hear, can't believe, but the world fades back in, strengthening my faith, because I'm looking down at Normal John, who's crumpled, sleeping with his eyes open, a small, black circle on the left side of his forehead that looks like a giant horsefly.

I look up.

Small wet bits of him running red down the beige wall.

It feels like I'm floating, with my mouth hanging open, breathing in the metallic stench of freshly spilled life.

Sixteen wheels screeching, chirping.

I stumble, trip, fall, land on top of 180 pounds of clay, still warm but cooling, as John and I slide along the floor of our suddenly stopping house, just sliding along the carpet to hit the sticky wall.

Furniture piles up against us.

Complete madness.

Breaking glass.

Splintering wood.

And then all is still and quiet again. »

I struggle to push a couch off of me and I tell myself that I am only covered in special effects makeup, like ketchup, like strawberry jelly. Not cooling, coagulating blood, but strawberry jelly.

Strawberry jelly!

Joe yells, "Flank!"

I raise up just enough to see Derrick climb out a broken window, as Joe cuts a gash in the plastic wall on the open wound side of the house and slithers out.

I hear unfamiliar, angry words, and then—

Bang!

Bang!

Nothing.

I am all alone in this broken home and I can't find my gun.

I take John's because he doesn't need it, and because I might.

I don't know what the reaction will be for what I've done.

And my mind tells me that I didn't kill him, that this is all just a movie, a game, that it was bound to be written into the script sooner or later, because it was inevitable with all of this R & R going on.

My mind screams *liar*!

Joe climbs back in through the opaque plastic wall, alone, and I'm wondering where Derrick is because I heard two shots.

I'm hiding behind the overturned couch, squeezing an old, dirty revolver, about to completely break down.

And Joe says, "Hey."

He asks me if I know how to drive a semi?

"N-n-n-no. . . . Please, I'm really sorry about—"

"Forget it," he says way too calmly, " Go help Derrick dig a couple of graves."

Never taking my eyes from him, watching him dial a

number on his cell phone, waiting for him to kill me, I climb through the rubble of broken furniture.

The only thing I hear him say before I back out of the broken window is, "Yeah? . . . Well, that's great news, but we're going to need another John before the ceremony."

thirty-six / rewind

STINK PULLS A KNIFE.

And I actually feel my face smile, can you believe it?

I'm still frozen, because fear and the general dislike of dying have reduced me to a spectator. It's like watching some strange nature show about the intellectually rationalized hate of human animals and the illogical spontaneous aggression it produces.

My mind narrates:

Notice how the young Stink sinks down defensively, making himself a smaller target. The knife raised high in his left hand, the wrist bent like a scorpion's tail. He is the territorial transgressor, the trespasser, the threat.

Observe the way Sandy Blue is now crouching down slightly, with all of her weight balanced on the balls of her feet, her skirt hiked up, her muscular legs tensed. She is the larger animal, older, wiser. She is the mighty lioness defending her right to the prey in question.

Wait a minute. I'm the prey?

I ask Sandy Blue to calm down for a second.

But she's locked in, ignoring me.

I tell her that it's OK, that this is Deirdre's son, and that I would really like to ask him a few questions.

"*Please*," I say.

Sandy Blue charges.

Stink charges.

No one screams.

When they collide, it's like some tribal dance or mating ritual. Face to face, they turn and twist and slide in a tight little circle of flesh, their arms thrusting, striking out, stabbing, slicing. The only sounds are soft, concentrated grunts, sharp breaths, a few small whines of pain.

Then they separate, backing away from each other.

Stink's hands are empty, his dark eyes shining with dirty adrenaline, his breathing loud and excited.

I notice Sandy Blue has his knife in her hand, gripping it tightly. It's covered in blood. She's leaking red from too many places to count.

I feel sick, tired.

I don't know what to do. I'm looking around my home for someone's help, because I know they're watching and recording this.

Sandy Blue drops the knife, drops to her knees.

"Somebody help us!" I scream.

Nothing.

No one.

Sandy Blue looks down at her own blood in dazed awe.

Finally I move to her and kneel down beside her, but I don't know how to help her. I'm afraid to even touch her.

Stink says, "It's over. Let her die."

He says it did not have to be this way, but it is.

He says mother.

I shout at him with what I feel is righteous anger, "This is *not* Deirdre! This is Sandy Blue, my . . . my . . . my lawyer!"

But Stink just shakes his head, telling me that she attacked and so she must be one of *them*.

Sandy Blue moans something indiscernible, scared, sad.

I stare down at her, feeling helpless, almost cruel. When I look up, Stink is gone.

Bloody hands reach up, tug on my shirt, staining it.

When I give in, when I lean down, Sandy Blue's breath hits my face like a bucket of wet pennies, coppery, as she asks me if I "sometimes . . . loved her."

I watch the bubbles form at the corner of her mouth. Tiny red bubbles chattering excitedly, popping, dying. And I just can't bring myself to kiss her.

"Yes," I tell her pathetically.

The light in her eyes is dull and glossy, as she shakes her head with great effort and says that's not my line.

"What?" And now I'm crying.

She asks me again if I sometimes loved her.

But I have no idea what my line is.

Her breath is gurgling like she's underwater, drowning.

"Someone help us," I scream out to my empty living room.

Nothing, just her breath gurgling.

Sandy Blue looks up at me like she's trying to hang on, like she can't die until I say my line.

Staring down at her sweaty, bloody, tired face, full of hope and determination, I say, "No . . . I don't love you."

My mind calls me a scumbag.

She shakes her head again, gasping for breath, pulling at me with bloody hands, struggling to speak.

"Look," I tell her, "Don't get me wrong. I really like you. I enjoy spanking you, swallowing you, but if I had a heart that was more than a muscle used to pump blood through my body, if it was more like a brain that released chemicals to create emotions . . . then that heart would belong to you."

Sandy Blue's eyes shine up at me, wet, filled with a

strong emotion that I mistake for happiness, as she smiles with pale, bloody lips and tells me that I am a great talent and that she'll really miss working with me.

I want to repay the compliment, but before I can speak, she closes her eyes and goes to sleep.

That's the word my mind uses: *sleep*.

I feel dizzy, tired, sick, and I close my eyes. I reach down to touch her flesh beneath the cold, tacky coating of blood, just under the hinge of her jaw.

Nothing. Lifeless clay.

But then I feel a thump and a thump and a thump, light and sporadic, but there. She's still alive! And I'm laughing, with tears rolling down my cheeks, running into my mouth, lukewarm and salty.

Normal John says the scene is over.

What?

I open my eyes, look up to see him standing over us wearing his FBI costume. In a cracking voice, I whisper that she's still alive.

"*Help* her," I beg.

But Normal John repeats that the scene is over.

"*No!*" I yell.

He tells the room, the mics, the cameras I can't see, that we need a recycle team. Stat.

"What the fuck is wrong with you people? She's still alive. You can't just throw her away like a piece of fucking trash."

Normal John blinks, his face expressionless, and he tells me simply that her part in the movie is over.

thirty-seven / fast forward

IDAHO, SAYS THE SIGN.

Outside the cab of our semi, the world passing by is surreal, grotesque. A post-nuclear orange envelops all that I see. Ash falls from the discolored afternoon sky in thick, swirling flurries, like snow, like dead skin falling from a psoriatic finally giving in to the constant promising pleasure of The Itch.

The radio tells me that 32,000 fires are currently blazing across America. Idaho is not the only state burning.

I haven't slept.

I'm tired.

I miss Deirdre so much that the chemical imbalance in my brain actually produces an aching in my chest.

The remaining three of us glide through the middle of nowhere in a free semi—you can't steal from dead people—and I'm the one driving, because Joe and Derrick are drunk and dreaming.

The script says we're heading for Skull Valley, Utah.

I have no idea where in the hell that is, but the semi's computer is much smarter than I am, and it produces a satellite image of where we are and where we're headed. Video-simulated progress.

Even so, I think I'm lost.

The ash keeps falling, filling this foreign orange world as it flutters down from a steadily purpling sky: a fresh bruise growing darker right before my eyes.

I'm lonely.

I don't really want to wake the others from their short, temporary deaths. It's so quiet and so peaceful—such a beautiful lie—with the giant green forests leaning in on me from both sides of the thin winding road that may or may not be taking us to Skull Valley.

And thousands of dead squid are washing ashore in California, littering the postcard beaches, disrupting the fantasy that everything is all right. The newscaster says scientists are baffled, that no one knows why this is happening.

I'm tired of touching myself to stay awake.

I think it's way past time for my medication.

And I laugh too loud, because if thousands of dead squid covering California beaches is not a natural occurrence, then isn't it obvious that *we* are the reason why this is happening?

But nobody wakes or even stirs in the cab's sleeping compartment, no matter how loud I laugh.

I wish Deirdre were here, so that she could drive, so that I could lay my head in her lap and breathe in her sweet-tangy-mouthwatering scent. She could explain to me why she's building another bomb in San Francisco.

Do you know what the scariest part of that sentence is?

It's not the word *bomb*.

No, it's the word *another*.

She is building *another* bomb in San Francisco, and nobody will explain to me what that really means. Even when I ask why, because it's a step, they just tell me that step three is to figure it out for myself.

Of course, that is impossible.

I can't even figure out what our next scene is about, because all that my single sheet of script does, besides tell me the destination of Skull Valley, Utah, is ask a question that makes very little sense to me (and by that I mean absolutely none at all): "What is the half-life of the Goshute Grizzly?"

When I asked Joe about it last night, while the third bottle of wine was being passed around, he said, "Eighty-five divided by twenty, multiplied by ten, equals tomorrow." He laughed so long, so hard, that he passed out in the back cabin, spilling the pungent red wine I can still smell.

And scientists have just cloned human DNA, it was just announced at some European-Council-for-whatever. This is what the radio is telling me.

But what it all means, I couldn't tell you.

Nothing?

Everything?

It could be either, but to me it seems like something as monumental as when the United States won the great space race, a long time ago, before I was born. The country shouted and cheered in swollen national pride, as it watched the grainy black-and-white footage of the tiny human animal bouncing across the moon's surface in its big puffy space suit.

I just don't get it.

Decades later, what has come of it?

It hasn't done a damn thing for me.

When I asked No-So-Little Joe about the script earlier, about Skull Valley and the Goshute Grizzly, he drained off one of the bottles of wine and looked at me with his evil smile and his dark, hooded eyes, saying, "It means you get to use a gun again. Since you killed my oldest friend, I have to shoot the second camera angle."

He spit the words out like he sucked them from a snakebite.

I had to turn away, to watch the road, to look at anything other than his bright red scalp filled with rage.

That was somewhere still back in the Bitterroots.

Now Idaho is a reddish purple night, and the tiny bits of fluttering burnt forests fall through the two huge beams of headlights, looking like television static.

"Cool, it's snowing," says Derrick, who yawns, then climbs up into the passenger's seat next to me, closing the black curtains behind him.

I guess Joe is still passed out.

I explain the illusion of the snow to Derrick, and he says, "Fire is a natural cleanser, same as the Black Plague. When a place gets too crowded to support healthy life, a natural cleansing takes place and a certain percentage has to die so that the rest can continue to live . . . or at least that's how it used to work, before technology."

I'm so happy he's awake.

I'm so happy we're alone.

And I say, "Yeah-yeah-yeah. Those damn vaccinations. I'm sure the earth will manage to score again with another beautifully horrible disaster. . . . But anyway, I really need to talk to you while we have a minute alone, because I'm thinking Joe wants to kill me since I shot John. But it wasn't really my fault with all of the R & R going on. I mean, it could have been any one of us, right? Right? Right?"

Derrick just shakes his head, his dark, wavy hair spilling over his brown eyes, and then he looks at me with wide-eyed, slack-faced compassion. "You know," he says softly, "It's not always going to be like this. We've had to rush you through a lifelong process in a short time, much faster than any of the others."

I cannot believe what I'm hearing.

"Are you . . . apologizing to me?" I ask, stunned.

"Not really," he says, "I just want you to know that when this is all over, when we're finished changing the world, you will have a lot of choices to make. . . . But the life available to you will be one of natural simplicity, where your rewards are tangible and fulfilling, rather than promised and digital and in another life, and ultimately empty."

"That sounds like a great fairytale," I say, "but what about Joe wanting to kill me?"

He tells me Joe knows that everyone who has ever lived, millions of people, for millions of years, have all died.

"It's no big deal," says Derrick.

Since it's just the two of us, and since he's actually in the mood to try and explain things to me, I ask him, "Why are you doing this? Why change the world? I mean, personally?"

Derrick stiffens, yawns, and says that he needs more rest.

I feel shunned and belittled, then angry.

He gets up and begins to climb into the sleeping cabin.

I grab his arm, dig my long nails into him.

"Ow!" he exclaims.

I can't take my eyes from the road, because I can barely see it through the static in the headlights, the falling pieces of burnt-up forests. I can't see his expression, but I growl, "Fuck the producers. Fuck the script. Fuck step three. And for one moment, just this one time, help me understand something that I cannot figure out for myself."

I can hear him breathing.

Breathing. Breathing.

I let go, giving up, as tears pool in my eyes, blurring the ugly burning world, because for one second I wanted to believe.

In what, I don't know.

Something. Anything.

"I'm doing this," whispers Derrick, his lips right up against my ear, "because in a world where every word, every idea, every action has been raped and exploited *ad nauseam* . . . a world where everything has been spoken and recorded and studied and explained, learned, understood, or at least pretended to be understood . . . this, what we are doing, is the last really original, really fun thing left to do."

What?

"You aren't trying to save the earth or something?" I ask.

He just laughs. Lightly. Quietly. Secretly.

He says, "Well, yeah. Sure. There's always that, too."

He disappears behind the curtain.

thirty-eight / rewind <<

THE RECYCLING CREW HAS COME and gone.

My carpet looks brand new, unstained: pristine.

Sandy Blue left with the clean up, with the stain. Now I feel more alone than I can ever remember, even though I'm not alone.

Normal John sits across from me on the couch, silently watching me, as he listens to someone on his cell phone. He hasn't moved for what must have been at least an hour.

There used to be a clock over my television, but it's gone.

And I'm wondering how much of my life I still control.

My mind says *the same as always, maybe five percent.*

When Normal John finally hangs up the phone, a sigh of tedium escapes him, as he pinches the bridge of his nose, rubs his eyes, and pulls out his gun.

My heart starts sprinting. I tell him, "My focus is fine. Really. Honest. It's my brain that needs fixing, I think."

But John puts the gun on the coffee table between us. He sighs again. He tells me to relax, that the day's filming is over.

What?

He says the bum-kid was unexpected. An editor's nightmare.

He says production is shut down for the night because of all of the rewrites the scene caused.

My usual confusion is spiced with intrigue. "Can't you just cut the scene?"

"No," he answers, "it doesn't work like that."

"Didn't you know that Deirdre had a son named Stink?"

"It's a lie," he whispers, not looking at me.

His jaw is clenching.

"She admitted it, you know. I mean, she didn't deny it."

John shakes his head, not denying either, yet showing me a look somewhere between anger and sadness as he says that those Bum-People are going to be a serious security problem.

"What Bum-People? There are Bum-People?" I'm trying not to sound too excited, but it's obvious.

"Deirdre's Bum-People," he half whispers.

I have to force myself to shut down, take a slow, deep breath through my nose, because I don't want to yell *what*? I don't want to disturb Normal John's dazed state. His eyes are pointing right at me, unclear, unfocused, and I wish I could see what he's seeing, remembering.

Patiently I wait, hoping, quietly breathing.

Silence expands, pressurizing the living room.

My ears are ringing.

Then John mumbles something that my brain translates as "Poor Deirdre," but could mean anything. So I pinch my nose, try to blow, and my ears pop.

I continue to wait, but it's killing me.

I feel like I'm close to receiving a huge part of the puzzle, a key to unlock one of the mysteries.

A sudden commotion shatters my concentration as several people—talking, laughing—walk through my front door and enter my home unannounced, uninvited. It jolts me like a needle trick, scaring the hell out of me.

Normal John grabs his gun.

We both snap our heads toward the foyer, the front door, and see Bob-the-agent, Karen-the-publicist and Team Image enter my living room.

All five of them stop in mid-stride, mid-laugh, mid-sentence.

All seven of us are on pause, and my mind tells me that two worlds are about to collide. I'm waiting for the screams to begin, the red dot, a gunshot, death to blossom before my eyes.

Nothing.

Pausing.

Normal John begins to laugh, slow and deliberate.

Others join in, forced and nervous.

It seems that the situation is defused, but then Team Image—which is three homosexual German nationals who always dress in black, always speak as one, and always say the same words at the same time in the same voice—ask in surround-sound idiocy, "Who is zis man wiz zee gun?"

Seriously, it sounds that fake.

I giggle.

No one else sees the humor.

John, who had begun to lower his gun, raises it back up, pointing it at the five sophists.

Team Image raise their hands up high.

I'm laughing hysterically, not entirely sure why.

But Bob-the-agent says, "Wait a minute."

He tells John that they know each other from somewhere.

What?

John squints his eyes and says, "Wrong answer." The veins in his gun hand grow.

The phone rings.

Everybody flinches.

But I have a delicious new thought, and before the phone can be answered, before Deirdre can be obeyed, I tell Bob-Karen-Team Image that this is my new lawyer/security guard. I say this is the newest member of our happy little dysfunctional family.

I say that this is John Zerbiak.

"What?" says everyone.

I'm smiling so wide that my second face is cramping. It takes every bit of my internal strength to keep from losing control of the insane laughter in my belly, because everyone, Normal John especially, is looking at me with expressions that say I just *cannot* do this.

But you know what? I just did.

I can't explain to you how incredible it feels to rewrite the script of your life, how much fun it is to re-create.

You should really just try it for yourself.

thirty-nine / fast forward

I CAN'T STOP laughing.

I can barely see the road through the tears.

I slam on the brakes. Tires screech, lock, chirp, and then Derrick and Joe yell at me in loud, faraway vowels I can't understand because my mind is opening as wide as a baby's first smile.

Epiphany.

In my entire life, I can't ever remember having one, but now I've had two in less than two days.

Laughing tears pour out of me.

My stomach cramps.

If I don't breathe soon, I'll pass out.

But I can't stop laughing; I can't stop thinking about something that changes everything.

Epiphany.

And maybe you've never had one, so I'm going to try and explain this wonderfully marvelous, super-spectacular sensation. It's difficult. Maybe the only way I can come close is by saying that it might be like getting hit in the forehead with a giant axe, where your entire brain is cut into two perfect halves, right down the middle; but just before you feel an unimaginable pain . . . a cool, soft breeze slides in to gently touch your mind.

It's like that, but not.

You should really just have one and see.

Finally, I start breathing, coughing. Phlegm or blood or something flies from the back of my throat to land somewhere inside the semi cab, but I can't see where because the world went away for a moment, before it began to ease back into existence. >>

The ink absorbs into the ether.

Not-So-Little Joe looks worried, frowning, which is his way of smiling, and he asks me if I'm going Lucy on him.

Not-Jewish Derrick leans into the picture frame and asks me what's going on.

I look at them both, with their genuine concern and their own ancient epiphanies somewhere inside them, and I say, "Meteor."

Derrick frowns.

Joe smiles.

"Meteor," I tell them, and start laughing again, only this time the lights blink out before I can really get going.

I wake up with a needle in my arm and the world full of sunshine outside of the moving semi.

Joe removes the spike.

I let the warming bright light shimmer through my body, as I look at the question in Joe's Groucho Marx eyebrows raised high on his stubbly bald head.

"You had one," he says. "Tell me."

I try to explain about how I was fed up, frustrated, pissed off because I can't figure out why everything is happening for reasons I cannot understand. Bombs. Civilization. Domination. Systems of control. Twelve steps for recovery. Changing the world. My wife. The producers. The half-life of the Goshute Grizzly. And then the radio cut in with a Special News Bulletin, telling me that a meteor the size of three football fields just narrowly missed crashing into the earth and wiping out every last living thing on the entire planet.

The punch line is that this happened three days ago.

Nobody—not the thousands of astronomers, not the scientists with their telescopes bigger than houses—saw it coming.

It passed right between the earth and its moon, the cosmic equivalent of a hair's width, but no one saw it coming. No one knew about it until it was way too late to do a damn thing but be dead.

Listening to me try to explain, Joe's smile grows too big for his own small face.

"And think about it," I say. "Here I am, stressing out over everything under the sun and, without even knowing it, all of this almost disappeared in the blink of an eye."

Joe, smiling so wide his eyes are just tiny dark slits, asks me how it feels to learn one of the only actual truths in this life?

I say I feel free. Alive. Lighter.

Driving, Derrick downshifts, double-clutches, congratulates, and announces that we are here.

I sit up, then look out the window at the deeply carved valley below us, with its small towns dotting the landscape with man-made sores.

Skull Valley, Utah.

Joe puts his hand on my shoulder and, with an enthusiastic joy so uncharacteristic of him, says, "Well my little superstar, are you ready?"

I'm scared shitless by his change.

Ready for what, I ask, trying not to shrug his hand away.

He squeezes just a little, fatherly, as he says happily, "Ready to kill the Goshute Grizzly."

forty / rewind

I CAN'T HELP IT.

I look away.

But still I feel the pinprick, the cold sliver of a needle splitting my skin and traveling a fraction of an inch, which seems like a mile, to puncture my vein with an internally audible pop that echoes through my body in icy waves.

This is the part I hate, dread.

Then the plunger comes down, euphoria comes down. My heart grows large, my brain goes numb, and when I finally take that first big fish-out-of-water-gasping breath . . . I feel so incredibly alive!

Normal John looks down on me, frowning, studying.

Bob-the-agent laughs at me.

Karen-the-publicist lets her fingers slide up my thigh, saying something about the muscle tone of my legs.

Members of Team Image each hold up a bottle with thirty-something-letter words on it. "Zis is za goot shtuff," they say in unison.

All I can do is giggle at them, because it's all so insane.

This is my life now, can you believe it?

This is the brand new development being brought to you by Bob-the-agent. Weightlifting. Bodybuilding. Because Bob says that people—and by that he means consumers—don't want normal, don't want themselves.

This also makes me giggle.

He says people want big, massive, huge, jumbo-sized, super-sized, larger-than-life, chiseled, cut, statuesque.

He says people want perfection: the opposite of themselves.

Karen agrees, saying, "They just won't worship for less."

But Normal John scowls, growls, announces with calm defiance that, historically, the majority has always been wrong.

I just cannot stop giggling, because Normal John is suddenly not so normal anymore. He's so out of place in this group. This back and forth bickering has been going on for weeks and it just keeps getting funnier. Because I can feel every hair follicle on my scalp tingling, humming. It feels like it's growing. Yes, it's true. I've been doing this for a while now, but every time I feel this rush, my mind says it will never be this good again, because it's never been so good, because it just can't get any better.

We are all in my bedroom, and I'm lying on a weight bench that is exactly where my bed used to be, but that's no big deal because I never sleep anymore. I can't. I've stopped trying.

Karen says it's my work ethic.

Normal John says it's the drugs.

"Ja," agrees Team Image, but with whom I'm unsure.

Bob-the-agent dials a number on his cell phone, listens for thirty-six beats of my enlarged heart, maybe five seconds, before hanging up. He says the latest polls are in and that 63 percent of Americans would buy my book, that 87 percent would pay to watch a movie based on actual events of my kidnapping ordeal.

I am truly happy, impressed, dazed, high on drugs—the names of which I cannot even begin to pronounce.

Team Image uncradles the thick metal bar above me, holding it there as my arms automatically rise to meet it. My freshly manicured hands clench it a shoulder's width apart. When Team Image lets go, the bar bends and sinks. My chest muscles flex, rip, tear underneath, fill with fire. The bar just keeps sinking. Sinking. Even though I'm pushing as hard as I can.

Bob says that 54 percent of Americans will buy underwear if I tell them that they look sexier, more desirable, less like themselves, while wearing them.

I would giggle but I can't breathe.

“Pusht,” yells Team Image.

But I can’t scream that I *am* fucking pushing, because I still can’t breathe. My face is too hot, too full of blood, shrinking my vision to a circle that grows steadily smaller.

Karen’s hand is stroking my inner thigh *way* too high, her long fake nails almost touching my happy place. She just keeps purring, in what she probably thinks is a sexy voice, saying, “Do it. Do it. Do it.”

But I cannot do it!

The bar is now crushing my chest, my lungs, my heart.

Bob says that 37 percent of Americans consider me to be a potentially good martyr for an as-yet-to-be-named cause, but that less than 1 percent would choose to die with me, even if it were really important.

Normal John looks very concerned as he gazes down at my probably purpling face. He mumbles that individuality seeks no justification.

But he is dimming, fading along with the rest of it.

Karen’s fingers have now crept up the leg of my shorts, the acrylic nails lightly scratching at the soft curly hair there, which does absolutely nothing to arouse me because she’s such a bitch and because I have no available blood supply. In desperation I blindly lash out with my foot, kicking her brightly painted face.

She screams.

Everybody starts yelling, as panicked as I feel. Finally.

A phone rings, stops ringing.

The weight is still crushing me, killing me, until it is lifted away by someone who is still lost in The Black, which is trying to pull me under. Then the air that finally rushes into my empty, burning lungs kick starts my brain.

“Are you trying to kill me?” I yell.

The Black dissolves.

Bob shows me his honest-officer-I-did-not-know-she-was-under-age smile, as he tells me, "No way." He tells me that before I can die, *all* of the percentages must be in the high eighties because, "When millions die it's only a statistic, but when one person dies it can be made into a tragedy. It's all about the storyteller left behind."

"This is everlasting life," says Karen.

"The trick," says Bob, "is to be a martyr for something. Lucky for us there's always a good cause, because a good god is hard to find."

He winks.

And I smile, because Normal John's expression is so silent, so angry, that I'm sure that Bob and Karen's part in the movie is almost over.

forty-one / fast forward

EVEN THOUGH IT'S FIRE SEASON, the Utah night is cold.

My breath is fog.

I bash the small crowbar against the steering column as hard as I can, then watch the plastic break away like an eggshell, falling to lie with the broken glass on the floorboards.

This is an old Plymouth Valiant.

This only works with old cars. The kinds of cars not run by computers. The kinds you can still actually fix yourself. More and more, these cars are harder and harder to find, but in a small desert town like this one, they're all over the place.

I rip at the rainbow of wires exposed inside the shattered steering column, then select two and strip them with my fingernails.

Black wire touches red.

Sparks.

The car is mine.

I shift into drive, with the engine coughing on the cold air, but I don't move, because for a split second, I actually think about the possibility of just driving away. Far away. I'm all by myself, getting the get-away car, and I could do it.

I could disappear.

I could rewrite the script.

And my mind is taking a step, asking why. Why am I doing all of this?

The answer that comes back surprises me: because Not-Jewish Derrick is right. I've never had so much fun. I've never felt so close to being alive.

Meteor.

Smiling wide enough to die happy, I smash down on the gas pedal, because I'm probably running late, because right around the corner, right down the upcoming street, Derrick and Joe should already be ringing the doorbell.

Plus the script says that we really have to hurry up with tonight's scene, because in less than two days, Philosophy dies.

Don't ask.

I still don't know.

Rolling slow now with the lights out, I see Joe and Derrick standing on the front porch. The door opens to reveal a huge, dark shadow in the doorway surrounded by the sickened, greenish-white glow of television static.

It must be the Goshute Grizzly.

A bright blue flash.

The huge shadow jerks.

And then they're dragging the Bear down the steps, across the overgrown yard, onto the street. I pull up and jack open the door for them. They toss their load into the back seat, and for some reason the dim dome light makes it look like a fat old American Indian taking a ten-thousand-volt nap.

With the camera attached to his face, Derrick hops in the back to ride with the Bear.

Joe climbs in next to me. He says he just got off the phone with the producers and we've really got to get this scene over with so we can get back on the road. We still have to visit The Gecko Tree and pick up Normal John's replacement before we change the world tomorrow night.

Whatever. Meteor.

I still haven't taken off yet.

Joe wants to drive.

Someone starts screaming from the house.

We quickly switch places, me climbing over Joe sliding under me. He hands me the icy dead weight of his dirty old revolver. The car lurches forward, tires spitting gravel.

The gun in my hand feels like a collapsed sun, a star system sucked into a black hole and condensed, poured into a metal mold of destruction.

This is how heavy it feels, how powerful.

Joe turns on the headlights and cracks the driver's side door, which turns on the dome light again. He says to me, "Pop quiz."

He asks me the question from the script, "What is the half-life of the Goshute Grizzly?"

I can't help but smile, because I remember Joe's drunken math from the night before; the answer to my question right before he laughed so hard he passed out. For once I know my line.

"Today," I say.

Air howls through the open door that Joe keeps propped open with his left foot, and I'm waiting for some kind of surprised congratulations for my first correct answer, for being a suddenly apt pupil, but Joe just asks me why. He says it's an important step. >>

Shit.

Silence declares my ignorance.

Joe growls, curses, mumbles something about time being a system of control. He tells me, "The term half-life refers to the amount of time it takes for half of the radiation in a radioactive isotope to decay."

He says the half-life of Plutonium-239 is 24,000 years.

He says it takes ten half-lifes for a radioactive element to be considered harmless to human animals.

He's yelling at me now.

I hate math.

Derrick takes over, spitting out facts: "To date, Western Civilization has produced more than 13 quadrillion lethal doses of Plutonium-239, enough to kill every human being on the planet two million times over. Plutonium-239 is not even the most common or deadly type of plutonium that civilization has made."

Blah-blah-blah.

I've stopped listening, because these numbers are unbelievable.

I mean that literally. I don't believe them.

But Derrick is going on and on, explaining to me how plutonium or cesium or strontium or any other -ium elements that humans have created basically knock electrons off of the atoms of the cells in our bodies when we come into contact with them.

Finally with my head beginning to pressurize, I ask what in the hell all of this nuclear crap has to do with the half-life of the Goshute Grizzly?

In the back seat, with me facing him, Derrick zooms in for my close-up and he points with his free hand at the sleeping Indian, saying, "Meet Fred Grizzly Bear Griswald, Chair of the Goshute Indians."

In the front seat, Joe tells me, "You're gonna kill him."

THIS I MAY REGRET as long as I live.

This I will never forget, never forgive.

But the medicine is really helping and I feel more at ease now. Joe's gun feels a lot lighter in my hand now.

I yawn, a nice long one that stretches my second face to its max and sends shivers up my spine, down my arms, into my scalp. Joe returns the empty syringe to his backpack.

With Joe on my left and Derrick on my right, the three of us are standing in the cold, in the dark, just outside of the old brown Plymouth Valiant, and looking in at the fat old Goshute Grizzly, sleeping and waiting for me to kill him.

Our semi is idling behind us, shaking the ground.

Joe says, "What the hell? Do it already."

I'm trying to find my character's motivation by thinking about the way this asshole-of-a-man signed a contract with the Federal Government, agreeing to store 40,000 tons of nuclear waste on 100 acres of land which that same government let him keep after taking this whole country from his people in the first place. But even that is not enough for me to kill him.

I just don't really care that much about any of it.

I picture the entire valley dying.

Trees. Little kids. Fish. Beautiful women. Deer. Birds.

I picture a vast, dusty crater, a dead zone, all because this greedy traitor took the money, and I raise the metallic death machine, sighting the fat, sleeping head of the Goshute Grizzly.

But it's still not enough.

Holding the gun as still as I can—basically shaking all over the place—I close my eyes and say, "Tell me again how horrible this guy is."

"Sold the health of ten thousand generations," says Derrick.

“He bought three new cars, two new trucks, and a motorhome! Just kill him already!” yells Joe. >>

My hand begins to tighten.

I open my eyes.

And the Goshute Grizzly is staring right at me, wide-awake, unblinking, without even the slightest show of fear. His mouth moves. He says, “I know who you are.”

What?

“I’ve seen you on my new satellite TV,” he tells me. “You’re that movie star that everyone felt so sorry for the first time, when you and your old lady were kidnapped. You’re on all of the news shows and the most wanted criminal shows now.”

I’m so happy.

I’m so famous.

“You stupid nigger,” he sneers. “Everyone hates your guts.”

Joe starts laughing, loud, abrasive, really enjoying it.

I’m, frozen, pointing the gun. I’m shocked, because I cannot even remember the last time someone called me that hate-filled word. But then it rushes into me. The shame, the hurt, the shrinking, dirty feeling, the memory of the pretty blonde cheerleader, her blue eyes turning watery in fear of my taboo attraction, using that dreaded word the day before I ran away to be a big star.

As the memory fades away, the shame growing into hot anger, I aim for the center of the Bear’s face. My hand is rock steady.

“They’re going to kill you when they catch you,” he says, a smug smile twisting the skin of his old face. “They are going to kill you, you stupid nig—”

Bang!

My ears whine. My hand is vibrating, tingling. I smell the acrid smoke of the burnt powder, as I take it all in and let it go. Breathing. Breathing.

The Bear's face is a rotting blood melon.

The back seat of the Plymouth is violent art, the bright red paint still wet.

And you might hate me for saying this . . . but how this feels, what is born inside me at this moment, is amazing. It is empowered and empowering, forgiven and forgiving, intoxicating, light as a feather and vibrating inside me so fast that I am blurring.

Derrick and Joe must know. They are silent, letting me flow.

My numb lips feel like I am talking through a kazoo as I ask Joe for one of his cigarettes.

When he hands it to me, I feel loved.

forty-two / rewind

A SMALL GROAN . . .

. . . of tedium escapes me and I have a thought that is really just a rerun—a common realization of minute proportions—yet this time it is persistent enough to force me into studying it in much greater depth.

I. Am. Not. Happy.

And I know what you're thinking. So what, right? Everybody is unhappy, right?

Well, you have a good point and I would usually do exactly as you probably do, what everybody else probably does, which is to ignore it, pretend it's not there, not true, or doesn't matter, but tonight my mind is taking a step all on its own.

Why am I unhappy?

I'm riding in a limo filled with people I love to hate. Bob-the-agent, Karen-the-publicist, Team Image, Normal John, and I are on our way to our red carpet arrival at the world premiere of a major motion picture based on actual events of my life. This is a movie I had absolutely no part in making, a movie I did not even know about until today, a movie I am told will make me millions of dollars and will solidify my Star Power for future projects, a movie I never gave consent to make, a movie that has me wondering who is signing my contracts because it sure as hell isn't *me*.

Yes, this is pissing me off, but it's not the main reason I'm unhappy. I think it should be, but it's not. It's deeper.

I look deeper.

But Karen breaks my concentration, putting her hand up my shirt and rubbing my nipple, distracting me as she leans against me, her face inches from mine. Her breath smells like gin. She whispers that I look yummy.

"I know," I tell her. Because it's true, I really do.

Between the drugs and the exercise and eating practically nothing, my body is lean, hard muscle wrapped in smooth, tight skin.

I look incredible.

I feel like dying.

Karen, she's a real live fame-o-meter. For years she treated me like crap, but the closer I get to true Stardom, the more she throws herself at me. It makes me sick, makes me hate her.

She is now pinching my nipple.

Before I can push her away, Team Image shrieks as only three flamboyant homosexuals can.

I wince.

Karen is pulled away, shoved aside, as six hands fix my shirt exactly how it will look on television tonight.

Corks are popped. Champagne is poured. A slender-necked sparkling glass is placed in my hand and Bob-the-agent says, "Superstar."

They're all holding up their glasses—even Normal John,

who is frowning and talking on the phone with someone I'm hoping is Deirdre, explaining how she will soon kill us all—when Bob announces that tonight is the night. He's watching me with a look of absolute satisfaction, like how Sylvester would look if he ever really ate Tweety Bird. I think the word I'm looking for is *maniacal*, but I'm not sure. Bob says I have the look, the feel, the story of a new god.

I'm just one step away from immortality, he tells me.

I guess it's a toast, because everyone drinks except Normal John, who hangs up the phone and stares at me with a well-hidden excitement burning somewhere behind his plain brown eyes. He's sitting across from me, locked in on me.

I silently mouth the words, "I. Feel. Nothing."

"Living is preferable to surviving," says John.

Bob hands me a book, which I drop because my hands are numb, but Karen picks it up and sets it on my lap. Face up. My face staring up at my face.

I'm a two-dimensional image staring up at an empty shell.

Bob and Karen explain to me that this is my book, that it hits shelves tomorrow, that I should carry it with me tonight for the photo-op.

"But . . . but . . . but I didn't write this book," I stammer, confused, anger growing inside me like the seed of a poisonous flower.

"Sure you did," says Karen. She smiles at me like I'm being silly or delusional.

"You dedicated it to your dead wife," says Bob. He flips it open to show me that, sure enough, I did.

"I did *not* write this fucking book. And Sarah is *not* dead . . . I think."

Bob frowns.

Karen says something in German which sounds like a belch.

And then Team Image is stuffing pills into my mouth. Green. Purple. Red. White. Yellow. Different geometrical shapes and sizes. Champagne is poured down my throat.

I gag, swallow, and cough, choking.

My eyes are watering, but I'm smiling.

Bob tells me to remember not to smile.

Karen says the look we are going for is *tortured.*

Normal John, who is now looking at me with this kind of intense anticipation, says, "The truth is subjective."

He says, "Others' perceptions should never define you."

He is excited now, expectant, waiting.

The drugs are pressing down on me like a liquid metal sky, drowning me, and all I can really think about is the fact that I am still not happy.

Bob tells John that perceptions are what you make of them.

John's face goes slack as he says that individualism is unjustifiable.

Karen jumps in, laughing her fake laugh and saying that she could not agree more.

John looks at me and closes his eyes, clenching his jaw.

"Ja," agrees Team Image.

I tell everyone that I think they misunderstood John.

"We're here," yells Bob.

The limo eases to a stop at the curb.

The scene outside the tinted windows is all about controlled stalking. The press is en masse, flashbulbs firing like a lightning storm.

This is what I've always wanted.

Why am I so unhappy?

I step out, blinded by the lights, holding my book in numb hands and trying to look tortured, which isn't really much of a leap for me. The noise of the crowd washes over me like static electricity, with tragically normal fans screaming my name and semi-beautiful people yelling questions. It is everything I have always dreamed of! Wished for!

But I feel nothing.

I am nothing.

Why does it seem like for every wish that is granted, another dream is destroyed?

Inside, and the movie is half over.

It's *all* wrong. Something is wrong with everything.

The characters, the people, me, Deirdre, Not-Jewish Derrick, Normal John, Not-So-Little Joe, my wife Sarah, are all way too beautiful, too tall, *too white*, too perfect.

The guns are too shiny, new, sexy.

The blood looks too real when I shoot Normal John on R & R.

Deirdre rapes me viciously.

They shoot muddy heroin into my arms.

I struggle too much, try to escape too often.

And sitting here watching this load of over-produced bullshit, I feel so fucking *used*, so utterly pissed off, that I almost feel sober. Blood pounds inside my head like a murderer's hammer, and when I open up my book, squinting in the flashing light of the screen, I discover that it follows right along with the movie, except that it is infuriatingly spiced throughout with huge paragraphs of italicized-romantic-hero thoughts.

I close the book.

I close my eyes.

I smell gasoline and burning orange peels.

I nudge Normal John, who's sitting right next to me. I

lean over and ask him, in a barely controlled whisper, "Give me your gun." >>

John asks why. He says it's an important step.

"I know it's a fucking step!" I yell.

And somebody actually shushes me, can you believe it?

This is *my* fucking movie and they're shushing *me*.

I hold out my hand to John, but he is a bullshit virtue, calmly waiting for me to take the step.

I take a deep breath. My hands are shaking. I'm covered in sweat, makeup running down my face, and—

Click.

This is the sound my brain actually makes.

Click.

"I am unhappy," I whisper to John, "Because I have spent my whole life trying to be what they told me I could be. Because *this* is not how I pictured me. This is not the wonderful life I was told is my right, my reward. Because—"

Normal John cuts me off, saying that's enough.

A particularly bright scene flashes across the screen, lighting up John's smiling face as he places the big, black, grimy revolver on my lap.

I finally inhale: deep, slow, forever. A nice easy breath fills my lungs for the first time in my life. My muscles relax. My body cools. My hand wraps around icy metal.

forty-three / fast forward

MADAM GECKO'S tree.

Do you know the story?

I don't.

But Not-Jewish Derrick says it was an amazing story that captured headlines around the world. The story of one woman's fight against progress, against big corporate destruction of the earth, as she risked her life to save just one tree.

Not-So-Little Joe starts laughing.

A vicious sound.

I tell Derrick it sounds vaguely familiar.

We're all standing in the most peaceful place on this planet, on the softly crunching forest floor, just as dawn gives birth to another long day in the monotonous parade of forever everywhere else. Being in a forest is entirely different than being in a city. In a forest it's like you're in a world where your problems don't exist, where nothing moves faster than the slow rhythmic pumping of your heart, and your brain kind of takes a break, because all of your words and knowledge would only get in the way.

You just see. You just smile.

Derrick says her name was Madam Gecko.

I look up, feeling dizzy, watching the light purple sky begin to wash blue, peeking through the thick canopy so high above us. I whisper, "Tell me her story."

Joe ignores us, digging around in the semi behind me.

Derrick says the logging company was heading right for this glorious tree, this living entity older than this country or its government, and Madam Gecko climbed high into the branches to make a small treehouse, where she vowed to stay until the company would agree not to cut down this magnificent tree.

Joe is cursing behind us, banging around in the cab, missing this great moment, this inspiring story.

But not me. I'm soaking it up.

I really need something like this.

I am full of gratitude for Madam Gecko's courage.

The light slowly breaks through the dense old-growth

forest, picturesque, in thin needle-like shafts, which change the murky shapeless shadows into a kaleidoscope of greens and reds and browns. Living colors. The growing light defining, the giant tree takes shape before me, more majestic than anything man has ever created.

Tears are spilling down my face, happy tears, because the brave young lady obviously saved the tree. I tell Derrick, "Thank you for bringing me here to visit Madam Gecko's tree. Thank you so much for this. . . . I remember her now. So young and beautiful and fearless. Such a strong woman. She really showed them, didn't she?"

But Not-So-Little Joe says, "Nice fairytale. Now let's bring it down." He walks past me to the tree, and begins to wrap some kind of thick white rope around its base.

What?

I tell Derrick I don't understand.

He starts laughing at me, not with me, as Joe disappears around the curve of the trunk that's bigger than our semi, and says he cannot believe I fell for that load of shit.

I wipe my face, smearing cold tears, confused, pissed off, coughing from all of the smoke in the air from another fire somewhere nearby.

California is also ablaze.

America is burning.

Joe comes around the bend, wrapping the thick rope around the base, telling me that Madam Gecko was an ugly little girl who wasn't content with only fifteen minutes of fame.

What?

I say, "But I remember her. How beautiful and blonde and—"

You remember what you want to, he says.

He disappears around the tree, wrapping, wrapping.

Derrick explains to me that *that* is how history is written, beautiful and full of shit so they can make movies and holidays. The truth is Madam Gecko raised over $100,000.00 and then turned around and gave it to the logging company so it wouldn't cut down the tree. Because the corporation was not going to give in. Because she was tired of living in this tree for more than a year.

But the forest is still standing, I say.

"See the ribbons hanging from the trees? See the paint marks waist high?" Derrick asks.

"Yes," I say. "I thought they were decorations put up to celebrate the saving of the forest; prayers put up by the defenders."

Derrick laughs. "The ribbons are markers put up by the timber company to tell the loggers which trees to cut. The paint tells them where to put the chainsaw."

I notice that all of the trees are decorated except for Madam Gecko's.

But she still saved the tree, I point out.

Joe comes around the bend again, out of rope, saying, "She makes twice that much money now on the Inspirational Speakers Circuit. And let's compare how much she makes to the ones who caught the bags of piss and shit she dropped to them late at night after the World News cameras left."

I have no idea, but I'm thinking the shit carriers aren't getting quite so much.

Joe says she wrote a book and talked to Congress.

"But what did she accomplish?" he asks me.

"She saved a tree," I say. "She raised awareness."

"Wrong answer," yells Joe.

They walk back to the semi, leaving me behind, so I hurry to follow them. Once we reach the rig, we all stop.

Joe pulls out a car alarm activator, like you keep on your key chain. He pulls it from his deflated backpack and growls, "That fucking story is everything I hate about environmentalists."

I'm just way too tired or stupid, because I don't get it. I

say, "What's the big deal if she had to buy it? They didn't cut it down, right? It's still alive, right?" ››

Wrong, says Joe. And he shows me a rare, true-blue smile.

He activates the car alarm an—

The force of the blast, the hot wind, shoves me into Derrick and onto the ground, as bits of five-hundred-year-old tree rain down on us. In the ringing silence, what sounds like firecrackers echo across the smoky dawn.

When I roll over onto my back and look up, I realize that it's not firecrackers.

I watch the ancient, magnificent symbol of everything Joe hates about environmentalists tear away from itself, first leaning, and then falling in super-slow motion. The ripping wood sounds like the tree is screaming. The tree crashes down with a noise that is twice as loud as the initial explosion, shaking the forest floor like an earthquake, vibrating every bone in my body, and hurting my teeth.

The loudest silence now.

Until Joe begins his vicious laugh.

Derrick, smiling like a new father, tells me that a tree without a forest is no longer a tree, and that saving one tree is like a terminal cancer patient getting a new haircut, anyway.

Joe climbs to his feet.

He helps me and Derrick up.

He says we'd better hurry, because Philosophy is dying tonight and we still have to pick up the new John.

forty-four / rewind

IF YOU COULD REWRITE THE SCRIPT, the movie of your life, would you do it?

If you were frustrated and tired, angered by doing what is expected of you, only to find out that your promised reward is death, just like everyone else, what would you do?

Would you say things you're not supposed to say?

"Liars," I howl at the screen, the people, the world. "Liars!"

Would you do things you're not supposed to do?

I stand up in the constantly changing shadows of the giant movie theater with the heavy, empowering weight of Normal John's gun gripped in my right hand so tightly it feels melded to my flesh, an extension of my hand, a long, black metal finger I point accusingly at the shocked faces staring at me in the flickering light.

If you were watching a movie of your life on a giant screen and you did not like what you saw, would you let it drag on, hoping it would get better? Or would you do something to change it?

I point my mutated finger—I point *death*—at Bob-the-agent's head. He's three seats away, sitting next to Karen, and they're both stuck on pause, awe-struck, star-struck. I close my eyes and see their faces captured on Deirdre's Polaroids so long ago, remember their shocked, bruised, bloody faces staring up at me from the goose down comforter.

I'm about to make Deirdre an honest woman.

If you reached a point where it was murder or suicide, what would you do?

I open my eyes, the screen flashing bright, and I pull the tr—

"Gun!" shrieks Team Image, in 3-D panic, no accent.

Hundreds of people start screaming, freaking out, scattering like frightened animals, which is not a simile. They scramble over seats, over each other, and I can't kill Bob or Karen because I can't see them anymore. I've lost them in the sea of tuxedos and black evening dresses.

But I have to shoot this gun. I have to.

I spin to my right and empty its loud poison into the movie of my life, punching big black holes in the screen, killing it. Then I turn to Normal John.

He's gone.

The crowd is running away, receding from me in waves, rushing out into the lobby, leaving me to stand alone in the rows of empty seats.

A man yells out, "Put your hands up!"

I choose a fire exit to the left of the screen, run to it, and shove it open. Voices tell me to stop, to freeze. I run into a dark skinny alley, throw the empty gun at a heap of trash that says, "Ouch."

What?

A bum rises up, saying something about the beach, but I'm not listening, just flying by him, kicking off my shoes and running faster, sprinting out of the alley, out into the street and looking right, looking lef—

The sound of tires screeching on asphalt and all I see is a silver blur as a Mercedes slams into me, tosses me into the air, tumbles me head over ass. I come down on the hood, my head bouncing off the windshield.

I sit up, scramble off, land on my feet next to the idling car like warm blood is not really running down my face in tiny rivers, like my left leg is not really a throbbing hunk of dead wood I cannot use to support my weight. I yell at my wife Sarah, "What the hell?"

What?!

Sarah looks at me in shock as I place my hands on the closed driver's side window. I lean in, press my face against it, squint, and try to make sure I'm not going totally insane.

She looks at me with those glacier blue eyes, her blonde hair grown out long and straight, her breasts heaving with each breath, barely contained in her black evening dress.

Time stops, is broken, drags on in slow motion.

I'm aware of the sirens.

I'm aware that she is alone in a car that I've never seen.

I try the handle, but the door is locked.

I hear the sound of heavy metal being dragged on concrete, of shouts far away, of echoing whispers much closer, and Sarah, my wife, who I thought was dead, then kidnapped, smiles at me with a strange happiness, a half-hidden sorrow.

Someone grabs my ankle.

Sarah mouths three words I no longer believe.

Several hands grab my thighs.

Suddenly I'm being dragged down, even though I'm standing straight up, rigid. I'm sinking slowly, steadily, like an elevator, like the fucking street is swallowing me whole.

Sarah doesn't move, doesn't look too worried, looks like she might be crying, and then, as I grow shorter, she disappears. I grab the door handle again, trying to pull myself back up, trying to fight the hands tugging me down as I scream her name, but the door stays locked, stays closed.

"Please help me," I yell.

The car begins to slowly pull away from me.

I try to hang onto the door's handle, but it's ripped away from me and I scream at the top of my lungs, scream at my wife, asking her why.

Why is this happening to us?

Why won't you help me?

My only answer is fading tail lights growing smaller in

the distant night, as I claw at dirty asphalt and am dragged beneath the city's surface into a darkness that is made complete when again I hear heavy metal being dragged against concrete.

The manhole cover clangs shut with a sound of finality.

Too many hands restrain me as I lie here, unmoving, with something that feels like a small rubber ball being shoved into my mouth to keep me from screaming. I try to spit it out, but it won't fit. It forces me to suck air in through my nose, which is no good because the holes are too small. I need more oxygen. And what's even worse, what's really creeping me out, is how quiet it is down here under the rest of the world.

Nothing.

Silence.

Except for the screams of my own mind, there isn't a sound.

I'm being kidnapped again. Can you believe it?

I try to tell myself it's only Deirdre, Joe, Derrick and John, but the one thing they are not is quiet.

No, this is someone else. Something else.

Fear consumes me, adrenaline rushes through me, as I thrash, writhe, push, pull, twist, jerk, kick, try one last time to free myself from these silent predators, but it's of no use.

I lie spent, unmoving, accepting.

"Everything is going to be just fine," says a voice.

I think I know who it is, but before my mind connects the dots, a flashlight clicks on and Stink's ugly, young, dirty face smiles happily, excitedly, as he tells me that his father wants to see me.

The flashlight clicks off, darkness swallowing all, and I think my eyes are still open, but I'm not sure because all I see is a picture solidifying in my mind, my brain's chemicals washing over it, details sharpening, the picture coming to life.

It is Sarah. My wife.

Underneath this odd mental picture is written the caption:

Friend or foe?

forty-five / fast forward

THE SCRIPT SAYS I'M BURSTING with excitement.

I feel like a zombie.

I'm told for the fifth time today that tonight Philosophy dies, but I still have no idea what it means.

I haven't slept in what seems like a large chunk of forever.

In the last two days I've managed to kill two people, dig two graves, blow up a five-hundred-year-old tree, and ride in the cab of a semi filled with enough uncomfortable silence to fray the last few fibers of sanity I had left.

But now I'm sitting in the back seat of a free Lexus—because you can't steal from dead people—and everyone is laughing and joking, teasing each other with inside jokes that leave me on the outside.

Already, I hate the new John.

New John is everyone's old friend but mine.

As we pass through San Francisco, it looks like every other big city, glowing in the night so bright that I can't see a single star.

Even though this thought registers and my mind comments, it doesn't really matter, because my mind never shuts up anyway, and all I really want to see, do, feel, taste is Deirdre. I miss her much more than Normal John, my wife, or my old life.

Finally, I just can't take it, can't wait for inclusion. I interrupt the three reunited amigos, asking loudly just where in the *hell* is Deirdre.

Not-So-Little Joe says airport.

New John tells me, for the third time, how great it is to finally meet me in person. He's showing me the kind of big-toothed grin that only people who actually hate you can pull off, with his perfect teeth and his chiseled jaw.

He reminds me of a pretty-boy quarterback. »

He slaps Derrick on the back and says it really is about time he was promoted to the Alpha Team.

I am so tired.

Eyes gritty, mouth chalky, lips chapped and splitting, my skin feels like it's shifting beneath my clothes, and it takes my mind longer to click than usual, but it does.

"What do you mean by *Alpha Team*? Were you with my wife?"

New John shakes his head, saying no, he wasn't, because that was Charlie and he was Victor.

Derrick tells him that's not his line.

Not-So-Little Joe says I am only on step six.

New John shows me that hate-me smile as he tells me that step three is to figure it out for myself.

Shit.

SFO is the emptiest airport I have ever seen.

I say as much.

Derrick tells me that it's twelve three one zero one, like that is supposed to explain everything to me.

Joe parks next to a long, black hearse on the second level of a huge monolithic parking garage, and I stare at myself in the dark pools of the funeral car's tinted windows.

What I see must be me.

What I see looks like a freshly resurrected savior/cadaver. Dirty. Skin and bones. Mostly dead.

I ask why we're meeting Deirdre at the airport.

The window I'm staring into slides down, my reflection slowly being replaced by Deirdre's face. First I see her short, blonde hair behind a black mourning veil; then I see her eyes, red and puffy from crying; and finally I see that she's smiling. She says we have to hurry because the ceremony is about to begin.

I have no idea what in the hell she's talking about, but I smile right back at her like an idiot, because she's sexy and faux fragile. I feel my crusty lips ask her, "What ceremony is that?"

"You haven't heard?" She mock pouts. "Philosophy is dead. And she gave so much inane comfort to us all. . . . The world will be shocked at her passing."

I tell her that I didn't really know her that well, but that I'm sure her spirit will live on in the hearts of millions.

Deirdre says that is a beautiful sentiment.

Joe says wrong answer.

And Derrick turns off the camera, announcing a wardrobe change.

I climb from the hearse, dressed in black.

My shoes are way too big, clip-clopping on the surprisingly uneven asphalt of the runway, and I can't stop shaking from the fear. Sweat slickens my hair. My throat keeps trying to swallow something that's not there.

New John winks at me and says I'm a phenomenal actor.

I cannot believe we are doing this.

I'm sure we will be stopped at any moment, sure we are about to die before this can be pulled off, and that is the *only* thing keeping me from screaming.

I stare at the tiny Lear Jet, so sleek and beautiful, and I manage a twitching half smile because I'm thinking there is just no fucking way we are getting on this plane.

But two pilots and a stewardess walk down its fold-out

stairway with somber expressions and generic condolences. They are so polite, so understanding, so sorry for our loss. >>

Right on cue, Deirdre begins to sob.

The stewardess consoles her, hugs her, leads her away, and they climb the stairway, disappearing inside the small jet's fuselage.

Holy. Shit.

Deirdre's inside.

A commercial airliner roars to take-off a mile up the runway, deafening, and I wait for the violence to arrive, with my heart beating barely enough to keep me alive. I think the word I'm looking for is *desensitized*, but I'm not sure. I'm never sure.

The two pilots say that the bottom cargo hatch is already open to receive our dead mother. They excuse themselves to go prepare for flight.

I am shock.

I am fear.

When the two pilots climb the steps and disappear, I ask Derrick where's the security. Where's the post nine-eleven hysteria?

Joe says private charter. Big money.

"What does that have to do with it?"

"The more money you have," says Derrick, "the fewer rules apply."

I don't know what to say. So I follow the others' lead and grab a corner of the shiny coffin as it slides from the back of the hearse on rollers. My hand slips and my corner dips, hitting the runway and splintering.

"What the fuck?" yells New John. "It's a bomb, damn it!"

"Sorry," I mumble, "I'm tired. Our dead mother is heavy." I pick up my corner, then grunt and stagger toward the bullet-nosed jet with the rest of them.

Not-So-Little Joe begins to chuckle, grunting that I'm

right, it's true, Philosophy *was* heavy, a fat, lazy whore that gave birth to and ultimately helped kill civilization.

Derrick says it's the best kind of irony.

I want to ask a question, but my mind is a mud puddle, murky, unclear, and the words just keep sinking. I can't stop thinking something is wrong here.

Another airliner roars overhead, vibrating me, hurting my ears.

We walk the casket to the back of the jet, shove it up the tiny ramp, being especially careful with our dead mother, Philosophy, the bomb.

Everyone stands around huffing and puffing.

Joe lights up a smoke.

I wish I had a gun.

I think maybe I should have run.

I realize we actually aren't going to die, so I begin to scream, "Cut! Cut! Cut!"

Everyone but Joe frowns, as he asks me what seems to be the problem.

I tell him I want a script change, a rewrite, that I need to speak with the producers, because this whole scene is no good.

"It's too late for all of that," he says.

"Well then I want you to at least tell me why, because I need to know, because I can't figure it out for myself, because—"

A bee stings my ass.

"Ow!"

The world floats, shimmers, blurs, and dims.

The last thing I hear is New John asking someone how the cargo hatch opens and closes.

The answer is lost in The Black.

forty-six / rewind <<

MOVEMENT IN THE DARKNESS.

The sound of scurrying feet.

The blindfold is yanked from my eyes, and I blink away the blindness, fearfully awaiting a new reality.

An immense room takes shape. Not really a room. More like an underground cave, filled with stalking shadows and changing soft light, smelling of candle wax and the desperate hope of secret prayers, unwashed flesh, animals, death. The walls and ceiling are intricately painted with scenes of devastation and war, like some ancient, deranged society's attempt at recording their dark history for the future to see. A warning.

My flesh chills, shrink-wraps tight to my bones, making me feel small and weak. Cold. Brittle.

There are figures hidden in the deep shadows, unmoving, figures that could be people, but they are so still, they could also just be more paintings, or statues. I stand alone, bare feet in cool sand, looking up and trying to figure out why the dragons painted high above me are wrapped in flags from so many countries and are falling, on fire, trailing blood and flaming entrails with—

"Welcome," booms a voice filled with authority and something stronger than confidence. A deep voice. A man's voice. Whiskey burned and filtered through a million cigarette drags. A voice born to sing the blues. "Welcome to the Chapel of the Truly Free, the Last Church of the Apocalypse."

The last word echoes on too long in the eerie half dark, in the numbness of my mind. Fear runs down my leg, trickling from my left foot into the damp sand.

It smells an awful lot like urine.

"Amen!" shout hundreds of voices in fervent unison.

I still can't see anyone, and the sound bounces off the

stone walls, filled to their capacity with murals showing death at every glance. War. Abortion. Suicide.

Light explodes, a single cluster in a far corner of the ceiling, flooding the room too fast, too bright, and I shield my eyes with a hand as if against the summer sun.

I squint, blink, tears pooling as I adjust.

What I see disorients, confuses, amazes, makes no sense to me at all, until I hear the gravelly blues voice say, "Welcome to the past and the future, the alpha and omega, the beginning and the end. . . . Welcome to what lies beneath the layers of civilization's concrete. . . . Welcome to the beach, my child."

The cave, The Chapel of the Truly Free, is maybe the size of a sports arena, though asymmetrical and ruggedly carved from the earth. The floor is entirely made of sand, and brightly colored umbrellas stick up from it like trees in a Dr. Seuss book. Cheap lawn chairs, dirty, broken ice chests patched with duct tape, bright blow-up beach balls, tattered and torn volleyball nets: all await the tourists, the holiday crush. I watch in amazement as men and women, pale and ugly, clad only in stained underwear, file like ants from doorways carved into the stone walls to fill the mock beach, as if it is the center of a giant labyrinth to which all tunnels lead. The destination that is their only reward.

A post-nuclear holiday.

An underground beach for the insane.

They are smiling, gap-toothed, so happy and deranged, with their tangled hair unwashed and unkempt, as they pick their spots and throw down torn sheets, blankets, and towels, laying out to absorb the fluorescent-sun rays. Children begin their games of tag and volleyball with their skinny legs, bloated bellies, gleeful laughter.

I am stunned, horrified.

"How can so many people have the same delusion?" I wonder out loud, watching at least two hundred people take part in group insanity.

But the gravelly blues voice laughs, a calm, lazy laugh that comes from the tall man walking toward me through the crowded nightmare beach scene. People step out of his way with reverence.

"You are mistaken," he says, "to dismiss these people as being delusional."

I can't speak, only smile and gaze up at the young face, which does not fit his damaged voice. He looks like the most beautiful painting of Jesus Christ I have ever seen.

He smiles.

And I know why Mary Magdalen stopped turning tricks.

"My child, we have so much to discuss," he says with that broken voice, that perfect smile and two eyes the color of fresh honey—the same color as his long, tangled hair and soft-looking, uneven beard.

I feel my mouth ask him if he's Deirdre's husband.

He throws back his head and laughs so loud that it booms through the big stone cavern. All of the dirty, sickly, pale people on the make-believe beach begin laughing also, even though there's no way they could have heard whatever I said that was so funny.

He stops.

They stop.

The echoes stop, giving way to silence, and he tells me that he loved the woman I speak of, but her name wasn't Deirdre and they were never married.

"I don't understand," I whine.

He is so tall that he has to bend at the waist to take my hand in his, but when he does his face is inches from mine. My legs go weak when he whispers, "Confusion is only the front step to the house of knowledge."

I nod in total agreement.

I believe him 100 percent.

And you're right: I'm *that* stupid.

We sit down on the slowly warming sand, with the bright lights hurting my eyes and making me sweat, and the pale half-naked people gather around us, opening their recycled lunch pales and their cracked ice chests. Food is passed around in stained tupperware and soiled Chinese takeout containers. Each person eats from each container with grimy hands, slowly, happily, before passing it onto the next person.

No one offers me any.

I am surrounded, sitting in the middle of a massive circle—maybe two or three hundred people now—enjoying a bum's picnic, as they all watch me with their tall vagabond-Christ.

"You wanted to speak with me," he states.

My mind is a blank.

I can't stop staring at his savior-face.

"What is it you are looking for, child?"

"Answers," I say.

And the faux-sunbathing bum-people scare the shit out of me by shouting, "Hallelujah!"

As the echoes bounce off the walls covered in flowing frescoes of death, the Bum-Messiah's golden eyes grow smaller as he tells me, "Wrong answer."

He shows me his teeth.

He's not smiling.

forty-seven / fast forward

"WE HAVE NO CONTROL over who our parents are. . . ."

These words ooze down into The Black, surrounding me, caressing me like a silken lover, a silken straitjacket, binding me, pulling me, and I begin to rise.

I struggle, fight it. >>

I do not want to leave, but am powerless to stop it.

These words have a voice, the voice a face, the face two lips which press against mine so soft and spreading, as I let my tongue slide between them to dance with another's in a tangle of gossamer lace screen.

I open my eyes and reality is too bright, unforgiving, making me squint. Deirdre backs off a bit to freeze me with those cold blue eyes, shining wet behind her sheer black mourning veil.

We are in a phone-booth-sized bathroom built for dwarves.

"We have no control over what race, city, state, country, sex, religion, or culture is our birthright. . . . We are *born* into a political system as well. . . . And it is up to every individual person to accept or reject the given terms."

I stare at Deirdre, saying nothing, just listening to her words with my mind bending, because this is much more stimulating than the usual fortune cookie wisdom I get from my own mind. This is heavy.

This is a brick.

And bricks are heavy.

I tell her, "Hey, I thought you said Philosophy died."

In this tiny bathroom, we are crammed so close I can barely breathe. Deirdre slowly nods her head, looks down, mock pouting, then says she is only trying to help me out because this is going to be a very difficult scene for my character. "It's all action," she says, "because this is what happens when Philosophy dies."

I think I have claustrophobia, but the script is unavailable.

I'm feeling rather vague.

I tell her that I really, really, really missed her.

And when she asks me if I need help with my focus, I say, "No. No. No. I don't need any R & R."

I tell her it's just that we are on a plane, with a bomb, and I'm very uncomfortable with the way this scene has been played out on television recently.

Deirdre frowns, bites her bottom lip, and decides something. Lightning quick, she grabs my wrists, leans into me, pins me against the wall with my hands over my head, and she is kissing, licking, and biting my neck. With one hand keeping me pinned, her other slides down my stomach, down my pants, and she spreads her fingers, stroking, rubbing, as she whispers her warm breath into my ear. "You have ten minutes to ask three questions."

What?

My . . .

My . . .

My mind stutters, then goes blank.

I don't know what to say or do, but then my pants are unzipped and pulled down, her skirt hiked up, and the *do* part is solved.

When she kneels down, her silky, warm mouth covering me round, her hand rubbing tiny circles, I moan loudly, ask if she loves me.

Shit.

I hold my breath, waiting for the pain, feeling stupid.

Deirdre lightly kisses my stomach, laughs, and says I'm stupid.

She says next question.

And I try to clarify her—

"Next. Question."

She starts up again, picks up the pace, momentum, staring up into my eyes with that look, panting through her nose, and I can't think of another question, because the first one is the only one that really matters to me at the moment.

I still don't understand her answer.

"Eight minutes left. Faster."

With her other hand moving between her own legs, she's racing me. So I thrust my hips to meet her as she groans, moans, growls, says it's all beach. "Alllll *Beach*!"

"Seven minutes. Hurry up. Come on."

"No fair," I say, "Time is a system of control."

She tells me that won't be true much longer.

She's giggling.

I'm losing the race.

The jet's engines roar to life, heavy vibrations coming through the walls and floor, through her and into me, as she lets loose with that odd giggle again that is my signal to catch up or be left behind.

My hips move faster as I ask her what we're going to blow up.

She says the bomb.

She says six minutes.

I moan with pleasure, curse with frustration.

"Last question. Hurry."

And she's hurrying, smooth, frantic, well-practiced.

I'm trying to keep up, but my brain is slowing me down, because I'm attempting to word the next question like a prison she can't escape, because I'm zero-for-two, because I'll probably never have this chance again.

The engines grow louder, vibrations deeper, heavier, thicker, and I can tell she is eyeing the finish line, so I ask the question.

"How is this bomb going to change the world?"

"Because," she groans, eyes closed, concentrating, "the bomb is a time machine."

What?

That was my last question, last riddle, and I say, "No."

"Yes. Yes. Yes." She is moaning.

"No!"

And I sink to the floor, grab her arms, pull them up, hold her hands between us, unmoving.

She squirms, wiggling on the vibrating floor, trying to finish without me, but with me basically sitting on her, she can't. When she asks me why, with fire in her eyes, I tell her that step three is to figure it out for yourself.

It feels wonderful.

I'm waiting for her to bite off my nose, slice my throat with the razor blade she keeps under her right index nail, but she surprises me by figuring it out for herself.

She says, "*Quid pro quo*."

Her sly smile is a challenge.

She says the time machine is an E-bomb.

If I speak, I'll crack, so I just loosen my grip a little.

She tells me that the E-bomb creates an electro-magnetic pulse by using a Flux Compression Generator she built from junk-yard parts and old television transformers.

I let go of her hands.

With one for each of us, she begins to move slowly at first, telling me that the FCG is just plastique in a metal tube, the tube wrapped with a copper coil, the coil energized by a bank of capacitors, creating a small magnetic field.

She stands up, pulling me with her, and I'm moving with her now because she's doing it all; because this is the best of both worlds.

Sex *and* truth.

She starts bouncing, shaking, moaning that when the plastique is detonated, the tube flares out to touch the copper coil, creating a moving shockwave, a moving short-circuit, a ramping current pulse, high frequency, microwave range.

Her lips brush mine, her hot, hurried words tumbling out of her mouth, gushing into mine.

She grunts, grunts, grunts, says ramp times of hundreds of microseconds, peak currents of tens of millions of amps.

And I'm only vaguely understanding her, but I say, "Yes!"

I say, "Don't stop!"

And she says, "Hurry, faster, do it now!"

She tells me that there is no target to hit, just boom in the sky over the city, an invisible wave of lightning.

I bite her neck.

She says it's the Compton Effect.

I'm grunting dirty words in her ear, licking, sucking.

She tells me it's harmless to animals—plants and humans included—but that it renders all technology useless. Broken. Fried. Irreparable.

She twitches, arches her back, shoves her chest into my face, as she yells out the name, "Arthur! H! Compton!"

The jet's engines begin to whine.

The plane begins to move.

And I'm moving with Deirdre's movements, but lose my balance, falling sideways to hit the wall. I try to straighten up without breaking contact or losing momentum. My foot lands in a puddle.

The toilet flushes, sucking down my shoe.

But Deirdre doesn't miss a stroke, because we are skilled professionals at work here.

The plane takes off.

Gravity tugs on our flesh.

Deirdre licks my face, bites my chin, announces that she is coming, as she frantically tells me that firing a stream of highly energized protons into atoms that have a low atomic number causes them to release a stream of neurons!

And I'm firing.

And she's releasing.

And I'm releasing.

And she's firing.

And we are melting together in the tiny bathroom of a jet carrying a bomb that's a time machine, flying over a city that is about to be returned to the Dark Ages.

And what this feels like is better than love or happiness or insanity. I mean, the sensation is inexplainable, indescribable.

You should really just try it yourself.

forty-eight / rewind

STARING AT THE CHANGED FACE before me, I have that same feeling you get the first time your father is angry enough to threaten you with violence, that dawning knowledge that you do not really know this man and that he could be capable of terrible things.

"I'm sorry," I tell the Bum-Messiah, "I don't know my line."

His teeth disappear as his face softens, returns to the calm faux kindness of his Christ-like beauty. He tells me, "You do not seek answers, child. Answers can be false. It is truth that you seek."

"Truth," yells the flock.

It makes my body jerk. I'm terrified. The façade, the strange spell I was under by this man's presence, his power, is broken. I look at the walls and roof of this vast underground church—deep under New York City—at the macabre murals filled with so many bloody, dying faces, and I think there are only four exits.

I'm wondering what these people are eating.

The Alpha-Bum, Leper-Messiah, says, "We are eternal. It is pain that is the illusion. We are the next step in evolution, eating *E. coli*, drinking cancer, waiting for the coming Apocalypse to wash away Civilization like the rain, so we can reclaim the earth. . . . We are the new millennium's primitives . . . and we will be the only survivors."

Holy. Nutball.

The pale, dirty, half-naked, fluorescent sunbathers, the insane congregations of bum-people, are in a frenzy, shouting, jumping up and dancing, bouncing off each other like the whole cave is a mosh pit.

I get up with them, throw my hands in the air, wave them around like I just don't care, like I am more than happy to be delusional.

The Bum-Messiah claps and smiles.

I shout to him, "Well, thanks a lot for enlightening me. Good luck with all of that. I'll make sure and tell Deirdre you said hello." I dance away, pressing against the shaking, stinking, filthy bodies, as I try to make my way out of the circle.

I am pushing, shoving, feeling like the winning sperm deciding this is not the egg I was looking for, but I'm getting nowhere.

They won't let me leave.

They smile so deranged, pushing me back.

As I turn around, I watch the circle close in on me, swallowing me in a gyrating mass of unwashed flesh. I try to fight it, to slide, to plow, to move away, but it's no use. I'm too weak, too small.

Cold, bony hands viciously rip off my clothes.

Leather straps are slipped around my wrists. My ankles.

Suddenly I am quartered—each limb yanked a different direction—as I'm stretched and hoisted high above the sea of screaming lunatics.

Like crowd surfing at a concert.

Like witch hunting at Salem.

Looking up, I see the painted dragons on the ceiling, which are wrapped in flags of all of the countries, falling, trailing blood and fire. France. Greece. Spain. Uruguay. United States. China. Israel. England. Dying.

Germany. Dying.

Italy. Dying.

The crowd parts beneath me, and the leather straps are yanked tighter. My joints pop and crackle, and I'm slowly lowered onto some type of stone table. Cool. Rough. Sticky.

My mind says *picnic table*.

It says *altar*.

I can't move even a little bit. The stone table, the picnic-altar, smells like sweat and blood and dead animals, and the Leper-Messiah is standing over me, raising his hands, bringing immediate silence.

In his right hand is an old rust-colored butcher's knife.

No. Not rusted. It's stained.

In the silence, with the demented flock mouth-breathing, panting, I say, "Wait! You can't kill me! I still don't know the truth and you said that you would tell me the truth, because that's what I am really looking for!"

The Bum-Christ shows me his teeth again, without smiling, and shouts, "Truth? You want the truth? . . . The truth is that you are not one of us, the discarded, the unwanted, the thrown away, because you are an *owner*. . . . But how can you own the world? How can you own chaos? Disorder?"

His hands slowly come down.

He's screaming at me.

"Do you know what the *owners* of the world have taught me? Do you know what I've learned down here in your sewers? I've learned that there is no such thing as 'throwing away' something."

He yells, "Where do you think it goes?"

And just to keep him talking, just to delay my own killing, I say, "I don't know. Away?"

"Where," he barks, his gravelly voice a dark growl, "Where do shitty diapers, obsolete computers, smashed cars, nuclear waste, unloved plastic dolls, broken dishes, used condoms, infected syringes . . . Where do these things go?"

The insane thrown-away followers yell, "Amen."

The Alpha-Bum rips off his sweat-darkened shirt.

Flaming red diseased blotches, black and purple cancerous moles, cover him like burns, like tattoos. I stare up at his twisting face of rage.

"Look at me," he howls, "This is the truth!"

As the words make me shiver, as they echo out into the fluorescent sunshine of this underground nightmare, Deirdre says, "Truth is subjective."

What?

Her voice says, "You never could understand that, Beau."

I lift my head, crane my neck, and frantically try to see her, to prove that she is really here. Deirdre. Queen. Lover. Torturer. Director.

But I can't see her.

Every empty, dirty, deranged, and mangy head is turned the same way, and finally the sea of bloated pale filth parts to my left.

The tendons in my neck are on fire, my head shakes from the strain. My naked body is soaked in sweat. I see her.

Standing alone in a lonely carved exit, she is as I first saw her almost two years ago. Short, curvy, black-clad, with those full lips smiling through the mouth hole of her ski mask.

Kidnapper.

A pair of well-used, long-barreled revolvers dangle in her delicate hands.

This silence stretches out so long that all of the confused, ugly faces turn back and look past me to their leader.

I turn to look, too.

Mouth open, eyes wide, his face fills with a shock he just can't hide. Then he slowly begins to recover. Cold, calm hate solidifies in his face.

"Well, well," he growls. "If it isn't The Holy Mother Whore. Are you still young and stupid and trying to change the world? Or have you finally come to—"

The shot is beyond loud.

The blood is the darkest red.

And for this sliver of time, this single clicking-frame of the movie, before anyone breathes or moves, before the chemicals of our brains flood to induce panic, we all just watch the beautiful color of life spill from his chest.

Click: His face unbelieving.

Click: His body falling forward.

Click: The heavy sack of lifeless clay comes crashing down onto me, leaking his liquid cancer all over my bare stomach.

Screams.

Gunshots.

The shattering glass of a dying fluorescent sun.

And in the darkness, with the frantic madness unseen and moving all around me, someone cuts the straps off my ankles. Someone cuts the straps off my wrists. The dead weight of the dead Leper-Messiah rises and I am scooped up in strong arms, throwing my own around some else's neck, someone's bald head.

Not-So-Little Joe tells me to let go or get dropped.

But I don't.

And he doesn't.

I'm crying on his bony shoulder, because I am so happy to be alive, so happy to be kidnapped this time. To be saved.

Maybe saved is the wrong word.

I don't know why they're here, or where they're taking me, or why any of this is happening to me.

But at least I'm alive.

forty-nine / fast forward

DEIRDRE HANDS ME her filthy gun.

I take it in my hand, a feeling of comfort, of power filling me, and I ask her why.

I don't need to tell her that it's an important step.

She unlocks the tiny bathroom's door, and says that if at any time this scene becomes too uncomfortable, I can use the gun to rewrite the script. It's that easy.

She tells me that nobody is going to die unless I do the killing.

She's not smiling.

She's looking into my eyes and I have this whole melting thing happening in my chest, but emotions are the biggest liars of all and I don't know if I can trust.

Truth or lie, I take the gun.

I tuck it into my waistband, cover it with my black blazer, and Deirdre uses her thumb and forefinger to pinch the skin between my nostrils hard enough to bring tears to my eyes.

"Ow! What the hell are you doing?"

She tells me it's a funeral, that crying is in the script.

Tears roll down my tired face as I follow Deirdre into the root of the jet, and instead of my mind screaming *What?* it just snickers cruelly.

The plane is deserted.

The big screen television is on, the wet bar is lined with caramel-colored glasses, still full, unsipped, and it feels like a lie. Trick. Dream. Movie. So I pinch the bridge of my nose, rub my eyes, blink it all away.

It doesn't go away.

And I remember that this *is* a movie.

"Where's the cast? The crew? The lights, camera, action?"

Deirdre tells me that the ceremony has already begun.

She sounds like a little girl, so excited.

I follow her to the front of the cabin, where she knocks on the cockpit door, a beat to a song I know but can't name, and the door unlocks, opens. We step through.

Derrick and Joe are driving, I mean flying, and the new John is filming, not them, but what is outside.

I gaze out the wrap-around window at the night, at the thousands of lights far below us that blink like conversing synapses, captivating and hypnotizing me.

I wonder how dark it will be without them.

I am dazed and confused, yet feeling euphoric.

The script says so.

We've been in the air for maybe fifteen minutes, but I'm not sure because I think I'm the only one not wearing a watch.

They all keep checking their watches.

My mind is temporarily stuck, gnawing on a chunk of flawed logic, something I recognize as a problem yet cannot name. Just like the song that Deirdre tapped on the cockpit door. It's hard to explain.

All I know is that something important has been overlooked.

I'm right on the edge of a cliff, staring down into the abyss of understanding, so fucking close, but then it's gone and I'm just stupid again.

Home sweet home.

Not-So-Little Joe says it's time for Philosophy's promised son to be born.

I feel my hand slowly inching towards my waist, the gun.

And when New John turns the camera on me, I smile. I can't help it. This is all just too surreal. It's so quiet, faux somber, yet the excitement is thick and intoxicating beneath the façade, cleverly disguised as tension.

My hand slides in my coat, wrapping around a cool metal handle that warms almost instantly in my clammy palm.

Joe looks at his watch and says, “Under a minute and directly over Silicon Valley.”

“Perfect,” says Deirdre.

Derrick announces that in Philosophy’s memory, he would like to quote a famous scientist.

Everyone laughs.

I don’t get it. I don’t laugh. I slowly pull the gun out and bring it down at my side with stealth you’d be proud of.

Joe gives Derrick the go ahead and grabs my left hand, my empty hand, pulling it to a lever on the blinking instrument panel.

The lever is marked “Hatch Release.”

I wonder what would happen if I shot him.

I wonder if Deirdre would kill me if I shot him.

Derrick says that the quote is from Albert Einstein, who once said, “I know not with what weapons World War III will be fought, but World War IV will be fought with sticks and stones.”

Silence.

My skin suit shrinks, tightens, tingling under my clothes.

Silence.

The camera zooms in on me, my heart pumping, air passing in and out of my lungs without my permission.

Joe tells me that I am the star of the show

He says the honor is mine.

I don’t move.

He says twenty seconds.

I am stone.

Deirdre’s lips are right at my ear, her gun in my hand, smashing up against her thigh. She tells me that the bomb will work even if I do not release the hatch. The only difference is whether or not we die.

For a reason I will never admit to another soul, not even you, I pull the fucking lever.

Everyone cheers and laughs, looking out the windows.

I am regret, shame.

Deirdre kisses my cheek.

I feel like God with a conscience, accepting the blame.

And when I lean over a happy Joe, thrusting the barrel of Deirdre's gun against his shaved skull, he doesn't even flinch.

"Rewrite," I say.

I ask him what happened to the real flight crew, the two pilots and the stew.

Joe just chuckles like a father at a silly child.

Through gritting teeth, I tell him to answer me, and quick, because his life depends on it.

I'm waiting for Deirdre to attack me from behind.

I'm waiting to pull the trigger.

But Joe says I need to lighten up, to pay better attention, because if I hadn't been screwing in the bathroom, I would have seen the unconscious flight crew and the stewardess get tossed out of the jet five minutes after take-off.

What?

He says it's really too bad they were wearing parachutes, because he didn't know his life would depend on it.

He asks me if this means he'll live forever, but I'm not paying attention anymore. I'm not interested, because my brain is screaming *Eureka!*

I know.

I know the name of the song Deirdre tapped on the door, the unnamed problem I recognized in their plan, the flawed logic, the missing piece of the script!

And it feels so good to finally figure something out for myself, to figure out something they did not. My eyes are clamped shut, cheeks cramping from a smile that is way too wide for my second face.

But before I can say anything, before I can rub my victory in their faces, I hear a large clap of thunder. >>

I stop smiling.

Everyone cheers, claps, yells quotable revolutionary slogans.

My stomach sinks, falls to my feet, as Deirdre hugs me and as Derrick pats me on the back. I shove them away.

They're frowning, confused, angry, and I'm trying to speak but I can't catch my breath. I can't make a single sound. Finally I manage to inhale, then scream the word, "*Idiots!*" so loud, so violent, that their faces cringe.

An invisible wave washes over the jet.

It feels like turbulence.

It's not turbulence.

I watch the beginning of knowledge dawn in furrowed brows.

The engines cut out.

The lights go out.

And we are standing in a dead chunk of technology, a dead hunk of metal that is about to fall from the sky like a meteor.

Meteor.

But I decide I don't want to die yet and I grab Joe, shaking him, digging the gun point into his head and screaming at him, "Where are the fucking parachutes? How many are left?"

Joe is calm.

"How many?" I yell.

His one word answer soils my black funeral suit.

fifty / play

TWO.

One is no longer the loneliest number.

New John drops the camera, keels over dead.

I'm freaking out.

We're all crammed into this tiny cockpit of a plane that is no longer flying, just falling, and I'm secretly glad that New John dropped dead, because I didn't like him anyway, and because it's one less person I might have to kill in order to ensure that I get one of the two remaining parachutes.

Hey, don't judge me.

This is survival, me or them.

And I still have Deirdre's gun pressed up against the back of Joe's skull. I'm *this* close to squeezing the trigger. I'm thinking now or later: what's the difference?

Joe spins around, elbow up, moving the gun, and his fist tells me that the difference is a broken nose.

Then I'm sitting next to New John, Dead John, on the floor.

Deirdre screams, runs over me, disappears through the door.

Derrick is pulling on the steering wheel—the flying wheel, whatever the hell it's called—trying to keep us out of a nosedive and failing. He yells that it's time to go. He asks what's wrong with John.

Joe says it's a pacemaker, an oversight, an easy rewrite.

Me. I'm holding my wet, flowing nose, stunned.

Joe bends down and takes my gun, tells me to grab the camera and follow him.

"It's broken," I tell him in my new, broken, nasal voice.

He says the nose will heal, it's no big deal.

"No. The camera, you idiot. It's broken. Just like the plane and John's pacemaker."

"No shit," he says, "but grab the tape inside of it, because this is a great scene. Action. Suspense. There's no need to scrap it."

Joe leaves the cockpit, shutting the door, leaving me sitting on the floor, bleeding, confused, waiting to die.

Derrick is still fighting the plane, fighting gravity, and he turns his head, looks down at me, his face beet red, cords standing out in his neck like thick ropes covered in skin, with beads of sweat pouring down his smooth face and dripping from his chin.

He is looking at me, staring, straining, unmoving.

I tell him, "I don't want to die. *Please* help me."

I'm trying to keep from crying, but tears spill anyway.

A softness shines in Derrick's dark brown eyes as he tells me that he will get the tape for me, that everything will be OK, that I'll see.

I'm so grateful for his kind words, his compassion.

He says, "Dying can't be as bad as we all think."

What?

And he laughs the craziest laugh I have ever heard.

That's it. I'm up and moving, scrambling to the door and pounding on it, screaming and yelling the word *no* over and over and over again, because the fucking thing won't open.

My brain starts again and I turn the knob so—

I'm sucked from the cockpit, flying through the air, out into the fuselage, tumbling, twirling, smacking against the headrests of luxuriously padded seats.

My foot catches an arm rest.

My hand snags a seatbelt.

And I'm floating in midair, hanging on for dear life, with the vacuum sucking at me so loud that my ears stop working.

It sounds like a distant waterfall.

My one remaining shoe is sucked off, gone.

I'm hanging on, but for how long?

The jet shakes, tilts forward, down.

And Derrick flies by me with the videotape between his teeth, his arms stretched out like fucking *superman*.

I drop my head, look underneath and behind me to see him get sucked out a black hole, open door, like soap scum down a drain.

Shit!

My mind is screaming at me to *let go*.

My mind is screaming *no*.

What the hell am I supposed to do?

All I want to do is live, but my brain is telling me that just cannot happen in a falling dead plane.

The pressure is incredible, tugging, winning.

My hand is slipping.

And before I can make myself let go, I let go.

I'm sucked into the night air so cold, my skin freezing. I'm having trouble breathing because there isn't enough oxygen up here. I fly through the darkness. Not really flying. Really falling. And I watch a jagged, moving rip in the night sky, our jet, quickly mend itself to reveal a blanket of stars which sparkle against the blackest midnight I have ever seen.

I have no parachute.

I am going to die.

I have never seen something so beautiful in my entire life.

fifty-one / play

I'VE BEEN FALLING forever, my whole life, at least three minutes.

At first I was unaccepting of death.

But not now.

No, now I am beyond denial. I am embracing the end with a determined enthusiasm which is total freedom from all things, total liberation from all I have ever known.

I am diving straight down, hands thrust forward, pointed together like a rocket, an arrow, headfirst into the wind, slicing through it, waiting for the earth to meet me, crush me, swallow me up, and the only unanswered question left in my mind is how big of a crater I will leave for others to discover.

It is an indescribable feeling.

You should really just try it for yourself.

My eyes are frozen open, but I see nothing. I feel nothing, only a curious excitement as to what will happen next, after, beyond all of this, and I'm really hoping that everyone is wrong.

Everyone.

Because whether it's nothing or something, I'm looking for originality. For new. For different. Something never dreamed of, never argued over or used to excuse mass murder.

But a tiny spark of light appears, moving toward me on my right, small and bright, growing larger, coming at me, and I'm hoping it's not an angel or a god or an alien or a fairy godmother.

Wait a minute. Am I already dead?

Do you feel the ground that kills you?

The light shoots past me, hissing, blazing, almost hitting me, shrinking in the darkness as it flies away.

Then there's another. Another. And another.

I aim my dive for their origin, because I've got nothing better to do, and no reason not to. If someone is shooting at me, then maybe I can take him out, take him with me by landing on him.

Someone shooting at me?

Who?

Why?

And just like that, I no longer want to die.

It could be Joe or Deirdre trying to tell me something, trying to keep me alive. I don't know how or why, but it's a thought that rapidly gains momentum. So I angle my body—aim my dive—toward where I think the . . . the . . . flares . . . they're flares!

Another one comes to life not so far away, shooting off the other way, and my mind screams that they are already on the ground, that this is their final trick, the last laugh on me.

But something rushes at me, dark and huge, hits me softly, giving, swallowing me, wrapping around me, and I bounce off of something hard. But I never stop falling. I'm still tumbling out of control, with something light flapping all around me.

My mind says *parachute*.

It says *idiot*.

I must have hit one of them, took the parachute, took them out, and, even though this means I'm still going to die, I find it to be a perfect ending. At least I took one of them with me.

I hope I killed Joe.

I would smile, but my face is frozen.

Something crashes into me, hard, heavy, taking my breath away, grabbing onto me, clinging to me, wrapping around me, and I'm spinning head over heels. But I level out with the wind at my back and someone on my chest.

The sound of metal and zippers.

I'm yanked so violently that bones pop from sockets.

I scream.

I yell.

I float.

The wind is gone and it's quiet now, as Not-So-Little Joe tells me that was a close call, that they almost lost me, that he seriously doubted I would be able to figure it out for myself.

I stammer, thank him, hate myself for thanking him.

He asks me where's the videotape.

When I say Derrick has it, he says nothing.

Floating.

Drifting.

"Did Derrick make it?" I ask.

He growls that we'll find out when we land.

I don't really know what else to say to him. He just saved my life in a probable-death-case scenario, which *he* created. His hands are iron vice-grips, clinging to me, crushing my arms. His legs are wrapped around me, flexed and bulging and keeping me alive. And in the swirling gray darkness, with my face way too close to his, I ask, "Deirdre. She had the other chute, right? I mean, she's going to be OK, right?"

He tells me yes, but who knows, because a lot of things can go wrong on a stunt like this. He's not sure if Derrick saw the flares and was able to follow them to her, or if she got a clean release from the first parachute after the initial collision, dove after him, was able to grab ahold of him and pull the back-up chute.

"But if you could do it," he says, "so could a chimpanzee."

It takes me a couple of breaths, but I realize he's describing exactly what he just did for me. I almost thank him again, but bite my tongue to keep the words from forming.

The coppery blood filling my mouth wakes me up a little, tells me that this is a movie, and since I'm not sure if we're still recording, I ask Joe how this one E-bomb changes the world.

"Good question," he says, "but bad math."

He tells me that the *one* is actually two hundred and seventeen, strategically placed in chosen cities around the world to assure maximum effect.

What?!

I cannot even begin to imagine what will happen when two hundred and seventeen metropolitan areas around the world are instantly reduced to a life lived two centuries ago.

Can you?

It makes me light-headed, excited, fearful, for some reason a little angry, and I tell Joe, "That's still not the whole world."

I'm waiting for him to say something like "It's a start," but instead he says, "The thing about these bombs is that when the electro-magnetic pulse, the shockwave, crosses a powerline or a telecommunications line, it latches on to ride the electricity as far as it will take it, leaving nothing but dead technology in its wake."

"In an everything-connected world," he says, "who knows?"

I'm trying to picture how far the ripples will reach, but I'm having trouble thinking where the shore would be.

I don't really feel anything at the core of me.

And the whole thing that's really bothering me is that this whole thing isn't really bothering me.

I still can't feel my face, but I think I'm smiling.

Because I'm not going to die.

Because it's not too often you get the chance to land on a different planet than the one you took off from.

Because, let's face it, this is new and original and exactly what I was hoping for on the other side of death, and I didn't even have to die to get there.

Out of the swirling dark fog, the cold wet firmament, the ground rushes up to slam into my feet, my back, shooting what feels like electricity up my legs and into my spine.

But electricity no longer exists, so I know it's just pain.

Good old hot, tingling pain fills my frozen bones, thaws my skin, stokes a fire inside me that is actually a metaphor for hate, because I know that after I see Deirdre again, after I see this new version of an old world, after this movie has almost reached its end, for the final scene I am going to have to kill these people.

It's not that I want to.

It's just that I know how this movie has to end in order to be accepted by the public, the consumers, to maximize the bottom line: dollars.

Joe lets go, is pulled off of me, dragged away.

When I sit up, slowly, trying to focus, trying to stay awake, I see that the ground I'm on isn't ground at all, but the roof of a car. I start to snicker, then howl with laughter, as I let myself slide back down to lie on the smooth, cold sheet of metal, because this car, every car, might as well be a giant rock. A prop. A tombstone. A dead, useless machine left to remind us of the civilization that once allowed us to think we ruled it.

In memory of . . .

And closing my eyes, I can smell the ocean's tangy salt. I can hear the waves crashing into the beach. Again. Again. Again. Far away.

It is the only sound left in the entire city.

It is all that I hear.

fifty-two / play

THE SOUNDS OF GUNSHOTS ECHOING through the empty, post-modern night snaps open my eyes, and I sit up on the sunken roof of a dead car that caught me falling from the sky.

And how long ago was that?

Was I just sleeping?

Again, gunfire shatters silence.

Wide awake now, heart racing, I roll off the car to land on feet made of wet concrete—soft, mushy, heavy, useless—and I crumble to the cold street, smacking my head, crying out, with my legs all pins and needles and pain.

What the hell is going on?

I force myself to breathe, breathe, breathe, trying to get a grip on it all, and I look up, look around, but the streets are completely empty.

It's beyond eerie.

I'm wondering where Not-So-Little Joe is.

As the blood pumps, as the pain recedes, I climb to my feet, my mind telling me that there is something wrong with the picture of the world it's attempting to process. But exploding bullets split the night, snag my attention, and I begin to stand up. I hobble in the direction of the warfare, because that's probably the best way to find Not-So-Little Joe.

Or Deirdre, if she's not dead.

Or Not-Jewish Derrick, if he's still alive.

And if there were such a thing as a higher power, you could say I'm praying they're not dead. And if language were not a system of control, you could say I'm hoping that they're still alive. Because at this point I have no idea what to do without them.

I gimp toward the sound of destruction, of death, of war pop-pop-popping in the night somewhere close by, in what appears to be the financial district of some major city I cannot be sure enough to name. I have to squint because the deserted streets are lit up like a parade of—

What?

These lights are shining so bright, nuclear bright, without electricity because electricity is dead, and my mind is screaming at me, yelling, "What does this mean?"

But there is no answer and I'm stuck on pause, standing on the corner in front of a store display window with the sickened greenish-white glow of computer screens and televisions spilling out onto me. It makes me feel nauseated, grimy.

I think I'm going to puke.

The giant display window shatters in slow motion and I try to move, flinch, dive, but it all takes too long, and by the time I finally get my back turned to the window, I'm screaming, panicking, a chunk of glass embedded in my right cheek, just under my eye, spreading fire through my entire face. When I reach up by reflex, my hand comes away covered in blood that looks like thick, black motor oil in this menacing fluorescent light.

Joe runs by me in a blur.

I look to my left and see Derrick and Deirdre sprinting toward me, hair flying, guns in hand, screaming the word *run* over and over. They pass me so fast, so close, that a strand of my long hair blows against my face where it sticks to tacky, black blood.

My brain kicks in.

Suddenly my shoeless feet—one bare, one socked—no longer hurt, because I'm no longer paying attention to them.

I've turned the mental channel to some kind of action flick where I'm running for what I'm guessing is my life, and somebody is shooting at me with the same poor accuracy you typically see in movies like this.

It's surprising how fast you don't realize you can run when your life depends on it, and I'm hauling serious ass as I sprint down streets which are somehow both way too bright and oddly dark, unnatural, like on a night-scene movie set where close-ups are needed for emotional effect.

I'm wondering where the cameras are.

I'm wondering if the bomb was a bomb at all, or if maybe it didn't work.

I'm wondering who's chasing us.

When I catch up to Deirdre, to run alongside her and Derrick, I ask, "Who in the hell is shooting at us?"

She actually laughs at me, can you believe it?

I mean, here we are running down the streets of a dead technological society with people trying to kill us, with bullets bouncing off of metal and concrete, with windows shattering all around us, with blood pouring down my face, with the boom of the barking guns echoing off of bright-lifeless-rectangular mountains of steel and glass, which reach toward the sky like modern-day towers of Babel . . . and Deirdre is laughing at me like a little girl poking fun at her girlfriend.

"You run like a girl," she says, and giggles at me with her short blonde hair bouncing, her eyes a violent shade of green in the garish light which should no longer exist.

It kind of pisses me off, but it also melts me. To see her alive and beautiful and unchanged. I ask, "Who's trying to kill us? And why are the lights still on?"

Not-Jewish Derrick, who looks like he's having just as much fun as Deirdre, says that only certain types of lights remain—mostly fluorescents—and the light is a chemical reaction to the electro-magnetic pulse we sent screaming through the atmosphere like an invisible tsunami.

Deirdre says, "Bums."

It takes me a second before I understand that Deirdre is answering my first question, because I was listening to Derrick and thinking about the lights, about how they remind me of me.

The lights are dead, but just don't know it yet.

We turn a corner. The guns stop barking. We turn left down a side street, right down an alley, then emerge onto another main street lined with slightly smaller buildings and stores. I have to swerve to avoid crashing into Not-So-Little Joe, who stands in front of the shattered window of a small shop, next to four bicycles.

Derrick trips over a bike, skids on concrete, sprawls on the sidewalk, emits a short sound of pain.

Deirdre jumps over him.

We all stop still.

My heart too loud, my face aflame with a bright red pain that seeps into my vision, I look at Joe. He's not even winded, not even sweating, just leisurely smoking a cigarette.

"Pick one," he says. "We've got to hurry."

Between ragged breaths from burning lungs, I tell him that I think . . . we . . . lost them . . . The Bums.

He ignores me, telling everyone to hurry.

Derrick gets up, gets on a mountain bike. Black. Sleek.

"Why," I breathe out in a burning gush of air, "Why hurry?" >

Deirdre hops on a ten-speed. Bright yellow.

This leaves me with a red BMX bike built for a ten-year-old, which I climb on to follow suit.

The lights go out. Not quickly, just slowly fading to black.

In the darkness, the darkest night I've ever seen, I look up to see more stars than you could ever believe exist.

That's when Joe, who I can't even see from ten feet away, says, "It's time for phase two."

He says it's time to visit the library.

fifty-three / play

WHEN THE FLARE SNAPS OUT, the darkness is total.

Without electricity, the middle of downtown, right in the parking lot of a giant shopping mall, in some major city—maybe San Francisco or San Jose—it's as dark as if I were in the middle of the wilderness.

I can't even see the concrete.

I'm sucking as hard as I can.

Deirdre snaps another flare. She returns to ripping brand new towels into tiny strips and covering them in baby oil.

Not-Jewish Derrick is popping corks and emptying wine bottles. He pours them into the gutter as fast as he can, then hands them to Joe.

Not-So-Little Joe's filling them halfway with kitty litter and lining them up, all in a row.

But me, I just keep on sucking. Waiting. Sucking.

This is assembly-line processing at it's finest.

We've been shopping.

Not really shopping, really looting. Or not even looting. More like gathering.

Since there aren't many rocks lying around downtown streets, the pockets of my funeral pants are stuffed with spark plugs, which everybody seems to agree work much better at breaking windows than rocks anyway. And now I've got a free pair of sneakers on my feet so I can walk through the broken glass without screaming or bleeding.

My cheeks are aching, cramping from all of this sucking, and finally the dreaded payoff comes: my mouth fills with cool gasoline, gagging me, choking me. I cough, spit it up, pull the piece of green garden hose out of my mouth and hand it to Joe. Gas runs down my chin and from my nose. The fumes burn my eyes.

Joe starts topping off the bottles.

I get up, stagger over to our bicycles, and reach into one of the shopping carts we've tied to the bikes with rope and bungee cords. I dig around, pull out a plastic bottle of Swiss water from some company that doesn't exist anymore, twist off the cap and with my head thrown back, empty the bottle onto my face. I swallow, cough again, spit again, rinsing out my mouth. Then I walk over to Deirdre to help finish stuffing the greasy bath-towel-strip-fuses into the wine bottles now filled with kitty litter and gasoline.

Homemade napalm.

My mind won't stop nagging, won't stop grasping, so I tell Deirdre loud enough for everyone to hear, "Let me get this straight. . . . We just killed every piece of technology, every machine within the blast radius or connected to a power source, and now we're going to burn all of the libraries? And this is going on in two hundred and seventeen cities around the world?"

Give or take a few failed efforts, everyone agrees.

It makes me lightheaded. I mean, I'm completely awed by how massive a scale we're talking about here. My mind won't flex enough to wrap around it. There are just way too many variables, way too may scenarios being played out inside my head without enough knowledge to follow any of them to completion.

I mean, can you?

Can you see how far the ripples go in an everything-connected world? Effect on the structure of civilization? Military action without any form of communication?

What happens when you get sick?

What happens when you get hungry?

All of these questions are just piling up in my head, clogging my mind, blocking the pathway to my vocal cords, and so I just keep on stuffing the oily rags into bottle after bottle, until we're done, until finally a question slips free, the words forming on my lips, spewing from my mouth, "How are six billion people going to survive without supermarkets?"

"They're not," says Deirdre.

"What?"

Not-So-Little Joe, who's loading up the bottles of napalm like he's a professional bag-boy, looks at me in the phosphorus glow of the flare lying outside the fire zone, and tells me, "Everybody wants to save the earth, but they're all delusional. They think they can have civilization and a livable planet, too. They've been taught to ignore limits, including limits to population. Even the radicals, the so-called anarchists, so-called revolutionaries, could never be honest about it and just admit that what we really need is not just to stop the clearcuts of trees, but to accept that the world is going to clearcut people: that the world needs a new start."

I am so stunned that I have to lean against the cold metal of the dead car from which we siphoned the gas.

"It's a moral hang-up," he says, "a part of Christianity they could never quite shake, even with all of their intelligent hate."

I'm staring at something I can't see, looking at nothing at all really, because my entire existence is losing feeling. I'm numb. I'm thinking. . . . New York. . . . Bejing. . . . Athens. . . . Madrid. . . . Paris. . . . Rome. . . . All of them dying.

Derrick says, "It's not as bad as it sounds. A few of the second-world countries and *all* of the thirds will be fine; in fact without the first worlders stealing from them, the people will be much better off, almost immediately."

I ask, "But what about? . . ."

"The more sophistic-ated"—that's how he says it, with a break in the middle—"and 'advanced'"—you can hear the quote marks—"the society, the more fucked you are."

He smiles wide, happy, proud, which is kind of creepy, because I'm only used to seeing half of his face.

I'm wondering where all of the cameras are.

He says it's the best kind of irony.

Deirdre announces that the earth will support as much life as it is meant to support without our cheating, and she gets up to walk over to one of the shopping carts, then rifles through it.

The flare snaps out. Instant nothing.

Another snaps to life, hissing, bright red in Derrick's hand, right in front of me, as he says, "It's just an even playing field now. Not only poor people will die of starvation or lack of medical care, because the rich have the same odds. This is an all-inclusive action. Race, sex, the size of your income and your bank account, none of this has anything to do with survival or quality of life anymore. That will be based on how well you get along with the land where you live."

I want to scream, but let it go.

Whatever. Spilled milk. Meteor.

Joe says we can have this discussion later, when we get home tomorrow.

Home?

He says we need to hurry up and get to the library before people start waking up and freaking out.

My mind fills with pictures of people waking up to curse their dead alarm clocks, empty coffee pots, broken water heaters. I see them walking out into the streets to squint at the bright sun of two centuries ago and complaining to neighbors they don't even know. But even as all of these images flicker through my brain's cinema-plex, it's only a silent movie to which I'm barely paying attention, because a single-word sound bite is playing over and over in Joe's gruffy old voice, inside my head.

Home.

Home.

Home. . . .

My legs are throbbing.

Lungs cold, wet, stinging.

My nipples are raw from my wet shirt rubbing against them.

And I'm pretty sure we're lost, because we've been riding through these city streets long enough to see the world go from black to purple to dirty-snow gray.

I still haven't seen a single living thing. Not a cat or a dog. Not a bum or a cop or a hooker. Maybe the thick fog that's swallowed this whole city, making everything slick and dripping, has driven them inside, but this is beginning to feel more and more like a closed set.

The cameras could be anywhere, everywhere.

I think the word I'm looking for is *denial*, but it could also be *sick* or *insane* or *intelligent*.

For the thirtieth time, I am about to ask how much longer

before we get there, but then we turn a corner, nice and slow so we don't flip the shopping carts we're all towing, and my eyes open wide, my mouth drops, because we're finally there.

I think we're too late, though.

There's a hole in the fog, like the hole in an overcast sky from a blazing sun, except that the sun is a giant stone building engulfed in flames, and on the rows and rows of front steps between Greek columns are a group of filthy, cheering street people throwing firebombs that break and splatter bright orange flames like fluorescent paint.

Bums.

Not thinking, I yank the brake, and before I can get my feet on the ground, my shopping cart slams into me, tips me over, knocks me to the ground. My elbow cracks against the cold, wet concrete.

I scream out.

By the time I untangle myself from the bicycle and the ropes and the bungee cords and the shopping cart, then scramble to my feet, holding my bloody elbow, gunshots are crack-crack-cracking, ricocheting off the street all around me with tiny blue sparks, crashing into cars, shattering glass. Some just disappear in the murky, gray mass behind me. I freeze, unable to move for a moment both somehow short and way too long. The moment stretches, stretches. I watch The Bums—hairy, dirty, screaming—charge down the street at us, emptying their guns and lighting their firebombs.

Derrick, who stopped right next to me, begins to dance. His arms and legs swing like some strange ritual or jazz dance as bullets puncture him, spin him around. He looks at me with his deceptively young face smoothed and relaxed, in shock.

His eyes stay wide, but something behind them blinks.

He crumples like a wet blanket. Mostly red.

And that does it. I move. I turn my back on it all. I sprint down the street and into the cool swirling fog. Because I never really cared anyway. I never cared about killing electricity or burning knowledge or changing the world by clearcutting people.

All I ever really wanted was to live.

To live and fall in love.

Live, fall in love and be happy.

Live, fall in love, be happy and popular.

Live, fall in love, be happy, be popular and—

All right! Fuck it! I wanted it *all*!

But now all that I wanted is all that is gone, and all I have left is all I ever really had to begin with. My life. My body, stinking, living, breathing, bleeding, and my mind, screaming and panic driving. My burning, tired legs are pistoning to keep me alive, for no other reason than it is the one thing I can still control.

But I'm slowing now.

Even my body is quitting on me.

Deirdre pedals up on my left.

Joe pedals up on my right.

Deirdre tells me to hop in the shopping cart.

"No, " I huff, "I'm tired of dying in small amounts. Of saving the earth instead of myself."

Joe starts to laugh, then says living is better than surviving.

Before I can scream at him that's exactly what I was fucking talking about, I realize that's exactly what he's talking about. He's agreeing with me.

Joe says it's over.

What?

Deirdre says it's time to go home, time to just live.

And me, I'm stupid enough to laugh and cry in relief, ignorant belief. I'm so insanely happy to hear that it's finally over, that we can go home, wherever the hell home is now, that I swerve to my left and hop up into Deirdre's shopping cart.

I lie there on bottles of water and clothes and food.

Stupid me.

I'm so content.

There are only three of us left.

It's an odd number.

fifty-four / play

"I'D RATHER DIE."

This is what I tell them.

Joe says that is always an option.

Deirdre just giggles her little-girl laughter, leans in against me, tells me that the movie is over and I can stop overacting anytime now.

"You can stop being so pathetic," says Joe.

Instead of telling him that I'm not overacting, which would mean I really am just pathetic, I ask him how the movie could be over without an ending.

"What about the conclusion?" I ask.

Joe says that only individual lives have endings: the same one.

Deirdre tells me that the conclusion is a legacy/new reality.

"Listen," she says.

I cock my head, concentrate, strain, but all I hear is a quiet nothingness. A light breeze whistling. A gull screeches overhead, close, but hidden in the thick fog. The lazy salt water laps at the soggy wooden dock moving rhythmically under our feet like a slow dance.

"I don't hear it. I don't hear anything."

"Bingo," she says.

And Joe starts going on about what I'm hearing is life,

without the constant hum of machinery, without the never-ceasing vibrations of electrical currents moving through our bones.

The worst part about what he's saying is that he's right. Once I notice it, I can't stop noticing it. This loud, peaceful quietude. The unpressurized silence.

But it doesn't change how I feel about the ocean.

"I don't care," I tell them. "I'd rather die."

You see, my problem is this: The ocean freaks me out. It's completely unpredictable. It can turn ugly and angry and kill you for no other reason than a change in the weather. And that's not even getting into the monstrous predators that cruise around beneath, hidden, just waiting for a free meal. For you and me.

I say as much.

But Joe says it's safer than flying now, and laughs at his own mind as he digs through his backpack, looking for something.

Deirdre puts her arm around my waist, pulls me to her, presses me against her hard little body, and tells me, "It's going to be just fine now. We're going home. And this is the fastest and easiest way to get there. OK?"

She's talking to me like young people talk to the elderly, like grown-ups talk to children, or men to women. Like I'm unreasonably scared or unimaginably stupid.

I've always hated that. It pisses me—

"Ow!"

A tiny pinprick, right cheek, and the numbness fills my ass as my body stiffens, but then it all drains, falling to my feet, leaving me limp and slipping away.

I fall in slow motion, stuttering single frames.

Lying on the cold, soft dock, I watch Deirdre and Joe look down on me with what seems like sad smiles, talking in muffled tones I cannot make out.

I think one of them said my first name. My real name.

And then I don't exist. Nothing does.

I am in that place which is . . . is . . . in between.

It is becoming my favorite way to exist, I think.

Somewhere between death and consciousness, not dreaming, not thinking, yet slowly becoming aware of my own being. I hear the heart, the blood sliding through me, the lungs taking in and letting out the air which surrounds me. My body doing the work to keep me alive, without my permission, without my gratitude. A thankless job.

It's kind of like being born again, only I'm smarter.

"Drink," coos the soft voice.

Soft fingers run through my long hair, caress my scalp, make me feel soft all over, as I exhale, long and deep, so happy and warm and not yet fully here. Fading back and forth, I am in that place which is . . . in between.

Deirdre sticks her tongue in my ear, hard, wet, forceful.

And I'm wide-awake. Eyes snap open. I'm lying here, uncovered, undressed, sweating on a waterbed, which I realize is not a waterbed because it's not moving beneath me. It is everything else that is moving beneath me, slowly. Softly bobbing, rolling like a ship at sea.

My brain says that I just took step three.

I hear waves crashing in the distance.

Nausea punches me in the stomach.

Fear expands in my mind, releasing chemicals that produce mental pictures of Moby Dick and Jaws pulling people under as they scream and gurgle, as the dark blue water runs blackish red.

My skin suit tingles, relaxes.

Sweat pours from tiny pores.

Heat flashes tumble through me, and I try to lick my lips, but they are dry, shriveled, plastic, jagged.

Deirdre is standing next to me, next to the bed, with a backdrop of darkly polished wood tilting back and forth. Back and forth. Her short, platinum hair distorts the shape of her head as it sways out to one side, then the other, in the same lazy rhythm.

I think I'm going to be sick.

My mouth floods with saliva.

Deirdre hands me some water.

Staring at the plastic bottle in my hand, watching the water level shift to an odd angle as the boat rolls, creaking, I have to suck the back of my throat shut to keep from vomiting. Between gulps of air, I ask Deirdre to please knock me back out until we land or dock or whatever.

"Until we get home," I plead.

But she just smiles, slightly tilted, and says we *are* home.

What?

Muffled waves crash harder up above.

She says I've been sleeping for two days and that we are home already, that we are just waiting for the tide to come in so we can anchor closer to shore and swim for it.

"You need to drink," she says.

I tell her that there is absolutely no fucking way I'm swimming to shore.

She sticks out her bottom lip, mock pouting, frowning.

I tell her again about the ocean. I tell her about the huge, hungry animals waiting to eat us, hunting the deep blue sea, looking for humans to devour because they hate us or are jealous or just plain don't know any better.

She starts laughing at me, can you believe it?

"Haven't you seen the movies? The brutal attacks? All of the terrible stories, the bloody news footage? Shark Week?"

"I have never seen it happen," she tells me in a soft voice, "so it does not affect me as experienced truth."

What the hell does that mean?

"Dropping anchor," yells Joe, above us, on deck.

The splash, the metal chain unwinding in its housing, sounds like a dinner bell calling out to every shark in a ten-mile radius.

I cringe.

Deirdre's face studies me, considering something. She tells me there are at least six hundred and thirty-nine phobias which are accepted by the old world's psychiatric community, fear of everything from spiders to foreigners to closed spaces and flushing things down the toilet by accident, and that these monuments to modern life will now fade away with the death of a frantic civilization. . . . The same with Attention Deficit Disorder and Job Performance Suicide. . . . But for now I need to drink my water, because the human animal can go sixty days without food, yet three days without water will kill you.

I stare, unflinching.

"C'mon," yells Joe. "Let's go down there."

Deirdre raises her sleek eyebrows in a question.

I shake my head.

Her sexy mouth smiles too wide, all by itself, her eyes blazing blue flames, as she turns and walks across the cabin into the rectangle shaft of light to climb the steps.

Shit.

I hear the anchor being pulled, the chain clinking.

The sails boom to life.

Shit.

The boat stops rocking, stops rolling, starts bobbing.

The crashing waves grow louder. The shore closer.

And a bright fluorescent life vest tumbles down the stairs to land on the dusty wood floor with the shaft of sunlight shining against it, turning the shadowed cabin a chocolate orange color.

Shit.

Even though I can't quite figure out what's coming, I think I'm about to go swimming, whether I like it or not. So I jump up, and the wooden floor, the hull, moves, drops, and I'm in the air, then crashing down, falling to my knees. I reach out to grab the vest, to throw it over my head, around my neck, and then I crawl up the steps, out into the blinding light of a red planet. A blood clot sun dunks into an ocean of fire which goes on forever.

I snap my eyes shut, but it's too late. I'm blinded.

Close behind me Joe yells, "Brace for impact."

I spin around and open my eyes, but all I see are black spots growing over one another, hiding the end of the world.

The waves are crashing too close, too loud, spraying me.

I reach out blindly, trying to grab something, *anything*, to brace for impact. I struggle to keep my balance on a bucking, bouncing, shifting floor that I can't see. And finally the world returns to me like some surreal watercolor painting, runny, blurry, yellow and red and black. A huge empty beach, the shore so close, so tantalizingly close, but we are—

The boat just stops.

Everything else in the world does not.

With the crashing waves and the shattering wood, I can't even hear my own screams as I stumble forward and hit the deck, as the boat rolls over on top of me, the water swallowing everything so quickly, so completely that the cold water is far beyond shocking. It steals my breath.

The commotion is far away, muffled.

The shark is much closer, sleek, coming my way.

I fucking *knew* it.

I'm so terrified that I am Zen, calm, smiling, because even though I won't be there to tell Deirdre in person, the blood on the waves will say it for me: I told you so.

I feel like the reddest red cape, a human floating in the cold, dark water, defenseless, easy, except that the bull is a shark, a sleek, gray missile of muscle and razor-sharp teeth wending its way toward me under the giant, white sail floating on the waves above. It has a machine's patience. A predator's grin. Two black eyes made out of coal.

Too slowly I begin to rise because of the life vest hanging around my neck, but time is broken and it's all in slow motion. I'm not going to make it to the surface, and even if I did, what would change? I cannot escape this hungry death.

I watch it cut through the water with such grace that it is almost beautiful. My beautiful disaster. My beautiful killer.

And instead of struggling or freaking out, I feel let down. Because I never got to meet the producers. Because I never got to find out why this whole thing happened to me. Because I never got a chance to try this wonderful natural life they've all been raving about, the one that sounds to me like a long, drawn-out, uneventful suicide.

The shark comes right at me, right up on me, and at the last second, nobody saves me. Nobody shoots it with a filthy speargun or stabs it with a dirty knife. It just turns left. It just wags its tail, then disappears into the deep.

I crack the surface, suck in air and salt water, and a wave sweeps me up, drags me, carries me, and spits me out onto the hard-packed sand of the shore.

I lie there, sucking air like a stupid fish.

I lie on my back with the waves washing up and over me, then tugging down at me as they leave, attempting to pull me back in. My butt fills with sand. I look up at the dark blue sky, bruising for the night.

Deirdre's face enters the view as she stands over me, looks down at me, and she says, "See? No monsters. You're fine, silly."

She smiles like the winner and says, "Told you so."

I call her a bitch.

She laughs at me and runs off.

And I couldn't love her any more if I tried.

fifty-five / rewind <<

DEIRDRE.

I missed her so much.

I love it when she does this, talks with her mouth full.

The vibrations rush into me, touching me where nothing else can, every muscle, even my bones. But then she stops, lifts her head up, pauses the action, and when she says the choice is mine, it blows my mind.

"What?"

"You have to choose. It's the next step."

She engulfs me, I her, and we are that number that reads the same both ways, that position which is my most favorite of all, with my body filling, brimming, almost overflowing with pleasure, with liquid electricity oozing, rolling through me in frantic, fuzzy, tingling waves. Then back into her, back into me. A closed circuit.

And the red lights are blinking in the darkness on either side of us, recording, making this moment eternal, caught forever.

With my mouth full of sweet-tangy-salty Deirdre, I say yes.

And she says yes.

And I say yes, yes, yes.

She starts humming my favorite song and I join along, with her hips bucking and both of us sucking, then coming, but we don't quit, because sex with Deirdre goes way beyond the point where normal people stop, past the point where you are sure that you can't go on.

Another song.

Multiple orgasms times two.

A few bruises.

And then finally she collapses on top of me, with her hair tumbling out onto my knees and her ass right in my face, with both of us no longer moaning or groaning, but laughing and wincing and breathing sharply through clenched teeth, our bodies twitching and shaking.

She tells me that she's happy, and it's good that I'm going to stay with them, to finish the movie, to change the world.

I almost say that I don't have much choice after pulling the gun at my movie premiere, but that's not entirely true. The choice is mine. That is not the reason I am staying.

She says tomorrow, day after at the latest, I begin my training . . . because such a beautiful bullet needs to be shot with precision.

I love it when she calls me that.

Her beautiful bullet.

fifty-six / fast forward

FREEDOM, THEY CALL IT.

A natural life is freedom, they say.

At first I kept track of things like days, but then I forgot to and it didn't matter. Because every day is a new day. It's the same, yet different in a way.

This kind of freedom, it's hard to explain.

At first I counted how many fish I caught each day in the river which empties into the ocean just around a bend in the beach, but then I stopped and only took enough to eat.

At first I looked at the tiny beachfront vacation house and tried to figure out how many square feet, but then I just smiled and called it home.

And do you know what this kind of freedom really is?

This freedom is . . . is . . .

Well, do you ever yearn? >>

You can be honest. No one is listening to you anyway.

You see, in my old life, in my old addiction to Western Civilization, I *constantly* yearned. I mean, I'd watch TV or walk through a department store or drive down the street, and I would just pine away. I'd want so desperately to own that brand new car. I'd yearn to live in that bigger, better, glorious house. To have sex with that drop-dead-gorgeous woman, have everybody love me like that superstar, have everybody respect me like that hero who saved the day.

But now, in this new version of an old world, the yearning is not so much anymore, because a brand new car would just be a shiny metal sculpture with seats. And even if it worked, which is impossible now, where would I go?

Now, a glorious mansion would just be a bigger, emptier, lonelier home full of useless space.

Now, sex with a beautiful stranger wouldn't please me as much as sex with Deirdre.

And now, I couldn't care less if everybody loves me or respects me, because I love and respect myself. Plus, there is no *everybody* anymore anyway. There is only us three. I can no longer see the rest of the world, and so they do not exist.

So, freedom is a life without yearning.

It makes me chuckle inside. It's like that faux-wise parable people say to you when you are frustrated, depressed, angry with your life and they are trying to be so *Zen*, proclaiming, "The key to being happy is not having what you want, but wanting what you have."

It's kind of like that, but not like that, because for Joe and Deirdre and others like them, this life is what they have wanted all along and they finally have it.

This is their desire, their creation: this freedom.

So maybe freedom is having what you want and wanting nothing more.

Another thing about it is there is no pace, no push, no rush. It's letting your mind empty of all of those facts, the useless knowledge about everything in existence. The names. The behavior patterns. The laws of science. Everything from the map of our solar system to the medical version of your own body, to the nutritional value of protein versus carbohydrates. Because when all of this cluttering, clogging, so-called knowledge falls away, you can watch a sunset just to see the amazing color and not describe it with words in your head.

So, freedom is killing the narrator of your own life story.

And I'm enjoying all of this freedom immensely, but with my mind crystal clear, basically empty most of the time, there is a single thought that I cannot seem to make disappear. It is not gaining momentum, but it's not fading either. And it has nothing to do with malice or hatred, it's just that cruelty is a memory that does not fade easily. And it's not that it has to be done soon, but that it has to happen eventually.

You see, lately I've been thinking about killing Joe and Deirdre.

The soft sound of her crying pulls me from my sleep.

I wake up with the summer sun shining noon-bright through the open patio doors. A slight breeze touches my face. I can smell fresh fish, campfire baked, for breakfast, yet again, and I wonder if we will ever eat anything else.

I've never been a big fish fan, but I eat to keep from dying now rather than out of boredom or unhappiness, and my body is lean, sculpted, hard, muscular.

All of that money wasted on diets, gyms, personal trainers, and all I had to do was change the world. Go figure.

>>

I scratch, stretch, flex, yawn, smile.

I get up to walk outside onto the patio, with the sand radiating heat all around me, and I see Deirdre sitting on the steps with her feet buried and her long hair moving in the breeze, her head in her hands, quietly crying, alone.

I stop and watch, torn, because the difficult thing about wanting to kill Deirdre is that I don't want to kill Deirdre. She is so different now. She is kind and helpful. She cooks and cleans more than me or Joe, which would normally make me feel like the man, but there is no difference in this life. There are no roles to play.

Sometimes she sings to herself, smiling.

Sometimes I think it would be great to raise a child together.

Standing here, listening to her cry, I want to hold her and ask her what is wrong. I want to make her happy again.

But I don't.

I've never seen her cry.

For some reason it is assuring, nice, encouraging, makes me want to forgive. To forget. To live.

She stiffens.

I do not turn away.

She turns around, twisting, looking up at me with the tear tracks streaking down her tan face in the sunlight, with a tiny snot bubble growing and shrinking in her left nostril, and she says, "He's gone."

"Who's gone?" I ask, even though I can count to three.

She reaches out and drops a single sheet of paper, letting the breeze tumble it my way, as she turns away.

I catch it with my bare foot, stepping on it, and I sit down on the warm wooden deck to read where Joe has gone.

Deirdre and Nikki,

I'm going for a long walk, probably to Asia, maybe to everywhere else as well. Enjoy the rest and pleasure as you re-create. You are both like daughters to me. Your strength, your recovery, the individuals you have become . . . It makes me very proud to have been a part of it all. Remember to live desire. Never forget that ecstasy is not temporal.

–J–

Holy. Shit.

Say it with me: *What?*

I can't believe it and so I read it again. And again. And again. Because I thought I had it all figured out.

Deirdre and I like daughters to him?

Finally I have to ask, I have to interrupt Deirdre's silent weeping, just blurt out, "Deirdre, I thought Joe *was* your father."

Deirdre turns to show me a look of confusion as she borrows my favorite line. "What?" she says, and she smiles so wide, so fast that her lips catch tears and track them sideways into her mouth.

She licks them away.

I say it again.

And then she laughs at me, the snot bubble popping, as she tells me that Joe kidnapped her too, just like me. "He saved my life. Twice actually. The first time from my father and the second time from his son, when we ran away and tried to start our own movement. . . . He left Beau in the sewers."

"What? The Bum-Messiah was Joe's son?"

"Yes," she says, her face returning to sadness, "We ran off together and had all of these plans to change the world before his father could, you know, just to beat him. . . . It was just the same plan really. We gathered some of the street people, adopted a boy who was on his own, and we started to teach them about how to bring down the system. But then for no reason, for some reason in his own mind, Beau began to think he was special, like he was the Chosen One or something, saying that the world could only be saved through him. . . . He basically went insane, megalomaniacal, like Hitler or Jesus or Mohammed, and when I questioned him about it in front of his 'congregation' he beat me so bad that I couldn't see for a week. I thought I was blind."

She's not even looking at me now, just watching the past inside her own mind. Fresh tears spill down old tracks.

I want to say something in the silence, but I'm still working out the equation of a new reality.

I'm thinking this is why the library was already burning.

I'm thinking that the baby in the FBI picture of Joe was Beau.

Deirdre returns to the now, to me, forces a smile and tries to laugh away the past, tells me she cannot believe I thought Joe was her father.

I do not laugh with her.

She says that Joe and she used to fool around sometimes, before she gave up on men altogether.

"And that's when I picked you," she says, her face turning bright and happy.

For the first time, I think I'm starting to see how some of the dominoes fell. "So I'm the first woman you ever had . . . a relationship with?" I ask.

"You're the first woman I ever wanted to fall in love with," she tells me, not smiling. She looks at me with her big eyes so wide and true, so white and blue.

I don't really know what to say now.

I don't really know if I feel it anymore.

So I say the first thing that comes forward from the back of my mind. "I never really liked men . . . never wanted them . . . never felt the need for them. Even when my father died, when I was just a little girl, I felt nothing. Except maybe relief for my mother."

One corner of Deirdre's mouth turns down, but she doesn't say anything and looks away.

Silence expands in the heat.

Trees talking in the breeze, I watch them sway.

And then in that low, sharpened-steel voice, the one I haven't heard since we got here, Deirdre says, "Get the guns."

I refocus, returning from my own thoughts to see her shielding her eyes and looking down the beach.

I do the same.

Three tiny figures shimmer in the heat, coming around the bend, heading our way.

The ghost of fear resurrects.

Heart thumping. Mouth drying.

Three shadows walking.

"Nikki," growls Deirdre.

And it shakes me, wakes me, snapping me back.

"Go. . . . Get. . . . The guns."

But just as my legs finally get my brain's signal to move and I get up, then spin around to run inside the beach house, I hear distant voices screaming those strange familiar words, and it stops me.

I turn back around.

They are closer now, jogging, waving and yelling the answer without the question that usually precedes it.

"The beach!" they yell.

And Deirdre stands, waves, yells the same thing back to them, like it's some sort of tribal greeting, a code word for a secret society of the insane.

I am diminished. It feels like I'm getting smaller as they grow larger, as they get closer, these three shadows in the bright sunlight slowly turning into distinct people, their characteristics sharpening, focusing.

A tall man in shorts, no shirt, all muscles, black hair.

I ask Deirdre, "How did they find us? Why are they here?" >>

Next to the tall man is his twin, only with breasts.

Deirdre says they're here for the gathering.

What?

The third figure is beautiful, with her long blonde hair, and she used to tell me to look into her eyes whenever I was about to come, because she used to say that it was the only part of heaven she would ever want to see.

I used to believe her.

Her name is Sarah.

I used to love her.

She used to be my wife.

But she's been dead, then alive, then kidnapped, then not, and I'm having a difficult time trying to figure out what I'm supposed to feel right now as she walks up with the other two.

I wonder what my face looks like to her right now.

But she's not even looking at me.

The tall guy says, "Los Angeles," like it's his name.

And Deirdre says, "Silicon Valley."

Cell introductions, says my mind, *targets*.

The Amazon woman asks if they are the first arrivals, and her voice is deeper than her twin brother's.

I don't hear Deirdre's answer because I'm not listening anymore. I'm staring at Sarah, who is studying Deirdre, ignoring me. I'm somewhere between throwing my arms around her in a big manic hug, and going to get the guns.

The guns are winning.

But then she finally turns to me, her eyes swimming, as she says, simply, "We really need to talk, Nikki."

She begins to sob.

But my eyes are gritty, dry.

I wish she wasn't here.

She is ruining my natural life of freedom.

fifty-seven / rewind

ANOTHER EMPTY MANSION.

Another empty day passing.

And as the earth revolves around the sun, filling this absurdly large dining room with growing shadows, the last shred of hope that my dreams may still come true falls away inside of me, for reasons I cannot really explain, don't fully understand, leaving me with only the single most powerful desire a person will ever know.

All I want to do is *live*.

This is what I have been reduced to, I'm thinking, because this time the decision to stay was mine, because all day I have had nothing to do but think. I have so much free time now that it seems not to exist for me anymore. It feels as if I have been separated from time itself. Because, if time marches on, is always in a forward motion, if humanity is constantly in a state of advancement, and yet I am in the massive dining room of an abandoned mansion, standing completely alone, completely still and forgotten, completely removed from all of this "progress" going on in the rest of the world . . . then I am basically left only to be concerned with myself, and time really no longer means much of anything.

I am a part of nothing bigger than myself, says the step.

The Big Black Book of Recovery tells me it is impossible to remain neutral on a moving train.

But I'm not entirely sure what that means.

All I want to do is live.

And, even though *funny* is the wrong word, the funny thing is that I'm beginning to understand things I never understood before. I think the medicine is helping.

The script says this is a very important scene.

Normal John enters the room, says it's time for step five. <<

I'm wide eyed, smiling, excited, because something is changing and growing inside of me. I can feel it. It's like knowledge, but better, and when John pulls the spike from my arm, my sinuses tingle, my eyes pool with tears of gratitude. Uninvited. Unwarranted. Inappropriate.

Normal John looks at me with what seems a very believable concern on his normal, everyday, professional, all-American face. He's one of those bit part actors you see in a ton of movies. He's a businessman. A florist. A cop. A teacher. A lawyer. An FBI agent or an accountant.

A main character's second-best friend.

He usually dies as a surprise or a turning point.

"How are you holding up?" he asks me.

"Fine," I say. Because that is what you say to people.

Manners. Another form of lying.

We are off camera. It's just the two of us, which is a first, because I've never been alone with any of them except for Deirdre.

"Step five," he tells me, taking my cold hands in his, "is very important for your recovery."

Step five?

I thought I was on seven, at least.

My eyes search the room. Its growing shadows make me squirm a little. I don't know where the others are. I'm half waiting for the incentive of pain to arrive. Education through domination. Subjugation. This is like high school all over again, with the chemicals and the hormones and the confusion, except detention is Russian Roulette with a dirty gun.

I ask John where everybody went to.

He says Deirdre is in the city having a meeting with our producers. Derrick and Joe went to kill a priest and get some pizza for dinner.

I laugh.

His face doesn't move.

Since we are off camera, all alone, with no visible weapons, I say, "Hey, can I ask you a personal question?"

His hands, still holding mine, relax a little, but he doesn't make a sound. He breathes and looks into my eyes, and his head moves so slightly that it might be only in my own mind.

"Why didn't you ever write a ransom note? Or contact any media to publicize your cause?"

He laughs, head thrown back, eyes closed, mouth opened wide. When he catches his breath, he looks at me again, shakes his head, and says, "This is not a cause. We are not concerned with the appearance of revolution, but rather the reality of our success in making a change."

I don't get it.

"Under the order of the dominant culture," he tells me, "perception of Self . . . clothes, likes, dislikes, appearance, speech, beliefs, dreams, desires. . . . These things are shaped by a seamless, ever-present stream of projected images that is external to the individual."

"You're losing me," I tell him.

He says, "Media."

He says it conditions us to believe that if an action is not visible, not talked about, not shown to all through television and newspapers, music, radio, then it is not real.

I think maybe for once I understand. It's like that whole if-a-tree-fell-in-the-woods-and-no-one-was-there-to-hear-it-fall-would-it-make-a-sound thing. "But how are you going to change the world if nobody knows what your concept is?"

He says it's not a concept. It's an action.

He says the dismantling of civilization doesn't need support, it just needs to be done.

"But how? I don't understand how. No one will tell me how."

"You have to be honest," he says, leaning in close enough for me to taste his stale, hot breath, his gaze leveled somewhere through my eyes, inside my mind, so intense, as he attempts to explain it to me, "You have to admit that you are frustrated with empty promises, empty calories, false beliefs, lies, while you break your back just to keep your place in line. . . . You have to admit to the pain it causes you. The ulcers. The insomnia, cancer, depression, loneliness, fear, alienation."

He's so out of character, so excited to help me now, that he's squeezing my hands so hard he pops three of my knuckles.

But I think I'm beginning to wrap my mind around it.

"Then you don't care about the media spin," he says. "In fact, you don't care what *anyone* thinks or says anymore, because you realize that even though you do what they tell you to do . . . you are not who they say you are."

He says it's a step.

His voice is getting loud, his words are all coming out in a strung-together rush.

"If I'm not who they say I am," I ask, catching his infection, "then who am I?" My breath comes quick and shallow, my heart thumps in anticipation, because I really want to know the answer, because I really have no idea.

I mean, do you?

Who are you when no one is looking?

Normal John tells me that I am me.

What?

He says, "Make *yourself.* It's a step."

"But I think I already tried that and it didn't work out."

"Who you are to the rest of the world," he says, "is just a role player, a stereotype, a single insignificant character in society's production of *The Game Called Life*, the giant spectacle that is a civilized world."

"You've lost me," I tell him. "Who am I again?"

"In your own life," he shouts, "in your own movie you are the superstar. But the trick, the greatest pleasure, the most important right that you have as an individual being is to shed your role like an outfit of clothing . . . to strip off your hopelessly type-cast life and to re-create yourself, to make yourself from scratch."

Suddenly it makes more sense, sounds like more fun than all of the useless psychobabble I have been told and sold my entire life.

I'm nodding.

I'm smiling.

I'm losing touch with the rest of the world's version of reality, and I think maybe that is also an important step.

fifty-eight / fast forward

FOR MONTHS THE THREE OF US have been eating seeds.

It seemed an odd theory when I first heard it.

You see, it works like this: You pick something you want to eat, something you really like, and you eat the seeds with each meal, like vitamins. Every once in a while, you walk out into some opening in the forest and dig a small hole with your hand. You squat and plant your green beans, your squash, your cherry tomatoes.

Deirdre is selecting a watermelon now.

The Amazon twins are digging potatoes up from the edge of the forest, which is our garden.

And I'm standing a ways off with Sarah. She just won't stop talking. Her story—taking forever—is basically similar to mine, except her "Deirdre" is the giant, Mr. Muscles, which means that she is in love with a *man*.

Can you believe this?

It's something like hours into this one-way conversation, if hours still existed, and Sarah's story has all of the momentum of a cooling lava flow. The kind that reaches the inevitable poorly located town of morons at the volcano's base and swallows it so slowly that no one screams or dies, they simply leave their burning homes, shaking their heads in dumbfounded disappointment.

I do the same, minus the dumbfounded, just disappointed.

I walk away.

She starts crying again.

Time passes ignored, which means it doesn't pass at all.

I don't count anything. I watch the giant eye in the inky night sky slowly wink at me, again and again.

Again.

Again.

And every day, every night, all the time, people are showing up, yelling about the beach. They introduce themselves as another dead city.

"Hello," they say, "We are Phoenix."

"We are Seattle," they announce.

Hi. Las Vegas.

Nice to meet you. Houston.

Chicago.

New York.

Washington D.C., Miami, Louisville. Hello.

I wake up and Canada is cooking pancakes.

A boat anchors offshore, next to the others, and China swims ashore to sunbathe with Italy, Greece, and Spain.

I play volleyball with Palestine and Israel.

No one keeps score.

A group of men show up one night in a big, green hot-air balloon, landing right on the beach, screaming about the beach, and they say, “Hello. We are the Soviet Union.”

They brought Turkey and Africa with them.

Talking with these people—not really talking, really just listening—I’m blown away by their stories of what they saw on their journey to reach us.

Special News Bulletin: The Collapse of Civilization.

Every day a dozen new reports.

It is the progression of deconstruction.

At first, Los Angeles and Portland tell us of the cities being chaotic war zones.

Then Oklahoma City shows up to say that the cities are now graveyards. The only sound is the flies.

Miami shows up to describe the same cities as being silent concrete jungles. Literally. With lions and monkeys, giraffes and elephants, walking around on the same old streets and park grounds that we all claimed to own once.

I look forward to each new arrival. Every time I hear someone yelling about the beach, I run to hear the news report. But the problem is that every time the special bulletin ends, the insane discussion begins.

These people talk and talk, nonstop, about who burned down all of the libraries before we could.

Deirdre never says, but of course she knows.

They talk for entire days about who might have freed all of the animals from the zoos, and what effect this may or may not have on the natural habitat of blah-blah-blah. . . .

I change the channel.

Because I don’t care.

Because even though it is obviously The Bums who have done these things, the real answer to all of their questions is *Meteor*. Because all I want is for these people to leave. I want to let my brain empty again, so that I can eat seeds and swallow Deirdre and watch sunsets and think of nothing.

Brazil shows up for dinner one night, saying that they stayed away from all of the big cities and that every little town they passed through seemed to be doing fine. The people were very nice. They smiled and talked about their theories of why this had happened, but were not angry in the least. They were not scared. They said it was solar flares or magnetic resonance from an asteroid belt, or they talked about some gods' not-so-infinite patience, but they were not sorry at all for what happened.

"The people in small towns," says Brazil, "were very happy."

I smile.

The discussion explodes about everything, nothing.

I turn the channel.

I do not fucking *care*, I want to yell at them.

Go *away*, I want to scream.

But I don't. I remain silent and smiling. I wait until they are eating or peeing or having sex, and then I ask them *why*?

"Why have you come here to the beach?" I ask.

They all shrug their shoulders, give me different answers to the same questions, say things like, "It's a celebration," or, "It is the gathering." A bright-eyed, happy, ugly woman from some country I cannot pronounce, somewhere I have never heard of, tells me that it's the last step.

But believe me, that is not the crazy part.

No. No. No. I wish it were, but it's not.

The truly insane part comes after I ask the next question, after I ask them, "Who told you to come here?"

They get this creeping smile.

They look around to see if someone else is listening.

They lean in real close and prove once and for all that I am *not* special. I am *not* smart. I am just as delusional as all of these other nut-balls.

I guess I knew all along that there was no movie. I mean, I shouldn't really blame it on the medicine. The truth is that it doesn't really matter, because before all of these people showed up, I was at peace. For the first time in my entire life, I was something beyond happy, beyond being merely content, beyond words.

"Who," I ask them, "Who told you to come here?"

And in conspiratorial whispers, with growing telling-a-secret smiles, with giggles breaking through, they say, "The mother ship."

What?

"Angels," they say.

What?

Aliens.

Their desperately missed, dead loved ones.

Drug dealers.

Their first loves.

Porno-stars.

And they are so happy, so proud, waiting for what they have desired for so long, waiting for their reward for completing their own steps or tasks, for changing the world or saving the planet or destroying evil. They are happy and free, stupid and delusional, just like me.

But not everybody is a follower, a clown, a puppet.

I quickly figure out for myself that there are two kinds of people here: the taken and the takers.

You see, sometimes when I ask that second question—about every fifth person or so—I get a different answer, and it's always the same different answer. They shake their heads and tell me that they honestly could not say who told them to come here because they never met them.

"We talked on the phone is all," they say.

If I say, "Producers," they smile knowingly, shaking their heads again, mocking one of the taken, *me*.

If I say, "Leaders," they tell me that there's no such thing.

And these people, the takers, are the calm ones, the older ones. They are respectful and quietly enjoying themselves, as they wait for something or someone. They will usually offer me food or wine or pot or sex or medicine.

I just walk away.

I'm not angry.

I'm patient.

I understand it's not their fault. Because like Sandy Blue once told me, "If it worked like that, it wouldn't work at all."

So I'm waiting.

I'm waiting to see who everybody's angels and aliens and porno-stars are, waiting to see who my producers are. I know there's a good chance I do not know them at all, that I've probably never met whomever it is, but for some reason, I think I feel I know that's not the case.

I begin to carry Deirdre's old, dirty gun with me.

fifty-nine / rewind

EARLY MORNING.

Deirdre breathes peacefully, sleeping on the carpet behind me.

I stare out the window, past the balcony, past the manicured multi-million-dollar property, not really seeing any of it because I'm busy thinking again.

Outside, all across this planet, people are living their own busy lives. And, although it's unpopular to admit it, they are for the most part not all right. They are not really happy.

They're waking up to marriages they've grown to dread.

They're driving to jobs they hate, loathe.

This day is just starting, but everywhere around the world people are wishing that it were already over so they could be back home.

But when they get home tonight, many will dream of being somewhere else, somewhere they've never been. They will dream of being far away from everything and everyone, as far as possible from their lives. Someplace warm and fun and relaxing, where there is no work, no heavy weight to carry, no burden of trying to survive, of trying to "make it."

The word in their minds is *vacation.*

The word in their hearts is *freedom.*

This is what *The Big Black Book of Recovery* is telling me.

This is what I've been reading—studying—for two days now.

And it says that all-day-every-day people struggle in every way, doing things they hate, things they wish they did not have to do.

"What are you doing?" asks Deirdre, sleepy, adorable, sexy.

Her voice startles me a little, brings me back quickly, and I tell her I'm just thinking about stuff. People. The rest of the world.

She yawns and tells me that today I begin my training, that thinking will only get in the way, and to come back to bed.

One in four women will be raped in her lifetime.

This is the headline.

We're all sitting around a table in one of those outdoor coffee houses. The kind filled with sunshine and people on their lunch breaks, with some funky little song I've never heard before being pumped into the air we breathe by unseen speakers, sounding like a thousand other songs I've heard my whole life. This is right uptown, complete with young college kids sporting piercings and serving fifteen-dollar espressos.

Deirdre dyed my long, black hair reddish blonde.

Normal John loaned me his FBI glasses.

Not-Jewish Derrick gave me a white T-shirt, too-long jeans.

Not-So-Little Joe flicked his cigarette butt at me.

Now that I'm here, out in the world, hiding, training, with the traffic clanging, horns honking, exhaust belching out onto me, with everyone around me talking on cell phones, sipping coffee, ignoring each other, I settle in and begin to study the woman at the table next to us.

Today's paper is open on the tables, hers and ours.

Same paper. Same page.

The big, black headline screams out that one in four women will be raped in her lifetime.

The woman sips her foaming latté. With her pinky finger sticking out, showing off her two-hundred-dollar manicure. With her sculpted hair and professional makeup job. With her cell phone to her ear. She sips her latté and tells someone on the other end of the line, "Did you *see* those shoes she was wearing last night? . . . I know, total knock-off Botticelli's."

I point my finger at the headline. I look at Deirdre and say, "Something is wrong here."

John, who is watching the woman, says she is blind on purpose, because if she doesn't see it, then it is not real.

"No," I say, "Not her. Something is wrong with this number. One in four? That can't be right."

Derrick, who's wearing a pair of non-prescription, black-framed, Buddy Holly glasses with a tiny camera built into them, snaps at me, asking, "What fucking number would be more to your liking?"

Spit actually flies from his lips and onto the paper.

"How many rapes are acceptable?" he growls.

"Well . . . less, I guess."

He's about to go completely off, his face scrunching up.

But Deirdre tells him this is not his scene.

He is rage on pause. He exhales, adjusts his glasses.

Deirdre tells me to pay attention, and points to the woman on the phone with the paper.

The lady turns the page.

I turn the page.

The headline: Slavery of children big problem.

The article says tens of millions of children around the world work in sweatshops, making shoes and cashmere sweaters and televisions, work for pennies, willing to be slaves in order to eat just one meal a day in order to survive.

The woman frowns. She covers the mouthpiece of her cell phone. She motions to the waitress and orders an éclair.

Joe starts laughing, billowing out clouds of smoke.

She turns the page.

I turn the page.

Headline: Nuclear storage in your back yard?

We turn the page.

Headline: Famine.

The woman takes a bite of her pastry, a dab of cream now on her nose.

Turn the page.

AIDS epidemic worsens.

Turn it.

Another serial killer.

Turn.

We're at war.

The woman puts twenty dollars on the table, on the open paper, gets up and walks off, laughs with her phone friend about a movie she saw last night.

I'm not laughing. My mind feels scarred. I feel depressed, void of hope, and I say, "This is why I don't watch the news or read the papers. . . . It's horrible."

"Closing your eyes doesn't make it go away," says Deirdre. She sounds sad. Bitter. Honest.

Joe lights up another smoke, and chuckles, phlegm rolling around in his chest. He says, "The first commandment for the great Western Civilization: Thou shalt pretend everything's OK."

"Step one is to recognize that there is a problem," says John.

"I recognize that there is a problem," I whine, so tired now, and feeling slightly ill. "I know the problems aren't going away by themselves. . . . But what the hell can I do? I'm just one person."

"You can change the world," they all say.

"Be reasonable," I mumble.

"Step eight is to be unreasonable," says Derrick.

What?

Deirdre tells me, "The problems in the world today cannot be solved on the same level of polite consciousness with which they were created."

I'm confused again.

She says tomorrow I start playing multiple roles in society, infiltrating, learning, unlearning, and before another autumn turns leaves this same color, the world will forever be changed.

Everyone is smiling.

I close the paper.

My mind takes a mental picture of the date in the upper right-hand corner, files it, remembers Deirdre's promise.

Nine one zero zero one.

sixty / fast forward

I HAVEN'T SLEPT SINCE I WOKE UP yesterday and Deirdre was gone.

No matter where I go, it seems every time I look up, Sarah looks away.

And all day long I'm wondering why the first one left, why the second one is following me, why every time I walk up to a group of people, they stop talking and struggle to keep from laughing.

All these people—all these dead cities and countries—are all very excited, buzzing about something that's purposefully being kept from me.

I think the word I'm looking for is *paranoid.*

But it could be *truth*, or *mistaken.*

And now, sitting here at the gigantic nightly bonfire, staring into the embers at its core to watch the sand turn to glass, with its heat touching my face like a sunburn, my mind takes a step.

Why am I still here if I'm unhappy?

Before I can answer myself, five hundred people stop talking. The silence is so loud that I start looking around at everyone looking around at everyone.

A sharp whisper rolls through the crowd.

No one except Sarah looks at me.

No one whispers to me, but I think it sounds like they're saying, "It's time. It's time. It's time."

But time is a system of control.

Time no longer exists.

And where the hell is Deirdre?

The crowd rises, stands, begins to clap, facing away from the ocean, looking toward the tiny beach house in darkness, but at *what* I can't yet tell. I push through them and their shouting, happy, foreign, hopeful faces shifting in the shadows of the dancing light from the bonfire, until finally I burst through the outer ring to come face to face with Sandy Blue.

What?

But she is . . .

I . . .

And she is so beautiful, so alive and breathing, in full character in her sexy-naughty-librarian costume. She stares at me and smiles so wide with those thin, soft lips which were covered in bloody popping bubbles the last time I saw her.

I am so fucking shocked that I say something stupid like, "You're alive." At least I think that's what I say, but I can't be sure because I cannot hear my own voice over the blood rushing through my body and the ringing in my ears from my brain trying to make sense of things.

I blink. I breathe.

"It's all over now," she says, smiling, happy.

I blink. I breathe.

She takes my hand like a child's, leads me up the slow rise of beach to the dark, dead, beach house in silence.

Everyone behind us at the bonfire is watching us, whispering, waiting, excited.

But for what, I just don't know.

When we reach the patio, I feel vibrations of movement from somewhere inside, and I walk on air, hanging on to Sandy Blue to keep me from falling over. My mind is trying so hard to figure it all out on its own, attempting to put all of the pieces together before I walk in the door, but it's just no use.

The door opens before we reach it.

Sandy Blue walks me into the darkness, into the house.

And I'm holding my breath, with my eyes wide and jumping all around, searching the black shadows that might be moving, which I think are moving.

They're moving!

Light floods the living room, bright, electric, impossible, shocking me, blinding me, as I try to blink it all away, until I see them standing there. All of them standing there.

Sandy Blue lets go and moves away.

Everybody is cheering, screaming, jumping up and down.

Normal John. Not-Jewish Derrick. Not dead.

Deirdre. Joe. Beau, the Bum-Messiah. All in tuxedos.

The buffalo guy, GQ-Man. The Goshute Grizzly. Not angry at me for killing them.

Bob and Karen, smiling, saying something slow, low, muffled, as my body stops working so hard to keep me alive, as my brain starts shrieking, as my heart seizes, stops, turns to hot lead, heavy and useless in my chest.

I can't breathe.

They are clapping, cheering, fading.

And I'm puking up thick brownish red egg yolk that must be blood, as I crumble to the hardwood floors. I must be dying.

As the people, the dead, the resurrected rush to me, crowd around me, maybe to perform CPR, maybe to get a better look at me dying, my head bounces off a floor so far away that I don't feel a single thing.

Through their shuffling feet and tan ankles I can see the dead television, which I never once tried to turn on. It's on.

What I see is me.

Me watching me on television.

Me dying on television, watching me die on television.

When they roll me over onto my back, I stare up at all of the familiar faces, the cameras, and I think that I wish my lungs would work one last time because I would really like to laugh right now.

Bob-the-agent pounds my chest, but I can't feel it.

Deirdre leans down and kisses me, pinching my nose, blowing.

But everything is fading, the whole world dying with me. >>

And then finally, as I'm sliding away, my lungs fill with enough of Deirdre's warm breath that I'm able to let out a tiny weak chuckle.

Because what else can you do with your last breath?

Because I remember Joe telling me one time that all great stories end in death.

Apparently my life is a great story.

And so the last thing I hear is my own laughter.

Then nothing.

Nothing at all really.

sixty-one / fast forward

WHITE WALLS.

White drapes.

White bed.

White smock.

Everyone inside wears soft, silent shoes.

Sarah keeps coming by to tell me that it's over now. Every time she visits, she tells me everything is going to be all right. Her shoes are so loud.

I wish I could tell her how very wrong she is, but I cannot speak. I cannot move.

They all say that I'm a big star now, rich, famous.

A nurse comes around to wet my eyeballs every half hour, and they hook my muscles up to electrodes so I can feel them twitch.

Deirdre comes by to say her name is not Deirdre.

John and Derrick come by to say they are not themselves either.

Joe never shows.

I want to get up and get dressed, to leave this place, but I cannot make myself move. Sometimes my nose bleeds.

Bob and Karen show me the contract I signed.

But all of them just do not understand. They go over and over it, again and again. They tell me it was all just Hollywood smoke and mirrors, that when Deirdre slit my wrist, it wasn't as deep as it looked.

And I remember how fast it healed.

They say I was never burned, just hypnotized and drugged.

They say there was no reconstructive surgery, just a little nose job, and I'm thinking that's why my second face looks so much like me.

They say I was in no danger falling from the sky without a parachute, because there were trained professionals all around me, wearing night-vision goggles, falling with me, in the dark night, so high, just above me, ready to save me if I could not save myself.

And I wish I could yell at them to *shut the fuck up*.

They talk of blanks and squibs and special effects that won awards, and they give me three Golden Spheres, which they tell me I have also won.

Even the doctors get in on the act, calling it reality-therapy, showing me the first week of the show, the big red-letter title, *Surviving Terror*, and they pause it on the opening scene after I tell the four ski masks in my bedroom, "I don't have time to make a movie. . . . I'm all booked up. . . . I just signed on for a new reality-TV series. . . . "

Stupid doctors. Poor acting, really.

The doctors tell everybody that there's nothing wrong with me physically, that it is mental.

I think the term they are looking for is *waking coma*. This whole thing is like a bad soap opera.

And I want to scream that I get it! I understand! >>

But I cannot scream. I cannot make myself move. I cannot return to this world, this way of being. I just can't.

Sleeping for me now is basically just dreaming with my eyes open, and the nurse wakes me up one day talking away, but the only part I catch is that she tells me my sister is here to see me.

I don't have a sister.

A woman I've never seen before walks into my room, but she is so tall and European-runway-model-thin that we could never be sisters. All leather, white half trench coat, knee-high black boots. Very mod.

The nurse leaves.

This woman says nothing for a long time, just stands there, looks at me through tiny dark sunglasses. Her long, black hair in thick rope-like braids, shiny nooses at the ends, her skin flawless. She is not beautiful, like Deirdre or Sandy Blue. She looks more like a human being. I have not seen one of those for a very long time.

And she is so tall that she makes the rest of the world look small.

She moves up close finally, towers over me, her face blank. She takes off her sunglasses and her eyes are coffee with too much cream, almost yellow, as she sits down on the bed next to me. She leans in so close that the heat from her skin touches my face.

She speaks slowly, with a thick French accent, saying, "I know why it is you cannot move, yes?"

My heart begins to pump harder, faster, shaking my chest.

She whispers in my ear, saying that what happened in the show . . . my American reality-show . . . it is going to happen soon in the real world.

My body flushes, tingling.

She backs off, her slender lips smiling wide as she looks down at me, past my body, into me, saying that she is going to change the world in reality, and that there are no steps, no rules, yes?

My eyes blink. Gritty. Sticking.

She says there is no hope, only action, only one step, one big leap into actual change, without a net, without cameras, without fear, yes?

My toes twitch, wiggle.

She says she is not Deirdre, that she is called Sasha.

I stare up at her standing so high above me. She's so tall. I feel so small. But my eyes are blinking faster now, beginning to self-lubricate, and my body is starting to wake, to move on its own, twitching, slowly coming to life, my bones tingling with the desire to end all desires that seeps out to fill me so warm, as I lick my broken lips with a leather tongue, readying my mouth to ask an important question my brain is still struggling to form.

Sasha takes a step backward from my hospital bed—one long step—and she's suddenly halfway across the room, still smiling in her mod clothes, the bright leather crinkling as she asks in her soft French voice, "Do you know what this is, that Sandy Blue should have wanted?"

I'm trembling all over.

"Herself, Nikki. You feel this now. Yes?"

I try to speak.

She says, "And she should have wanted for herself to be free. For the world to be free. For you to be free."

I want to understand, to stand, but I can't. I just can't. Not yet. Because how can I believe again, trust again?

Her wide smile is nudging me toward step three.

But she said there are no steps.

Her long curving eyebrows raise, playful, encouraging me.

And my mouth opens, empty, just hanging there dry, with my body shaking violently. I'm pushing inside, trying to force it out, and finally my voice croaks, rusty, too deep, the sound barbed and scratching my throat, sticking there, then popping out, "I can't . . . love lies again. . . ."

There is more, but it won't come.

And maybe that's enough.

My body sags, deflates, the bed's gravity resurrected.

Sasha's smile frowns, her large, thin face tenses, jaw clenches, as she drops her chin down, her big yellow eyes going wide and open like only a woman's can, so vulnerable, showing me all that is behind them. "You wish me to say that this is not the next season? Not another trick? . . . But I will reveal something much more better for you, what you really want to hear."

I blink, tears spilling, surprising me, so light and warm, moving so quickly down my face and dropping off as my body sits up in bed, just pops right up. This huge fragile thing growing inside me, craving to be named.

Sasha takes another easy, giant step back.

She's far away, by the door.

"Nikki, it is this. A love without complexities? Without domination? Yet strong and fierce enough to change the world. . . . And that I will give this to you freely. . . . But more important is that this is your choice, and you can leave when you want."

It bursts in me.

Rolls through me, so clean.

And I am laughing, crying, reaching out for her from my bed with heavy-aching-hungry arms, saying, "Yes. Yes. Carry me, Sasha. I am too weak."

She flies to me with her loud boots, fifteen feet, two steps.

She bends down, scoops me up, stands up straight with me in her arms, and I am featherlight, melting against her like a sleepy child.

She is that big.

I feel that safe.

She hugs me to her, squeezing just hard enough, and her voice says something in French, something beautiful and lilting, not meant for me.

The lights go out.

Someone screams down the hall.

Something explodes far away.

And she is turning, spinning, running.

And I am smiling again, nuzzling into her neck, happy again.

Sasha is laughing, running through the dark, down the halls, squeezing me against her. She bursts through a door out into the bright, blinding sunlight, and leaps into the air, gliding through the open side door of a red van.

The van jumps, revs, takes off, tires chirping.

I am alive, so excited, because I know what awaits me, I know what is underneath the world's concrete.

Another explosion, miles away.

Mmmmm. . . . It's all beach.

I'll meet you there.

acknowledgements

Thank you,

NOT-SO-LITTLE JOE, for teaching me. For saving me. For being a complete asshole. And for being more of a father than I ever had. (I'm so sorry.)

NOT-JEWISH DERRICK, for your kindness. For your love. For being my brother. For giving me more than I really know how to say. For helping me create this tombstone for civilization. And for redefining for me what a true friend is.

NORMAL JOHN, for your perseverance. For not giving up. For your long rants. For listening. For explaining. And for being smarter than I.

DEIRDRE, for showing me that what I want is not you. For giving me hope and snatching it away. For the pain. For the abuse. And for carving into me the understanding that sex has nothing to do with love.

SASHA, for awakening me. For showing me that love is the only thing that can kill monsters. For being strong. For weeping openly without shame. For showing me that action is caring. And for being more beautiful inside than out.

TIIU RUBEN, for being more talented than I can express, for believing in this book, for pushing so hard for it, and for helping to make it real.

Everyone who helped me. Without hesitation. Without even knowing me. For your kindness. For your belief. For your effort. **NITA CRABB**, for your intelligence and ability to catch the tiniest error. **MILAKA STRAND**, for your extraordinary suggestions. **LOUIS HAZARD**, for improving the ending. **BILL CELEGUR**, **REDWOOD LEAVERISH**, **ARIC MCBAY**, and **KEVIN WEBENDORFER** for an excellent job of proofreading.

MARY, for helping me make this dream a reality. For giving without expectations. For caring only because you feel it. And for being like sunshine on my rainy days.

CHAOS, for teaching me to crave solitude.

PAIN, for teaching me how to heal myself.

SORROW, for helping me to recognize joy.

HATE, for giving me the capacity to love.

EMPTINESS, for allowing clarity.

FEAR, for proving to me that I can beat you.

And finally, thank you **CONSEQUENCES**. For giving me enough time to find out who I really am. For teaching me that I am stronger than I ever knew. For doing your best to break me. For showing me that you can't. And for taking everything I ever loved from me so that I learned to love myself. (P.S. I understand now. I'm a different person. Can I please go home?)

Casey Maddox lives in Crescent City, California, at Pelican Bay State Prison, where he is at work on his next novel, about a man and a woman who seek out God to kill him on national television, and find love along the way.